Love's Justice

Rionna Morgan, author of *The Wanting Heart*

CRIMSON ROMANCE

F+W Media, Inc.

This edition published by
Crimson Romance
an imprint of F+W Media, Inc.
10151 Carver Road, Suite 200
Blue Ash, Ohio 45242

www.crimsonromance.com

Dedication

FOR MY BIG BROTHER, DANIEL B. ROBINSON.

JUSTICE THAT LOVE GIVES IS A SURRENDER . . .

—MAHATMA GANDHI

Dear Reader,

The journey of Sarah and Justin has been a great one. The idea for this book came in a single thought, a single question. My brother and I were at a restaurant one quiet afternoon. I'd been thinking about *Love's Justice* and I asked him, "How can I kill someone in a prison and not be seen?" My big brother, who'd grown up with such questions, answered me without even a blink. (I'm not going to tell you what he said. I don't want to ruin the story.)

I've had so much fun writing this with all its twists and turns. I even got to spend an evening with an FBI agent who read the completed manuscript, giving me pointers on what it is to be a federal agent. (Again, I won't tell you more. It was highly suggested that I not share beyond what I have.)

Along the way, there have been others who've helped create this story. My writing group, The Montana Romance Writers, have been an amazing support. Casey, Danica, Pam, Clare—thank you. My editors at Crimson Romance, Jennifer Lawler and Jerri Corgiat Gallagher. You ladies are the best! (Jerri, I wish there was a way to keep all your smiley faces!)

To my family, my husband, my children—there aren't enough ways to say thank you for all your cheering. I love you.

To you, my friends, thank you for dropping by for a visit. I am very honored and excited to share *Love's Justice* with you. And if you're ever at a restaurant some quiet afternoon and you see a brown haired man talking with a red-haired woman about *murder*, don't worry, it's just me plotting my next book.

All the Best,
Rionna Morgan

CHAPTER 1

A sweet whiff of carrot cake and the final strain of the "Happy Birthday" lyrics met Justin's senses as he walked into the brightly lit office.

"Well, that's not something we'd hear down at headquarters," he muttered under his breath as the glass door swished closed behind him.

Being in a profession clouded with intrigue and stereotypes himself, he didn't really know what to expect of a private investigator's office in downtown Portland. Frankly, he didn't give a damn. This was just a rent-a-cop shop anyway. As he settled down in one of the thickly padded chairs, he couldn't believe he'd actually come. It was like lowering himself. His surveyor eyes glared at the tasteful waterfront pictures gracing the walls and the interesting choice of reading material laid out on the end table next to his seat. He wasn't expecting a dim, smoke-filled room smelling of old liquor and yesterday's newspapers, but he hadn't expected this, either.

"God, what a sissy place." He picked up a photography magazine. "For the wife-cheating crowd no doubt."

Resigning himself, he flipped to an article and used his pretended engrossment in it as a cover for his thoughts. It had taken him months to get here. He'd had to endure the pain of burying his mother. He'd had to nod his head as the doctors explained that she really was healthy, but that she'd lost the will to live. Dying of a broken heart wasn't too hard to believe, Justin had thought as he'd stood at the edge of his mother's freshly covered grave and his father's aged one.

He'd made arrangements for his family's long-time butler to stay on at the ranch-style house in Austin that was now his. And as he'd hung up the phone in his Dallas apartment, he'd figured he was through with details for a while. But that's when the message had arrived from his father's lawyer. Following the directions in the message, he found his father's journal and the folder. They, or rather the contents, were what had brought him to Sarah Johnson's door.

In his mind he could see her picture in the folder he'd left locked in his safe. She looked to be about sixteen when it was taken. Her hair was a delicate blond, her cheeks rosy, and her eyes looked blue or gray—he couldn't be sure which. She looked young and innocent, yet so did her mother. But who better than him knew that looks could be deceiving?

In a few more minutes, he would see the daughter of the woman who was responsible for his father's death.

"Mr. Breslow?"

"Yes," Justin looked up into the face of the voice. The woman had brown, almost frizzy hair and green eyes.

"I'm Annie. I just wanted to let you know that S.J. will be with you in a moment."

"Thank you."

Annie nodded.

"Have you checked him out yet?" Annie asked as she walked into Sarah's office, folding her arms over her chest.

Sarah cleared her throat. "Yes. But I've been busy wrapping up the Hansen case. So I didn't have time to study his file. And, I didn't know for sure if he was going to pursue this any further than a phone call." *And I'm not sure if I'm going to let him poke into my life.* "If you want to read through the file, here you go." Sarah handed Annie the papers clipped neatly in a folder labeled Justin T. Breslow.

Sarah straightened her navy linen pantsuit and wished fleetingly that it were really a T-shirt and a pair of shorts. She wished she held a pair of running shoes in her hand and not her notebook and pen and that she was about to take a nice run on the beach and not the winding professional walk she had to make to the waiting room. *But this is what I love,* Sarah thought. *Maybe I'll take the vacation I keep promising myself, next year.* She put a smile on her face and opened her door.

The smile was what Justin saw first. Sure he noticed her walk. It was more of an easy jaunt and not just the simple one-foot-in-front-of-the-other. He cringed at how carefree she seemed. He also noticed her fancy outfit and quickly calculated the money it would have cost. *Looks like she's benefiting from rich wives looking for their cheating husbands,* he thought as his eyes were drawn back to her smile; pretty white teeth wrapped gently in full, lightly tinted lips. *Damn woman,* he thought in a blink. *It's been months since I've smiled just for the hell of it.*

As she got closer, he stood with a smile of his own. He schooled his features and made sure the smile reached his eyes. Briefly, he wondered if the long, blond hair framing her face was from a bottle, or if it was naturally that brilliant, and if her eyes were blue or gray.

"Mr. Breslow, welcome to S.J. Investigations. I'm Sarah Johnson." She held out her hand. In the time it took her to take her next breath, her eyes scanned, cataloged, and recorded his appearance and her impressions. He stood calmly, waiting. His white, button-up shirt and blue jeans looked well-worn, as did his black leather jacket. Most people looked at their clothing as an accessory for their personality. But Sarah had the impression that this man needed no accessorizing. His clothes were an afterthought. A worn-very-well afterthought.

"Justin Breslow." He nodded as his hand touched hers and held. *Her eyes are . . . gray,* was the last thought he had before he sank into them.

Sarah's smile faded as the warmth in their touch traveled up her arm and fluttered around her insides. She grabbed her hand back, fully intending to ignore the sensation.

"Mr. Breslow, it's nice to meet you in person. What can I do for you today?"

"Sorry. I'm just not used to be being surprised."

"How's that?"

"Your eyes are gray."

"Yes?"

"I just thought they'd be blue. You know blond hair, blue—never mind." Justin shook his head. *I sound like an idiot. Get it together.* "I'm sure you're really busy and didn't plan on spending your afternoon talking to a reporter from Dallas about the color of your eyes."

"You're from Texas?"

"Yeah, I guess I didn't mention that when we talked on the phone." *No wonder; the conversation had lasted about a second,* Justin thought. "I've done some freelance work, but now I work for the *Dallas Herald.*"

"I hear the accent." Now it was her turn to be surprised. She never missed things like that. She knew it was the similarity between Justin and her mom that had thrown her. "I've done some thinking about what you asked me, and I decided to at least listen to what you have to say."

After they were seated in Sarah's office, and after he was finished mentally chewing himself out for getting distracted, Justin began his prepared speech. "I was a huge fan of your mother's for years. Who wasn't? She's a hero in the journalism world."

Sarah nodded.

"I've begged my editor for this assignment since I knew he wanted to run the series."

"Why don't you describe what the series is, exactly." Sarah's eyes wandered over the pictures on her desk. They settled on the last picture she and her mom had taken together. It was at a cross-country meet in high school. They stood side-by-side, arms wrapped around each other. She was dressed in her running shorts and top while her mom was clothed in a classy suit. Sarah could still feel the pride and warmth she felt from being clutched in her mother's arms.

Justin wasn't sure what she was looking at, but he knew he didn't like the sad look on her face. And he sure as hell didn't like the need he felt to reach out and comfort her.

"It's a series of articles on your mother's life and her final assignment investigating the treatment of women prisoners in Alabama." He noted the confusion and hesitancy that flitted across Sarah's face. He had to pull this off or his plan was ruined. "Sarah, listen. Your mother was wonderful."

"I know she was."

"She won the Pulitzer Prize."

"But that's not why she wrote." Sarah crossed her arms and leaned back in her chair. *Hmm, this should be interesting,* she thought. *Let's see how much this guy can come up with. Let's see if he's found the truth.*

What else? Justin wracked his brain for remnants of what he'd planned to say. "She died when she was on assignment in Alabama and deserves to be honored, remembered."

Sarah glanced back to the picture of her mother.

"I would like to do that."

"Why?"

"Because she was—"

"No, I mean why you?" Sarah asked.

"Like, my credentials?"

Sarah shrugged.

"Well, I have a Masters in Journalism from—"

"No, you know what? I don't care about that." Sarah leaned forward. "I want to know why *you* want to do it."

Justin took a deep breath. Here it goes. "We, meaning you and I, have sort of a personal connection. My father and your mother grew up together in Texas Hill. It's probably through him that I learned to admire your mother so much."

Sarah raised an eyebrow. "Who's your father?"

"He was Thomas J. Breslow, but everyone knew him by Tom."

"Hmmm." Sarah tried to remember if she'd heard anything about this Thomas Breslow in her youth. *Maybe.*

"Yes." Justin bent his head. The anger was so fierce. He needed a chance to get it under control. "He died when I was young." *Your mother killed him.*

"I'm sorry."

"No. It's just that my mother recently passed away and it's—it's hard to relive the whole thing." Justin looked up. He saw true concern and sadness in her eyes. The woman was making him sound like a sap. "When I was going through my father's papers, I found what might be a connection between my father and your mother beyond their friendship when they were kids."

"What kind of connection?"

"That's where I'm not certain and would need your help."

"Would I be able to read and approve the articles before they go to press?"

Ah, hell. I knew she'd ask that. Justin cringed. He knew his cover might not be such a good idea. He hadn't written anything for a long time. He'd have to figure something out.

"Yes."

"Good. When do you want to start?" Sarah asked.

"As soon as possible. I want to focus on her life for the first few articles and then delve into her final assignment at the Alabama Women's Prison. I would really like your help—with all of it, if that's possible."

"I can definitely help with her life. But we'll have to talk to my Dad about her last assignment. He knows about the details and will be able to help more than I can."

"I've already talked to him. He's who sent me to you."

Sarah frowned. "What'd he say?"

"That he'd be willing to meet with me. But, that was about it. He said if I wanted help, I'd have to ask you."

"You haven't met with him yet?"

"No." Justin shrugged his shoulders.

"I'm leaving this afternoon to spend the weekend with him. It's my birthday." Sarah motioned to the streamers and banners sporting the message, "Happy Birthday S.J."

"Sort of figured that."

"He and I always spend some time together for it." Sarah looked at the man before her. He was a little taller than she was. He had brown hair and blue eyes. He looked average, but something in his eyes held her. She felt as if she could trust him. He seemed to be telling the truth, at least part of the truth. It was the other part she was concerned about. She needed to know what that other part was before agreeing to work with him. Coming with her might not be a bad idea. And if he came, she'd be able to watch him and make sure he didn't upset her dad. "Would you like to come with me?"

"Yes." Justin nodded with surprise and smiled.

"If you give me a number where you can be reached, I'll call before I leave."

"Great." Justin shook her hand. He was careful not to look directly into her eyes this time. But her sexy, intoxicating scent delivered a quick gut punch. Damn woman!

*

Sarah looked out the window and watched Justin get into a cab. Her instinct told her he was trustworthy, but there was something . . . The feeling she had when she just touched his hand told her she should walk the other way.

"S.J.," Annie called.

"Yeah, Annie." Sarah turned to her researcher and friend.

"I read through that info on Justin."

"So you know, huh?"

"I talked to his editor, Patrick Walker, at the *Dallas Herald*. He said Mr. Breslow's assignment is to write a series of articles on Helen Prescott."

Sarah thought, *if only it were that simple.* "I know." Sarah rubbed her hands over her face. Her mind traveled back to her sophomore year of high school. Her memories raced through track meets, award ceremonies, and old boyfriends. But the moment she remembered the most was the day she'd come home from school and met her father in the yard. Seeing his anguished face, she'd stumbled into his arms. As the mist of the evening had settled around them, he'd told her what had happened. While his body had shaken with sobs, he'd told her there had been a fire at the prison where her mother had been on assignment.

"She's dead, honey. She's dead."

Sarah wiped away the silent tear. "Happy Birthday, S.J.," she mumbled.

*

Outside, Justin hailed a cab. Grimly glad to have his own investigation underway, Justin dialed FBI headquarters in Dallas. Only when he was inside the cab moving away from S.J. Investigations did Justin press send to talk to his partner, Pat Walker.

CHAPTER 2

"So how long have you been a PI?" Justin asked. He had to do something to fill the silence. And he didn't think grabbing Sarah by her primly ironed collar and kissing her until she moaned with pleasure would quite do the trick, although it was something he'd felt the urge to do ever since she'd picked him up. *Dear God! What am I thinking? I don't like her. How could I? She's not only a wanna-be cop, but her mother killed my father.*

"Looks like you've been busy researching my mother and not me." Sarah steered her full-sized SUV through a winding curve that led to her father's house in McMinnville, Oregon.

"Why?" Justin scowled at how easy Sarah's long, tapered fingers gripped the wheel.

"I'm not a private investigator. I'm a psychologist, a profiler."

"Oh." Justin rolled his eyes. Great.

"It's an odd thing, what people think when I say I'm a profiler. Is she a quack, psychic, or just plain crazy." Sarah brushed her hair behind her ear. "Actually, I'm more of an observer."

Justin shifted in his seat. "I'm a reporter. I'm an observer, too. Does that make me a profiler?"

"Perhaps, but I observe different things than you do. You observe human nature for how it will make a good story. I observe human nature on the elements that make them who they are."

Justin let out a breath.

"Just like now. You're uncomfortable. Maybe because of me, but more likely because you're not used to being a passenger. You'd rather be driving. And I'm thinking, not a car. You must drive a motorcycle or something."

Justin scowled. How the hell did she know that?

"Now you're wondering how I know that. Well, I don't *know* it, know it. But I can tell you're uneasy. You have been since you got in. You're not exactly plastered against the door, but you're not sitting contentedly in your seat, either."

Justin shifted and tried to seem at ease.

"As for the motorcycle, I noticed this afternoon that you have calluses on your hands, where your thumb meets your fingers. Either riding something with handlebars, like four wheelers, motorcycles, or bicycles, is a pastime or provides your main mode of transportation. I'm guessing motorcycle?"

"Hmm. No kiddin'."

Sarah looked over and smiled. Justin felt as if the car had lit up. What a smile! Beautiful and sweet and innocent. What a combination. He shook his head. *I should've ridden my motorcycle. At least that way I'd be able to glide through each bend on this road with the wind whipping my jacket and not be looking at this beautiful—damn—woman beside me.*

"So." Justin cleared his throat. "How long have you been a profiler?"

"About ten years."

"Really."

"I haven't always been on the third floor of that office building. I've only been there about five years."

"Where were you before?"

"In a small basement office I rented."

"So what do you do? Find cheating husbands and all that?"

"No, I mainly focus on uncovering political scandals and illegal corporate transactions."

Justin looked startled.

Sarah laughed, taking pride in her success as well as Justin's surprise at it. "My first case was a little girl looking for her mom. She wanted me to help her dad find her." Sarah remembered how hard she'd worked for weeks, excited at the prospect of finding the truth.

"Did you find her?"

"Yeah. But sadly, the mom had run off with an old boyfriend and both had been killed in a car accident."

"Rough."

"The dad was pretty shook up."

The silence was back. This time it should have been the uneasy, sad silence that filled people with yearnings and caring thoughts. Looking at Sarah's face, Justin watched for sadness but didn't see any. She just concentrated on the road ahead.

"I met your secretary briefly, but do you have any other people working for you?" Justin asked.

"Is this article you're writing about me or my mom?"

"Sorry. Guess I'm just curious. Goes with the territory—you know, reporter and all. Observer."

Sarah nodded. "Annie, the woman you met, is my researcher. She'd belt you if you called her my secretary. But besides her, I have two other investigators working with me. They really help out when I'm researching and can't get into the field. Which is a lot lately." Sarah glanced at Justin. He'd forgotten his act of relaxing and his hands were back to being held tightly in his lap. She smiled. "So tell me about this motorcycle. What's the best thing about it?"

"They're great in traffic jams."

Sarah tried to envision Justin on the back of a motorcycle zipping in and out of traffic on the hot streets of Dallas, his brown hair blowing in the freedom of the wind. Beneath his sunglasses, his sharp blue eyes would squint. He'd lean with the speed and power of the bike as he maneuvered between cars. She could believe it. It fit him perfectly. "Sounds adventurous."

"Believe me, four thirty on a Friday afternoon, it gets pretty hairy."

"How long have you been a reporter?" Sarah asked, wanting to change the subject. She wasn't exactly comfortable with the images of Justin in his white T-shirt and snug blue jeans that her mind kept creating.

"I guess about nine years."

Sarah steered through the next curve. "Did you always want to be a reporter?"

"Yeah. I like finding out the truth and informing the public of it. I feel like it's my duty to educate the people about the injustices in life. Even if the injustice is just beyond their door."

"You sound like my mom."

"I know." Justin did know, too. He'd memorized that from an interview Helen did after she'd won the Pulitzer. "She was great."

This time Justin could feel the car fill with Sarah's sadness. "Who all's going to be at this party of yours?" He asked, wanting Sarah to think of something fun.

"My dad, Eric, of course, and my aunt Lainey, if she's in town."

Justin paused. "Is your aunt your mom's sister or your dad's?"

"She's actually my mom's twin. Dad doesn't have any brothers or sisters." Sarah clicked her blinker on to turn down a long, wooded street. "Carla and Nathan will probably be there, too."

"Who are they?"

"Carla is my dad's next-door neighbor. She's kind of a leftover-hippie type, and Nathan is her son. She and I never really got along very well. She sort of weaseled her way into our lives. You know, single mom living next door to a single dad. But Nathan is great. They moved in when I was still in high school. Nathan was just a couple months old. I babysat when I could. Carla always ends up giving me something." Sarah cringed, thinking of the gift from last year, a certificate for a new pair of running shoes. It had been too much; anything from her was too much. "I hope she doesn't get too extravagant this year." Sarah brought the vehicle to a full stop and unlatched her seat belt. "We're here."

As Justin shut the door behind him, he experienced the first surprise of the weekend. He saw Sarah, the professional woman he'd been riding with, laugh full and loud as she ran into, what he could only guess was her father's arms. Justin, of course, had seen pictures of Eric Johnson and expected him to look like the retired grocer he was. But what he saw widened his eyes. He'd expected the aging man to cordially pat his daughter in a birthday hug, not grab her and twirl her around and around in his front yard.

"Happy birthday, Sugarplum." Eric placed Sarah back on the ground and, spying Justin, tugged her toward him. "So you've brought a boy for me to meet?"

"Dad!" Sarah laughed. She couldn't help it. She was so glad to be home. It had been months since she'd been able to come. "This is Justin. He's—"

"He can tell me who he is." Eric walked toward the man leaning against Sarah's vehicle. His mind quickly evaluated his stance, his clothing, and his intentions.

"I'm Eric Johnson."

Justin blinked at the strong, firm handshake.

"And you want something from my daughter."

Justin wasn't quite ready for what Eric had said. He really wasn't prepared to be tagged so easily. This guy was supposed to chop lettuce and wash tomatoes. *I guess you never can tell about people,* Justin reminded himself.

"Yeah, I guess you could say I want something from your daughter. I'm Justin Breslow with the *Dallas Herald.* You and I spoke a few days ago. I'm doing a series of articles on Helen. I want to honor her and—"

"Mmm-hmm." Eric patted Sarah's shoulder.

"Sir, I want Sarah to help me research Helen's last assignment as an undercover reporter at the Alabama Women's prison. I would like your cooperation and help, if that's possible, as well."

"We'll see." Eric grabbed Sarah's hand and pulled her into the house, leaving Justin standing flatfooted in the front yard.

Justin swore under his breath, "What the hell? *He's* who sent me to her." He followed them inside the two-story, white house. He didn't have the audacity to take the bags in. He didn't know if he'd be staying.

If the first surprise of the weekend was Sarah's response to her father, the second definitely had to be the greeting Justin received from Sarah's aunt. He wasn't sure how he'd react to seeing a woman who looked like the one who'd caused his father's death. As soon as he'd received an introduction, she grabbed him in a hug to welcome him. Her warmth and appearance put his worries to rest. She looked nothing like Helen. Normally, he loathed women with high, beauty-parlor hair, red nails, and spiked shoes, but he couldn't help get a kick out of her. Soon he found himself ushered into the living room where Sarah and her dad were already seated. Lainey, whose real name he found was Elaine, motioned for him to sit next to Sarah on the sofa. He smiled as Lainy arranged presents around Sarah. Zipping here and there, she made sure everything was as perfect as she could make it. "Here honey, you open this one from Carla and Nathan first."

"How are they?" Sarah asked, hoping her dislike for Carla didn't come through very much. She really was too old for the aggravations of childhood to be bothering her now.

"They're good. Carla made the cake." Elaine's voice had turned serious.

"Nice."

"You're not seventeen anymore," Elaine said. "And it is nice."

"I know." Sarah nodded and sat up straighter. She wondered if families ever really saw the adult kids as true adults.

"Nathan's playing baseball, so they couldn't come. He was thrilled when the coach asked him to be pitcher."

"I'll be sure to stop in and say hello." There, that should do it.

"Come on! Come on. Open your present," Elaine laughed. The mood lifted to celebration-level again.

"Aunt Lainey, it's so good to see you." Sarah ripped the balloon-decorated paper, to reveal a camera from her father. "I wasn't certain you'd be here. I thought you'd be off in the Caribbean or something." Sarah looked at her aunt's big eyes. They were shadowed with just the right amount of blue makeup to make it too much.

"I just got back from the French Riviera. Like my tan?" Elaine tilted her shoulder and pulled her shirt down.

"God, you're crazy." Sarah chuckled. "Yes, I see it. I love it. Stop. You'll embarrass our guest."

"Oh, yeah. Sorry. Somehow I always seem to do that. It's just been so long since you've brought a man home, I've forgotten how to act." Elaine looked at Justin, eyes dancing. "I'm so sorry, darlin'. You're just going to faint dead away at the sight of a woman's shoulder." She batted her eyelashes.

Justin couldn't contain his laugh any longer. He let it spill out of his lips and fill the room.

"Well, it sounds like we're all having a great time," Eric said as he walked in from the kitchen.

Now, he looks like a grocer, Justin thought as he looked at Eric. His shirtsleeves were rolled to his elbows. A dishtowel was jammed in the waist of his pants and another lay flicked over his shoulder.

"Dad, I would've helped with the dishes." Sarah looked up from opening another present.

"I left the cake plates since we didn't eat it all yet. So you and Justin can do those later." Eric winked at Justin.

Justin nodded. *So that's the way of it. Now you're nice to me. Okay, old man, I'll play it your way.*

"Oh, Justin doesn't want to do dishes," Sarah said.

"Sure I do."

"He'll help. After all, you guys have some planning to do." Eric wiggled the edge of a towel in their direction.

"Planning?" Sarah asked.

"Yeah. You two have to figure out what you're going to do with the gift I have for you."

"But I already got a camera from you."

"Nope. I'm not talking about the camera. I'm talking about this." Eric held up a set of keys. "These are keys to our beach house in Bandon. I'm giving you a month off for your birthday."

"A month!"

"Yup. I'm taking your place at S.J. Investigations for a month. Well, sort of. I ought to be able to at least answer the phones and get the mail. Annie and the guys can do the rest."

"They knew about this? Why didn't they tell me?"

"Because they knew you wouldn't do it."

"You're right. I won't. I have clients who are expecting me to—"

"No. You don't have clients. Any that you think you have don't exist because Annie made them up or assigned them to Ben."

"But I thought Ben said he didn't have any—Dad, you can't do this."

"Yes. I can, and I have. You need a break. You're going to run yourself into the ground if you don't take a rest. I'm not going to have that. Plus, you'll have time to help Justin with his project. Now, are you going to do as you're told or not?"

There was a long silence where Eric looked at his daughter and she looked back. What passed between them was a message. It was the same one that had been there since her mom died. *Sugarplum, we promised we'd look out for each other, remember? Do this for me. You're all I have.*

"Yes." Sarah knew she had to do it. Wasn't she here with Justin because of that very promise?

"Yes—what?" Eric smiled at her.

"Yes. I'll do as I'm told." Sarah moved to hug her father. She didn't know how she was going to spend all of the free time she was forced to have, but she'd think of something. "Thanks, Dad."

*

"So what are we going to do?" Justin dried the last dish and placed it neatly in the cupboard.

"What do you mean *we*?"

"Your dad said we had a lot of planning to do. I was just wondering what you wanted to do, so I could say whether I agree or not." Justin folded his arms and smiled at the conflicting emotions crossing Sarah's face.

"I don't think he exactly meant *we*. I think he was just being nice and including you in the—"

"Nope. Didn't you hear him say—'help Justin with his project'?"

Sarah wiped her hands on the dishtowel and threw it on the counter. "What if I don't *intend* for you to come with me? What if I want a peaceful vacation without any snoopy reporter hanging around? What if I want to do the research on my own?"

"What if I didn't go as a snoopy reporter?" Justin closed the small space, successfully trapping Sarah between the refrigerator and the counter. "And just went as a man with you on vacation?" With a smooth shift of his body, he slid into an amazing fit against her.

Sarah drew in a quick breath. The air-cooled kitchen suddenly became a furnace.

His hands gripped the counter on either side of her. His face was so close she could see her reflection in his eyes.

"That is exactly what I don't need."

"Don't need, but maybe want?" Justin moved closer. Their lips were just a breath apart.

"Don't," Sarah breathed. Her heart rapped hard in her chest.

Justin smiled, enjoying watching her eyes cloud to darkness.

"Don't what." His lips brushed hers. "Tell me. Don't what?"

Sarah fisted her hands in his shirt. To pull him closer or push him away, she wasn't exactly sure. Panic and need and she didn't know what all tumbled around in her stomach. Instead of taking the time to decipher what to do, she just acted and tugged him to her.

He caught her bottom lip, soft and warm, between his teeth. He felt her body give against his. He savored the taste of her, the warmth.

"I'm going with you," he whispered against her lips.

She nodded her head, but his words never registered.

My plan is working perfectly, he thought as he pulled her deeper into the kiss.

CHAPTER 3

I can't believe how stupid I was, Sarah said to herself over and over as she ran. She and Justin had been at the beach house in Bandon a week, and every morning on her run, she relived the "little scene in the kitchen," as she'd been calling it. She'd tried to convince him that she'd never agreed to him coming with her. But then he wanted to know what she was agreeing to, so her options were let him come or let him believe she wanted him to kiss her. So he came. Damn!

She had to admit he was being very helpful. He'd helped bring in and sort all of her mother's research from her last assignment. Which was great. He'd made breakfast every morning. Which was great. *He hasn't even tried to kiss me again,* Sarah reminded herself. *So that's great. Sort of. Stupid. Stupid. Stop thinking about it! Just run.*

The small town of Bandon, Oregon, was nestled snuggly in the crook of the Pacific Northwest's long arm. While the Oregon Coast was famed for rugged rocks and wild waves, Bandon's beach had the luxury of smoother sands and soft winds on the mellow days. Sarah had been coming here with her family since she could crawl. Some of her first memories were of finding starfish and sand dollars tucked in the gentler tide pools.

She barely remembered the grandfather who had left them their home, which looked out on the ocean, but she remembered finding those treasures. As Sarah's feet made soft, thumping sounds on the sand beneath her running shoes, the sun began to rise. It sent out streaks of light, quickly replacing the gray-pink of the morning with a brilliant red. The power of the Pacific was calm in the light. The tide began its twice-a-day journey. Saran ran at the edge of the world, along the ever-changing line where the earth meets the water. The air quivered just enough to whisper a breeze. It smelled of salt and mystery and a pinch of seaweed.

The piercing calls of the gulls didn't destroy the peacefulness but perfected it. They swooped and danced, excited for another day of begging bread from the tourists. Shortly, people in wide-brimmed straw hats, with coolers and sunscreen, would scurry out to the beach. But if the old adage, "red sky in the morning, sailor take warning," were true, the day would be ruined and foul weather would soon banish the idea of picnics and kite flying.

Sarah's breathing was rhythmic and steady from years of training and habit. But she was restless. Her mind worked over all the progress she and Justin had made. Following her dad's notes, they'd arranged all the shipments from the prison from first to last. They'd spent the week reading notes from her dad and mapping the locations of recording devices her mom had hidden in the prison. Today, they planned to listen to the first recording. The anticipation Sarah felt pushed her forward a bit faster. Her breath stayed even as she ran, and the burning of her working muscles made her feel strong. She'd wanted to do this for years. She even got out some of the boxes after she graduated college, but couldn't bring herself to follow through. Having Justin here made the project somehow easier to handle.

During the last few paces, she could smell whatever Justin was cooking for breakfast drift from the open windows. If her nose didn't lie, they'd be having waffles. She stopped for a moment to stretch. As her legs pulled taut, her eyes scanned the white shutters that clung to each window, which were now banging against the house in the slight wind. The bright blue paint was beginning to fade in the salty air, but the house was still beautiful, and Sarah could feel its arms open wide in welcome. She took a deep breath, filled her lungs with the tangy air and maple syrup and took a step inside.

"Hey, how was your run?" Justin looked up from the waffle iron. He could have made a million waffles this morning and not known it. His mind was on other things. Well, one thing—Sarah. He'd watched her run each morning until he couldn't stand to see her compact body move in its fluid, graceful pace any longer. Or until he'd started to feel as if his new hobby was that of a Peeping Tom.

"Great. I was all by myself today. There weren't any old fishermen out staring at the water like yesterday." Sarah smiled. Justin was frankly adorable in his ever-present T-shirt and blue jeans. His toes, masked in their gray socks, poked from beneath the hem of the jeans. A dishtowel was slung over his shoulder, and in one hand, he held a plate of waffles. In the other, he held a fork.

"We're ready to eat anytime."

"I'm just gonna go shower real quick. But you can start without me. There's a storm coming, so I'm going to close the upstairs shutters." Sarah took the stairs two at a time, pulling the hair band out of her hair as she went.

"Yup, that just what I need. Being stuck in the house during a storm with the picture of Sarah's body, naked and wet, in my head." Justin stabbed the fork into the center of the waffles. "God, I need another hobby."

*

Justin thought he knew all the ways items could be smuggled out of a prison, but he learned a few things from Helen Prescott Johnson. She used the items she made as a method to transport information. If she carved a wooden box or pencil holder, the recording chip, which had hours of conversation, would be hidden inside the wood. But the question remained. How?

Justin and Sarah cleared the table after breakfast and were working in the kitchen. The view outside their window showed a dark sky and pounding waves.

"This is really high-tech surveillance equipment. Where'd she get all this?" Justin asked as he looked at the first, small, gray recording chip, which looked like a square button, and the playing device, which was similar to a television remote. Fifteen years ago, it would have been next to impossible to get any of it. Even now, it wasn't available to the public. He knew about it, because he'd been trained with it and the Bureau used some of the same technology.

"She knew someone in the military. Elvis was his name—well, not his real one—and I don't think she ever actually saw him. They always talked on the phone, and then she'd receive a package in the mail," Sarah said, hoping that would appease him for a while.

"I can't believe how much your mother was able to do in such a short time. She'd have been a great FBI agent . . . "

Sarah looked up. Did he know? She wondered.

" . . . or something," Justin muttered quickly.

He was impressed at how well documented everything was and how cleverly it was organized, but his opinion of Helen was still the same, questionable. He really wanted answers. Who was Helen Johnson? In fact his curiosity about her was heightened because of the devices on the table in front of him.

"How did she even know where to begin? Where did she—?"

"She only had one more week. Then she was coming home." Sarah held the playing device in her hand. "It was her last assignment. She and Dad were going to retire together."

Justin noted the sad tone in Sarah's voice.

"We can take a break if you want. We've been working pretty hard." He thought he might need a break himself. Thinking of Helen as Sarah's mom, someone she loved, was difficult. Since he'd learned about what she'd done, all he'd ever felt toward Helen Johnson was hatred. It was hard to separate the two.

"No. I want to hear the first recording." Sarah pressed play.

A voice sounded from the recorder, *"Oliver is a damn jackass for puttin' me in here. He's a filthy, lying, no-good son-of-a-bitch."*

"Oh God." Sarah dropped the player. Her mother's voice kept talking.

Justin was so intent on hearing Helen's voice, hearing the voice of the woman who had caused his father's death, that he hadn't paid any attention to Sarah. Seeing the player hit the table had him looking at her, but he didn't catch her before she was out the door.

"Ah, hell," he whispered as he raced after her. Sarah's crying could be heard above the wind for only a moment, so fast were her steps, which took her beyond the yard. She ran as if she was being chased. She *was* being chased, by the memories of her mom and the voice she'd just heard. Her heart pounded with her feet, as she curved around the sandy bend to an overhang of rocks. She crawled to the back of the covering and let the pain wash over her.

"Where the hell did she go?" Justin swore at the edge of an outcropping of rocks. The wind whipped against his body, battering him with its anger. He tried to listen for any sound, but all he heard was the roaring of the waves. Following his instincts, he looked at his feet. Footprints in the sand in front of him led into a cave. Shaking his head, he followed and ducked into the opening just as the sky opened to pour out its fury.

Justin's breath caught when he saw the strong, confident woman he'd known huddled in the corner of the cave, her body rocking back and forth.

He didn't know what to say. He'd never been any good at coming up with the right words. After his father died, his mom would go into his father's study and cry. Justin could hear the weeping from his room, so he'd go down to her, but he didn't know what to say to make her feel better. So he did the only thing he could. He'd hold her until she fell asleep, and then he'd pull a cover over her, hoping to warm her, and let her rest.

The sound of Sarah's sobbing made something in his heart shift, and he needed to help. But he didn't know what to do now, any more than he'd known with his mother. So he did the only thing there was to do. He gently pulled Sarah into his arms and let her cry.

CHAPTER 4

As the ocean crashed and the wind lashed the world beyond the cave, Sarah's emotions were caught in a storm of their own. She felt as if she were again the young girl who had to face her teenage years without her mom, the mom who had always been there with a kind word, an ice cream cone, or a funny story. As the tears raced down her cheeks, the anger she'd always felt at how unfair it was to lose her mother worked its way to the surface. She wanted to pound on the ground and scream at the injustice of it.

Seeping into the anger and confusion was another feeling, the feeling of comfort. She could sense warmth encompassing her. From somewhere inside she knew that couldn't be right, not with the storm that had been brewing this morning. Working herself out of the misery she was in, she sat up and looked into deep blue eyes. They held a questioning look of concern. She had no idea how long Justin had been holding her, but only a little while was too long. She never let anyone see her this way, not even her father. She felt shame and embarrassment immediately warm her face.

"Justin, what are you doing?" She scrambled away from him toward the opening.

He wasn't quite prepared for the anger in her voice. "I am helping you."

"I don't need your help."

"What was I supposed to do?" Justin wasn't mad, but he was working up to it. "When you went running out into the storm?"

"Leave me alone." Sarah wiped the drying tears from her cheeks. "Just leave me alone." She didn't think she'd ever felt this humiliated.

Sarah ducked out from under the overhang and wished she could just disappear for a while. *He probably thinks I'm some frail, prissy girl,* she thought as the first burst of rain hit her.

"What the hell are you doing?" Justin grabbed Sarah and swung her around.

"Leave me alone." Sarah yelled above the wind.

"Why? So you can run off and do something stupid?"

"Now, I'm stupid?" Sarah's eyes shot anger.

The sight of it. The sight of *her,* standing with her hair whipping around her face, her wet clothes plastered to her body, and those eyes . . . gray, angry, and holding all the fury of the ocean behind her. He felt as if a dam was breaking when he looked at her, and he didn't try to stop it.

"Yes, damn it." Justin yanked her hard against him and devoured her. Her lips, warm and salty from her tears, were inviting. He didn't think about the danger of the storm around them; all he felt was the hurricane of emotions ricocheting in his system.

Sarah felt his body, hard with anger, connecting with hers. Her senses shifted from shame to anger to want in the time it took her to take a breath. In him, she found need and intrigue. Winding her arms around him, she took what he gave.

It was wonderful to feel the sensations and textures of tongues meeting tongues. She couldn't help but wonder how it would be to be beneath him feeling his hands move over her body with nothing between them. The thought shocked her, and she pushed him back.

"Let go." She whispered through clenched teeth, trying to rationalize her actions and thoughts.

Kissing her before was a nice treat. This, Justin thought, sucked at his control. He was still trying to get his mind to function when she started walking away.

He watched her determined strides take her toward the house until she disappeared. He could even imagine he heard the door slam behind her.

"Get a grip, Breslow," Justin muttered to himself and scrubbed his hands across his face. "Or this is going to get complicated."

Justin made sure he was quiet when he walked in the house. He wasn't prepared yet to have the fight he knew would probably be waiting for him. He drew an easy breath, when he heard the shower running above him and was glad that he didn't have the same thoughts he'd been having all week. *Maybe I'm over her,* he thought. *Good, that'll make my job easier.*

As he punched the numbers on his phone that would connect him to the FBI headquarters in Dallas, he ignored the twinge of disappointment he felt.

"Hey, Pat, this is Justin," he said into the mouthpiece and then made a mental note to monitor his language when he heard the shower shut off and footsteps move around upstairs.

"Well, shit. How you doing?" Pat answered in a voice heavy with a Midwestern accent.

Justin laughed. He'd gotten good at masking his Texas accent, but Pat didn't care how many people knew the location of his birth. He was damn proud to be from Minnesota.

"Everything's going fine."

"Well I didn't ask how everything was. I asked how you were, but if that laugh was as real as it sounded, you're doing better."

"Yeah." Justin heard a step on the stair and moved to the other room so he could still talk in semi-private. "The articles should be coming your way pretty soon."

"She's there, isn't she?"

"So?"

"What's she look like?"

"Oh, hang it up. You're married."

"And loving every minute of it, but come on."

"Like her picture." Justin grinned at the groan he heard from his oldest friend. "Anyway, I was just calling to check in and let you know everything's right on schedule."

"You still going to do it?"

"Yup."

"Geez man, carrying around all that anger isn't good for you."

"I want some answers, too. The boss still saying it's okay for me to be gone for a month?"

"Yeah, he even thinks you should take some more of your personal time and go on a real vacation when this bereavement stint is over."

"Maybe. Right now I need to focus on this." Justin didn't want to hear Pat tell him what his conscience had been saying since he'd met Sarah. So he worked toward ending the conversation. "Tell Marcy hello and give little Becky a hug for me." Justin smiled, thinking of Pat's wife and their new baby.

"When you come back into town, why don't you come on over and we'll barbeque some hamburgers and drink a few cold ones."

"Will do." Justin hung up the phone and turned to look at Sarah. He'd felt her watching him for the last few minutes.

His eyes skimmed her form. Her face was scrubbed clean, and her hair was pulled back in a hair clip. A fresh T-shirt hugged her body, and a pair of ancient pants were snug against her hips. She looked like a college kid getting ready to put in an all-nighter. *Well, so much for thinking I'm over her,* Justin thought when he felt his blood begin to run hot.

"I wanted to say I'm sorry. I don't usually behave that way." Sarah looked at the knuckle she'd skinned sometime while she was outside. "And I'll understand if you don't want me to work with you on this anymore. My dad might change his mind and help."

"Why would I not want to work with you?" Justin asked and noticed the raw scrape on her hand.

"My mom was brave. She could do anything. I can, too." Sarah raised her head defiantly. "This is difficult for me." She hadn't expected her emotions to backfire the way they had. She really thought she'd healed. She thought she'd gotten over her mother's death.

Justin walked over to her. He knew what she'd felt when she'd heard her mother's voice on the recording. It was the same thing he'd felt when he'd read the words in his father's journal. It was shocking and extremely painful. "I can't think of anyone who wouldn't have a hard time hearing the voice of a loved one . . . who'd been gone a long time."

"But the thing is it wasn't really her voice. I mean, sort of, it was, but not really. She sounded mean—like a convict."

"That's who she was being."

"I'd never even heard her swear. She never used that tone of voice."

"If you want, I can listen to them alone." Justin wanted to kick himself for that idea. Without Sarah there to ground him, he knew his anger at Helen would just take over.

"No. I want to do it. Maybe if I listened to some of it by myself, I might be able to work through it."

"Okay, I'll go upstairs and clean up, and you can listen. But if you need me, you can call me." Justin lifted the wounded hand to his mouth and brushed his lips across the red welts. "You take care of yourself." He winked and started to leave.

"Justin, wait. There's one more thing I think we need to talk about."

"What?"

"Kissing."

Justin smiled and moved closer to Sarah. "Yeah?" He was amused at the innocent, flushed look on her face.

"Not kissing."

"Oh, and why's that?"

"I don't think it's a good idea. You have an assignment to do and I don't want to get in the way of that."

Justin wrapped his arms around her waist and pulled her to him, a whisper at a time. "You don't want to kiss me?" He nipped at her bottom lip.

"I didn't say that. Yes . . . no." Sarah stepped back. "No. I don't want to kiss you. I don't think it's a good idea."

"You're not a very good liar." Justin reached out and brushed the pad of his thumb across her lips. He smiled when her eyes fluttered at his touch. "And you're not in my way."

Damn. Sarah let out the breath she was holding as he walked out of the room. *You handled that really well,* she chastised herself. *Why didn't you just say, "Hey, Justin throw me on the carpet and do what you will." You might as well have. And besides, don't you remember from psychology that the thing people want most is in the world is the thing they can't have?*

"I'm surprised he even left the room," she muttered as she walked to the kitchen.

While Sarah mulled over the idea of making a fresh pot of coffee, she remembered there was something else she wanted to ask Justin. She thought it a little odd that his editor wanted to know what she looked like and made a mental note to ask later.

Justin wandered around his room, after his shower, sort of killing time so he didn't have to go down and face the woman in the kitchen. He wanted to know if Helen was responsible for his father's death. He wanted to know how she was. All he had to go on was a letter from Helen in an Alabama prison envelope date stamped *received* the day he died. If she were responsible, Sarah would be hurt. He hadn't thought of that. Didn't want that. *God, this doesn't even make sense. I just need to stick to my original plan and get this over with as soon as possible.*

Sarah decided that making coffee was just an avoidance ploy. She made herself sit at the table, flip to a new page in her notebook so she could take notes, and start the player.

Her mom's voice still sounded angry and mean, but soon Sarah could let the private investigator part of herself take over. And eventually it was as if she was just listening to some surveillance tapes, trying to unravel the clues to a mystery.

The people on the tape—her mom and, Sarah guessed, her mother's cellmate—were having a conversation. They were talking about various jobs in the prison and who was assigned to what and why, nothing really interesting until her mom asked the other woman where she went at night and why others girls went with her.

"That's none of your damn business. You just work on scrubbing those pissers every day and don't worry about the rest of us."

Sarah double checked her notes on the Mary Freeman Women's Prison in Alabama and found no reason for prisoners to be gone at night.

"I wonder where they went?" Sarah asked aloud to the empty kitchen. "And why?"

CHAPTER 5

Sarah backtracked to play that piece again for Justin when he came in.

"Further on, it sounds like some of the inmates disappear for days at a time."

"It was probably just a fluke thing."

"I don't know. My mom had pretty good instincts. I listened to this whole thing, but nothing really popped out. It was just information on the layout of the prison and different schedules of who worked where.

"Well, let's listen to a few more," Justin said as he sat down next to Sarah and tried to ignore the scent of her hair. It had been hard enough standing under the spray of hot water, looking at her bottle of shampoo, but sitting here next to her, knowing that her hands had been full of the soapy mixture, lathering it, some of it slipping, sliding down her . . . my God! *This is getting out of hand,* Justin thought and slid his chair away from her and grabbed a pad to take notes on.

"Ready then?" Sarah asked and wondered at the cross look in Justin's eyes.

"Yeah."

They listened to more of the recordings, but only a few things were really noteworthy concerning where the women went, but otherwise it was just a report of the miserable conditions the prisoners had to live with.

"I can't believe anyone would put themselves through all that." Sarah shook her head and sipped her cold coffee.

"She was a reporter with a story to tell. The piece she did on the prison in Louisiana sure changed life for those prisoners."

"It's not like I think it should be a walk in the park for them, but I don't think rat- and disease-infested facilities are okay, either."

"My dad used to say that Freeman Prison was "one frog's hop away from hell." But I guess it's a lot better than it used to be."

"That's only the second time I've heard you mention your dad. What was he like?" Sarah asked. "If you don't mind? I'd like to know. I don't ever really remember Mom talking about him, but I was only sixteen when she died."

"I don't mind. I mean I was relatively young when he died, but there were some real specific things I remember about him." In Justin's mind, he could see his father sitting tall with pride and being in total command of his courtroom. "He was fair. He thought if someone committed a crime, they ought to pay for it. And he didn't mince words. Not even at home." Justin could almost hear him hollering up to his room, "Boy, you get your butt in the kitchen and help your mama do the dishes." The memory made him smile. The next made him sad. "He was a good man and that made him an even better dad and husband. There wasn't anything he wouldn't do to protect his family . . . or the people he loved."

Sarah wanted to know how he died but figured that was really too personal. "I'm sorry. I didn't mean to make you sad. I just got to thinking that your dad had to be a good man . . . to raise such a—Anyway, I never did thank you for going out into the storm after me." Sarah looked into his eyes. "So thanks."

Justin raised his eyebrow in her direction. What was she getting at? "Such a what, Sarah?"

"I don't know. A good guy, I guess." Sarah looked at the player; it had stopped. "Do you want to listen to the next recording?"

"Sure." Justin didn't want to push it, but he couldn't help but feel good that she thought he was a good man. That made him smile, and it kicked his guilt into overdrive.

"We only have three left. I hope this gives us some sort of clue." Sarah pressed start on the player.

"You know we could take a rest. I don't know what we can do to solve this. It's almost fifteen years old. I doubt we'll find anything that will tell us why the prisoners were disappearing."

"I know, but I feel like my mom was on to something. And I want to set it right. For her. Finish what she didn't get to."

"It's just that this kind a thing happens all the—," Justin stopped at hearing Helen's whispered voice.

Eric, I think I stumbled onto something today. It was a business card from a hotel in Atlanta. I put it in Sarah's lamp that I sent for her birthday. Can you take it out before you give it to her.

"Do you think he took it out?" Justin stopped the player.

"No. It says on his inventory that he hadn't listened to this recording yet."

Justin picked up the list of notes Eric had taken.

"He usually kept up with everything, but if I remember right, he had a friend who was ill. Whenever he wasn't at work or with me, he was with his friend. Aunt Lainey even stayed with us for a while. And then after Mom died, he couldn't do it anymore."

"Do you have the lamp?"

"Yeah. I had Dad bring it out here. It hurt too much to have it in my room," Sarah said as she went to the guestroom on the first floor.

"While you get the lamp, I'm going—" Justin broke off as he walked into the room after Sarah. Seeing her lying across the bed and reaching behind the nightstand to unplug the electric cord, had Justin swallowing the rest of his sentence.

"What?" Sarah asked as she sat up.

Splash some water in my face, ice water. Justin shook his head. "Is that it?"

"Yeah." Sarah looked at him. "What's the matter?"

"Nothing."

Sarah immediately felt the change in the air. It was as if it radiated static. Justin stood with his arms folded, leaning against the doorframe. Sarah sat at the edge of the bed. Her gray eyes searched his blue ones. The need she saw in them looked very much like anger. She looked away. Pulling off the base of the lamp, she could still feel Justin's intense gaze and willed her hands not to tremble. She felt relieved when she found the business card curled up in the center beam.

"The Confederate Regency, Atlanta's Finest."

"What's it say on the back?"

Sarah flipped the card over and read her mom's precise handwriting, "Ask TJB about SN and BL. I wonder who TJB is?"

"Thomas Justin Breslow is my father." Anger and pain slammed through Justin, so strong and so fierce he had to take a deep breath to bear it.

*

"That was Annie. She says she's faxing the list of everyone who worked at the prison during the time my mom was there." Sarah said as she hung the phone up and looked at Justin. She was pleased to see the anger from yesterday gone.

Justin sat with his arms crossed and his legs stretched out before him. Their notes, cold coffee cups, and crumpled papers with dead-end theories covered the table behind him. Sarah's eyes couldn't help themselves. Any woman's eyes would enjoy the scene before her. They traveled over his bare feet, up his well-muscled legs, over his waist; they paused just a moment to admire his arms, and then they skimmed his jaw, his cheek, and finally settled on his eyes. Which were shining with humor at her assessment. Damn! She cursed her libido. He smiled as her slippered feet stomped to the sink. Turning her back on him, she grabbed the coffeepot.

"Well, that should give us some answers." When the fax machine beeped, Justin said, "I'll go get those pages."

Sarah dumped out the old coffee and rinsed the pot without focused thought. She measured the beans into the grinder, pressed the lid, and was glad when the chopping began.

I've got to get a grip, she thought to herself. *I can't go around looking at him like that. I can't notice that he wore a black shirt today rather than a white one, or that his jeans are faded in all the right places, or that his feet are sexy. Who would've thought toes could be so . . . damn!*

"She sent a partial inmate list too. There's a note saying that's all she could get for now." Justin said.

Sarah jumped. She didn't know how long he'd been standing in the doorway of the kitchen, watching her, but seeing her flustered was undoubtedly great for his ego. "Oh yeah?" She looked at the fine powder she'd made out of the beans and rolled her eyes. *This is good though. A strong cup of coffee is what I need*, she decided.

Justin studied the pages in his hand while the coffee brewed. When it was done, she sat down at the table, mug before her. He took a seat beside her.

"SN and BL," she said, thinking of the writing on the card they'd found last night. "I wonder how long it will take us to figure out who they are?"

"Not long." Justin said as he pointed with the tip of his highlighter. "SN looks like the prison director and BL looks to be the warden. My dad knew Newell."

"Simon Newell and Becket Larson." Sarah looked closer at the list. She sensed rather than saw Justin's arm move to the back of her chair. She knew if she sat back, his hand would brush her hair. But instead of commenting on it, she looked at the yellow circles surrounding Simon and Becket's names. "How would your dad know anything about the prison director?"

"Simon was my dad's best friend from college. He'd come around at least once a month to visit and tell stories." Justin remembered a tall man, not as tall as his father, who would bring ice cream and bananas in the summer for dessert. He could remember laughing at his off color jokes and listening to his opinions on the legal system. Come to think of it, Justin held some of the same opinions. "But I don't know who Becket is."

The thrill of finding the truth to an unanswered question brought a smile to Sarah's face. "Well, we have one more recording to listen to. If that doesn't help us, then we'll go ask Simon and Becket what they know. I'll call Annie so she can find out where they both live."

"Simon lives in Texas near my grandfather."

"Great. I'll just call her about Becket then." Sarah jumped up to get the phone.

While Sarah's voice gave the facts about what they'd found to Annie, Justin scrubbed his face. Seeing the smile on Sarah's face warmed his insides. It was intoxicating to see that excited flash in her eyes. But, as an agent, he was wary. He'd seen too many good investigators lose their lives because the excitement of the moment overpowered them. Which brought him back to being a man. He wanted to protect Sarah, from herself if that was necessary. That wasn't in his plans at all.

"Annie's on the track-down," Sarah said. "So let's listen to that recording." When Sarah sat down, she noticed the dark look on Justin's face. "What's the matter?"

"Nothing."

"Right."

"Just old memories I have to deal with," Justin lied.

"We can talk about them if—"

"I don't. Let's get this over with." Justin pressed play.

Scuffling and scraping could be heard on the tape. Justin picked up the player to see if there was a problem with it but set it down when another voice started talking.

"Listen to me. Don't you start asking questions around here. You may not like the answers you find."

"You're a bitch, Sherry, you know that?" Helen replied. *"Now let go of me."*

"Yeah. I'm a bitch all right. Just do your time and you might get the hell out of here alive."

Empty static followed. Justin skipped forward looking for more, but there was nothing.

"This is a new chip," Sarah said as she took it out of the player. "Why did she send it with only this on it?"

"Don't know, but she told us a name. Sherry." Justin picked up the inmate list.

"Is a Sherry on there?" Sarah leaned closer to him.

Justin ignored the sweet, spring, vanilla scent of her. He wanted to block out the sound of her voice, her breathing. He read the names that began with, "S…Sandy…Sally…Sharon…Shirley…Shelley… no Sherry."

"Who is she?" Sarah sat back against her chair, feeling deflated at the prospect of facing another dead end.

"Well, it looks like we're off to Alabama. Maybe that'll give us some answers. We need to get a full inmate list too. That might help." Justin hoped it would. He needed to be somewhere else. Being cooped up with Sarah in this place was beginning to wear on him. He was afraid of what he would do if they stayed. He glanced over and saw her excited smile. Yes, he was definitely afraid.

CHAPTER 6

"Annie said she arranged for a rental car to be there when we land." Sarah stretched and dug in her carry-on for a piece of gum. "She told Dad where we're headed too so he doesn't worry. He suggested that we us aliases. Do you think we should?"

"Probably," Justin muttered, totally exhausted. He'd thought a red-eye flight was a good thing. He'd thought they'd both get settled in their seats and then sleep the whole way to Montgomery. He'd just assumed that the flight would be straight through with maybe one layover. That's what you get for assuming. He groaned and shifted in his seat.

He should have looked into the flight arrangements instead of letting Annie handle it. Because it became very evident in Detroit, their first layover, that Sarah loved them. She loved the airports, the foods, the people—just all of it.

In Charlotte, she'd squealed with delight when she saw a woman with a dog and went over and sat beside her. He'd tried to get her attention and tell her that wasn't what you did in airports, or anywhere for that matter, but right away she began talking to the woman, but not with her voice. He was startled when he saw her fingers moving rapidly, her facial expressions shifting, indicating how much she liked the dog. The woman spoke right back with questions and answers of her own. He noticed them gesturing toward him, but he only waved and went back to reading his magazine and rocking in his white rocking chair. At least that's one good thing about this airport.

"I didn't know you knew sign language," Justin said when she sat down in the chair next to him.

"Yeah, it's one of my languages." Sarah waved as the woman moved to greet one of the exiting passengers. "She's meeting her daughter, and they're going on vacation together. Isn't that nice?" Sarah smiled as she watched them hug.

"One of your languages? What's another one?"

"French."

"Really?" Justin sat up and massaged his chin. "So what'd she say about me?"

Sarah laughed, "Oh, just that my husband was very lucky that I like animals."

"What!"

"But I told her you weren't my husband," Sarah said quickly.

"Oh." Justin didn't especially know what to do with the bafflement he felt. Husband? Why the hell would anyone assume that?

Hours later, Justin vaguely heard the pilot over the loudspeaker, informing the passengers to put their seat belts on in preparation for landing at Montgomery Regional Airport. He could still feel the low hum in the pit of his stomach when he thought about what the lady in Charlotte had said. And then looking over, seeing Sarah rubbing her sleepy eyes made him clench his teeth, becoming all the more determined to forget about it.

"Do you want to go to the prison now, or do you want to rest first?" Sarah looked at her watch, noting that it was after lunchtime.

"I don't care. I'm kind of tired. But we can grab something to eat and then go if you want." Which wasn't true, tired was not the word. They'd been traveling all night and half the day. He was exhausted.

"Great." Sarah smiled.

Apparently, she felt completely refreshed and was looking forward to finding out who Becket Larson and that Sherry girl were. Gathering her things, she stepped out onto the walkway, wanting to get off the plane as soon as possible.

Justin huffed out his breath and contained himself from rolling his eyes.

"My wife's like that, too," said a voice behind Justin.

"What?" Justin looked at the guy as he pulled his carryon out of the bin above him.

"My wife. She can fly all night and feel completely ready to go. Not me. I have to sleep first."

Justin glared at him and raised his left hand. He wiggled his fingers in front of the guy's face, wanting to make sure he saw there wasn't a ring.

"Oh, sorry. Girlfriend then."

"Yeah, whatever." Justin walked off down the aisle. What is it with people at airports, anyway? Why do they always talk to you about things that are none of their damn business?

Finding Sarah was easy. She'd already found baggage claim and was waiting with her arms crossed, smiling at him. Justin saw her excitement and noticed her foot tapping, which reminded him that he needed to talk to her about keeping her head on her shoulders and that sometimes things weren't as they seemed and to be careful!

Sarah watched Justin make his way toward her and thought, that in the time that she'd known him, he always looked well put together. Well, as well as a T-shirt and blue jeans would allow. But today was a surprise to her. He still looked good. His hair may have been a little mussed, but that only made him more handsome, if that were possible. She would have expected all of him to be wrinkled and wadded as she was, but no. He looked as if he'd just taken a quick hop from one city to another instead of the all-night flight across the United States.

She could tell by looking around his eyes that he was tired, but that was only because she knew him. She smiled about it as he stopped to help a woman pick up souvenirs she'd dropped, probably ones she'd bought for all her grandkids back in Arizona or something, but the smile froze on Sarah's face when she felt her stomach hitch and flip. *You will not do this, Sarah, she lectured herself. This is no time to think about your attraction to him and what that might lead to. We're busy. We have things to do.*

It's not like that. I just like him, she argued with herself. *He's a good man. Why wouldn't I?*

Working out the reason why she reacted the way she did helped, but it didn't keep Justin from asking what was wrong once he reached her.

"Nothing. I guess I'm just hungry." Sarah smiled. Her stomach didn't flip this time. Maybe it had been just a onetime thing. Good.

"Well, let's get that car and find some food."

*

Having a meal inside of them improved both of their spirits and by the time they drove north to Freeman City, they were ready for exploring.

"Oh, my God," Sarah whispered as they drove past the dilapidated, Welcome to Freeman City sign. "Look at this place."

The dripping heat of the afternoon seemed to suck what life there was from the day. The tall grasses along the roadside bent their wilting heads to the earth. Shards of broken glass glinted in the sun on the other side of the highway's white line. *It's a worn-out place,* was all Sarah could think.

"This is horrible," she said.

"You're not kidding," Justin responded.

Sarah shook her head as she continued to look out the window. The scene before her was such a contrast to anything she'd ever known. When she thought of the South, she thought of *Gone with the Wind,* her mother's favorite movie. Beautiful homes with wide expanses of lawn and tall, white pillars. She didn't think of this. She'd seen pictures of places like this, but they'd been old pictures. It was hard to believe that people lived in what she was looking at. She thought she'd see not only those big plantation houses, but typical suburban houses as well. Houses that she was used to seeing, maybe brick with white trim or painted, cute houses tucked under some trees. But everything here was different than what she expected.

As they drove around the next bend, she saw a house that startled her. A sinking roof barely covered the patched boards of a small dwelling. Gnarly, winding vines grew up and through an old worn-out truck with the windows broken out. A sad willow tree hung in the stifling heat. At first glance, it didn't look as if anyone lived there. But seeing a long floppy-eared dog and an ancient man in overalls resting in the shade of the porch said she was wrong.

This is the South no one talks about, she thought. *But this is what we should see. So that we know there are places in our own country that need us.* At that moment, Sarah knew why her mother had done what she did. It wasn't for the Pulitzer that might grace her career. It was for the people of her homeland. She'd always heard her mother talk with pride about the people of the South, their giving nature, their kind smiles, and the humor they found in their own lives.

Now, as she looked out her window at the roadside shadowed by tall leafy trees and sprinkled with sunlight, she saw the rundown houses and abandoned cars differently. She smiled as she saw a group of kids playing baseball in an empty lot. She smiled and waved and was pleased to see them stop and do the same.

"How about we find that hotel Annie put us in first and then go out to the prison?" Justin suggested.

"Sure." Sarah dug through her bag. "It's called The Governor."

"Did she give directions?"

"No." Sarah looked at Annie's notes on the fax in her hands and read it aloud, "The hotel manager said there would be no problem finding the hotel. Just follow the road into town and you'll see it." Sarah looked over at Justin, who had an amazed look on his face.

"I'll be damned," he said. "Will you look at that!" Justin drove into the parking lot and turned off the car.

A brick building towered to the sky, dwarfing all that was around it. Shining, white-washed shutters looked down on the town. A long, narrow span of grass circled and twined with yards of sidewalks, each linking one small flower garden with another.

Roses of every shape and color grew from the well-tended beds.

"Wow. No wonder it's called The Governor." Sarah said as she got out. A hot blast of air hit her as if she'd just stepped into a very humid furnace. The pungent aroma of roses filled her nose. The scent was nearly too sweet.

She was thankful the foyer in the hotel was air-conditioned.

"We're Adam Plummer and Abigail Barry checking in," Sarah said giving the alternate names Annie had made their reservations under to the man behind the counter.

The man's pressed shirt and gold nametag, which showed William, Hotel Manager, went well with the marbled floors and lofty white walls.

"This sure is a nice hotel," Justin said as he leaned on the counter.

"Yes, sir," The man said in a clipped manner. "But there is a small problem with your rooms."

"Problem?" Sarah asked.

"The air-conditioning is out in one room." The man shuffled through his papers. "And the shower is out in the other. I am sorry. We are in the process of renovating, and there's been an incident." He said each word slow and practiced.

"Can we have other rooms?" Justin asked.

"No, sir."

Sarah knew he went on to explain why they couldn't, but his Alabama accent was so thick, she couldn't understand him. But Justin stood there and chattered away with the guy in an accent just as thick. Where did *that* come from, she wondered. And she was really curious when they started laughing. What could they be laughing about?

"Well, we'll just stay here," Justin said in the voice Sarah recognized.

"Thank you, sir."

Justin nodded and walked away, pulling his suitcase.

Sarah grabbed hers and followed Justin down a long corridor. "Are there two other rooms?"

"No."

"There has to be at least a hundred rooms in this place."

"There's a group of people in town and they have a bunch of them."

"Another hotel then?"

We'd have to go back to Montgomery.

"So what rooms do we have?"

Justin nodded toward a door and handed her the key.

Sarah grabbed it, opened the door, and was blasted by hot, stale air. "Augh! It smells like dirty feet." She went over to the window, opened it, and even hotter air came in. "Good grief!" she said and slammed the window closed.

"Here," Justin pointed to an attaching door. "My room's probably better."

"Your room?" Sarah followed Justin through the open door. Cool air met her senses. Relief. "Why is this your room?" Sarah shut the door on the hot air.

"My shower doesn't work. And I figured with you being the woman, you'd want the shower."

"That's a sexist remark." Sarah scowled and crossed her arms.

"Is it true?"

"Well, yes. But I don't want that room. It's sticky and hot and it smells. Let's just go back to Montgomery. We can find a hotel there."

"If you want. But it took us about two hours to get here. Are you sure you want to do that?" Justin hoped not. He was dog-tired. The plane trip across the country, the too-close proximity to Sarah; it was exhausting.

"Fine, we'll stay here. But can William send up a roll-away? 'Cause I'm not sleeping in there." Sarah pointed to the other room and made an ugly face.

"No. They're all being used."

"Well, where are you going to sleep?" Sarah asked as she started putting clothes away in the oak dresser beside the bed.

Justin shook his head. "On the bed, sweetheart." He dropped his duffle on the floor. "Right now." He shrugged out of his T-shirt, kicked off his shoes, and flopped on the bed.

"Good grief," Sarah said, thinking that phrase should be her mantra, especially when she heard Justin snore and said it again. After she finished with her clothes, she was anxious to get going. First things first. She wanted to take a shower but crinkled her nose at the other room's door. The idea of a fresh outfit was so appealing she decided taking a shower in the stinking, hot room would be worth it. She felt silly dancing back and forth from one room to another, holding her nose, washing up, and getting dressed, all the while making sure she didn't wake Justin or let any hot air invade the cool room where he slept. With that done, she grabbed the keys and left to find the prison. She couldn't wait to see what she could dig up.

CHAPTER 7

Driving out of town on the same road she and Justin had driven coming into town, Sarah found the prison easily. It was the only structure within five miles of anything. The long L-shaped building, with tall, wire fences topped by nasty, razor-wire curls, looked as if it had grown up out of the ground. Sarah drove around it and followed a winding road into a well-lit parking area. It was beginning to get dark.

She didn't plan on going inside tonight. Couldn't have at any rate. She needed the prison inspector badges that Annie had prepared for her and Justin to use. Sarah just wanted to look around. "Know as much as possible about an opponent" was a leftover thought from track in high school. Tonight, on this case, with every case, she was not on the home team. In the parking lot across from the main entrance of the prison, Sarah turned the car off and got out, taking note of the mounted security cameras tracking her every move. Looking along the narrow dimly lit sidewalk and up to the entrance, Sarah couldn't help but wonder what it had been like for her mother to be hand-cuffed and escorted through the doors as a prisoner. No one, not even the warden, had known she wasn't a convict. It must have been terrifying, Sarah thought.

"How could my dad let her do it?" she whispered and walked to the other end of the parking lot toward a two-story brick building looking lonely in the eerie twilight.

A large, historical-site sign had two spotlights shining on it. Sarah stepped forward and read the inscription.

"Fob Wyatt Piskin, first Governor of Alabama, always joked that being married to his wife, Mary Freeman, was like being incarcerated. So, in 1818 when the first brick was laid, he named it after her. In 1820, when the prison was completed, it was the first Women's

Correctional Facility in the State of Alabama. This building is the original structure and the new facility still holds the same name."

"Interesting bit of information," Sarah said and got back in her car. "Wonder what else I can find out." She pulled out of the parking lot and headed back to town planning to make a few more stops before being done for the night.

By the time Sarah got back to the hotel, she'd learned that The Governor was such a nice place because when old Piskin died, he left a huge sum of money for the continual restoration and upkeep of his hotel. Which was sort of funny, Sarah thought, but more importantly, she'd learned his family still ran it. That was wonderful information, because she had, right at her fingertips, a great resource. They'd been here a long time. She just had to figure out how to get them to talk to her.

The other bit she'd found out was that the group of people taking up half the hotel was a prison-inspection team. That was going to put a hitch in their original plan.

She was smiling, enjoying the challenge of trying to resolve a problem, when she twisted the key in the door of the hotel room. She had no time to react or defend. She was yanked inside the room.

"Where the hell have you been?" Justin's voice was deep and angry.

Sarah felt his breath on her face. But in the shadowy room she could barely see him.

*

"I was out, doing research."

He was angry and scared, but he focused on the anger now and shook her. "Don't you ever do that again! This isn't a goddamn game."

"I know that. Let go of me. Now!" Sarah yelled.

Justin stepped back.

"What's the matter with you?" Sarah straightened her shirt.

"It's not safe out there by yourself."

"What do you mean, not safe. I was perfectly fine. I only saw a few people."

"That's not counting the ones who saw you. For God's sake, look at you. You're all dressed up in your fancy city clothes and you smell good. You're a goddamn gold mine."

"You're acting like it's the nineteen-thirties or something!"

"You don't know what goes on down here."

"Oh, yeah, and you do?"

Justin thought about his last assignment. The little girl he was supposed to find who wasn't so little. And when he found her, she didn't look a thing like her glossy senior picture. She was bloody, beaten, raped, and very much dead.

"Yeah, I do!" Justin couldn't take any of it anymore. The lack of sleep, his conflicting feelings over Sarah, the need for her were all piled as high as any man could take. Added to that was all the worrying he'd done and the helplessness he felt being stuck here in the hotel room, not knowing if she was safe or where she was. He would've called the police, but he didn't want to alert anyone that they were here. So he had to wait. Now he was done waiting.

Sarah started to talk, but whatever she would've said was lost as Justin approached her. Her eyes grew dark and wary, but she didn't stop him as he moved in close. Her mouth opened a bit and her breathing quickened. Slowly, he pinned her against the wall and brought his head down to hers, crushing her lips with his. She mewed, but moved sinuously against him, making her need as apparent as his.

He'd tried to keep his hands off her, but now all he could think about was all the places he wanted to touch. *God, she's perfect,* he thought. And he pressed his body to hers until he could feel the pounding of her heart through her shirt.

"You scared me," Justin whispered.

"I'm sorry." Sarah swallowed against the frantically building pressure in her throat.

His lips molded to hers.

Her body instantly reacted. There was no time to think. She felt as if she were at the mercy of a lightning bolt as each hot strike of fire shot through her. His hands were everywhere, molding her, shaping her. She wound her fingers through his hair, latching on and guiding his mouth on hers.

He felt like an animal was prowling inside him. He coaxed her tongue with his and found it craving more. He gave more, demanded more. His hands trailed up her hips to her breasts. He made his fingers lazy as they explored, relishing the fact that they strained against his palm.

"Justin," Sarah breathed.

"Hmmm?" He didn't move away. He just changed the angle of the kiss and pulled her legs up and around him.

He knew he moaned when he felt the heat of her core come in contact with his.

Sarah unclenched her fingers in his hair and moved her hands down. Feeling his muscles bunch and move on his back thrilled her. She spent several seconds enjoying the feeling, but soon realized that his back was bare. That was all it took to jolt her out of the kiss.

"Justin!"

"What?"

"You're not wearing a shirt." She knew that sounded stupid, but she couldn't quite think yet.

"So?" His voice was bleary like his vision. He felt as if he was drowning in a dark lake and was looking for the light.

"So put me down." Sarah still felt heat and need as her feet slid slowly to the ground. It wouldn't take very much to pull her back into another scrambling kiss.

"You're down." Justin grinned and nipped at her bottom lip with his teeth. "You worried me."

"That's a heck of way to show me you were worried." Sarah

tried to move away from him, but he kept her pinned. "And I was perfectly safe."

"This time." Justin held her face with his hands. "Don't do it again, Sarah."

*

"Well, you might as well tell me what you did," Justin said. "Since we're not going to get any sleep."

It had been decided, by Sarah, that they would share the same bed in the air-conditioned room, but she'd got the extra blanket off the shelf in the closet, rolled it and stuck it in the middle of the bed. With a firm, stay-on-your-own-side look.

"I went to the prison first and just looked around outside." Sarah twirled the fringe from the bedspread in her finger. "I didn't see much."

"What else?" Justin had his hands clasped in his lap. If he could have stood back and looked, the scene would have been funny. Two fully grown people were sitting on a small bed in a tastefully decorated hotel room in the deep South with only a rolled-up blanket between them. He would have howled with laughter, in fact. He knew the guys at the Bureau would never let him live it down if they knew. But instead he listened intently as Sarah went on with her story.

"Then I went to a bar or little restaurant downtown—"

"You what!" Justin shook his head. "Never mind. Go on."

"Anyway, when I was at the restaurant, I overheard some old timers talking. I didn't listen at first. I thought they were just gossiping about, you know, what old timers gossip about, but then I heard them mention prison inspections. So I ordered some pie and stayed a while."

"What'd they say?" Justin sat up.

"Through all their ums and ahs, I learned that the present governor, Virginia Evans, is cracking down on mistreatment of inmates and has sent out teams of inspectors to evaluate each state prison. Freeman Prison is one of them."

"Damn, that's gonna mess this whole deal up. Did they happen to mention when the inspectors are due at Freeman?"

"Sort of. I don't know if they knew for sure or if they were just making bets. But I think the day after tomorrow."

"That gives us one day."

"I think we can do it. All we need are the recording devices my mom hid in the kitchen, bathroom, and in her cell."

"And we need to know who her cell mate was."

"Right." Sarah huddled down into the covers, knowing that she needed to sleep but not wanting to; she was excited for tomorrow. "Good night, Justin," she whispered and closed her eyes.

"'Night." Justin rolled over and punched his feather pillow a couple of times. But it didn't make him feel better. He thought about his dad's saying, "Freeman's one frog's hop away from hell." Justin figured in this instance it could mean two things. One, they were in for a hell of a surprise tomorrow. This whole trip may turn into more than they'd bargained for. And two, he knew he was in hell right now. Sarah's soft body was just a few inches away, and he couldn't do anything about it. He stared at the light across the street until his eyes started to sting.

*

Across town, in the backroom of a dimly lit bar, stood a man with a towel tied around his middle. Smoke from the customers who sat drinking their beers seeped underneath the door and spilled around its edges. The sickening smell of seafood, deep fried in grease, coated every inch of space. The man saw someone he'd known for years, but hadn't seen for more than a decade. He felt shock, when the cloaked figure walked to the back of his bar.

"What the hell do you want?" The man asked the figure, who wore a long overcoat and hat.

The figure's gloved hand pulled a pad of paper from the pocket of the coat and wrote on the clean white sheet. *There are two people in town who could ruin everything.*

"It's been almost twenty years. We can't be traced." Sweat beaded on his upper lip and the man wiped it away with his makeshift apron.

The gloved hand wrote again. *You just watch them!*

"Fine. Where are they?" The man grew impatient.

At The Governor.

"I'll watch. Now get the hell outta here!" The man demanded in a hoarse whisper.

The figure tucked the notepad back in the coat, turned, walked out the door, and disappeared into the night.

The man in the apron watched the figure go. He'd often wondered who that guy was. He'd never seen his face, or any inch of skin, for that matter. He'd even tossed around the idea that it might be a woman, but he didn't think a woman could be as ruthless and cold-blooded as this guy. Probably a dirty politician or something, thought Becket Larson as he scratched his beard and went back in to serve his customers.

CHAPTER 8

"Sarah, listen. Before we go to the prison, there's something I want you to think about." Justin sat on the edge of the bed and finished tying his shoes.

In the light of day, after a few hours of sleep, the hotel room looked nicer than it had yesterday. The walls were taller and brighter. The pictures scattered about the room were elegant prints of Southern scenes, long fields of cotton swaying in the breeze, wide rolling lawns hugging the edge of a commanding white plantation home, magnolia trees lit by the moon

"What?" Sarah asked from where she sat at the table going over her notes.

Justin waited to talk until she looked up. He wanted her to take this seriously. When she did, he said, "You know, not everything's the way it looks." He paused at her confused look. "I've been an investigative reporter for a long time and I . . . run across people all the time who aren't who they say they are." *Yeah, like you.* Justin cringed. "I know this isn't making much sense, but I just want you to be careful who you trust and who you share information with."

"Geez, Justin, you sound like my dad. When he called this morning, he said the same exact thing." Sarah put her papers in her satchel and buckled it. "You know, I've been doing this for years, too. And it all hasn't been scandals on paper and research. I've been in some tricky situations." Sarah patted him on the shoulder. "But don't worry. I think quick on my feet."

"That's what I'm worried about," Justin muttered as Sarah left, taking her bag out to the car. He had stood to follow her, when his phone rang. Looking at the caller ID, he smiled.

"Hey Pat, what's going on?"

"Nothing here, buddy. Same as always. Just wondering what you're up to."

"We're in Freeman City, Alabama."

"What the hell for?"

"Sarah decided she needed to do a little research on a case." Justin didn't want to say too much more because there was never any way to know who might be listening.

Pat recognized the tactic. "You need anything?"

"Not as yet, but I'll keep you posted." Justin paused when Sarah came back in. "Yup, next week sounds great. I'll have that first draft to you by then. Bye." Hell, why'd he say next week? How in the hell was he going to write a believable piece on Helen Johnson in seven days when he knew he couldn't write a bad one in twenty?

"Was that your editor?"

"Yeah. He wants to see a first draft soon. So I've got to get back to my computer pretty soon." Brilliant idea, Breslow. Justin mentally patted himself on the back. He didn't have a way to write the piece here, so no worries about that.

"Where's your computer?"

"Dallas." Justin smiled. A long way away from here.

"Maybe when we're done here, we can go to Dallas. Anyway, you said you'd let me read anything before you sent it in. And we can maybe go visit your dad's college buddy, Simon Newell."

"Right." Justin nodded and wanted to kick himself. "Sounds like a good idea."

*

Pulling out of the hotel parking lot, Justin looked in the rearview mirror. He hadn't seen anyone suspicious, but it didn't hurt to be wary.

Sarah sipped her coffee in her carryout cup from the hotel. She hadn't realized that pie at midnight wouldn't hold anyone over till morning and she was hungry. So she was glad to see the array of choices the hotel had for their breakfast. Actually, it was more like an all-you-can-eat wonderland of food. Beyond the normal breakfast foods of eggs and toast, there were piles of bacon and sausage and ham. She couldn't resist the beautiful arrangement of hash browns and scooped a few on her plate. She did skip the biscuits and gravy, even though the biscuits looked buttery and flaky. The fruit was ripe and delicious, especially the cantaloupe.

It was kind of strange to sit across from Justin in a hotel dining room, eating eggs and toast. Not that they hadn't eaten breakfast together before, but as she sat there this morning, she couldn't quite get over the fact that they felt like a team. That he would go where she went and she would do the same for him. It felt good to know it. Letting her thoughts wander, she remembered something she'd wanted to ask him. "Why would your editor want to know what I look like?"

"What? Why would you think that?"

"When we were in Oregon, I overheard you say, 'she looks like her picture,' and I just wondered why your editor would want to know."

"Because he's an idiot." Justin laughed.

"What?"

"He and I've been friends all of our lives, practically. When my family and I moved to town from the ranch, he lived four houses down from us. We went to college together, joined the B—joined the basketball team together." *Whew, talk about thinking quick on your feet. You're the idiot.*

"You played basketball in college?" Sarah asked, eyes narrowing.

Justin looked away from the question in them, thinking she must be wondering about him stumbling over his words. "No, just a local block league. No uniforms or anything. We used to round up all the players and have playoffs. It was fun."

"But that still doesn't answer my first question."

"Right. Well, it's the same old story. I was best man at his wedding. He and his wife just had a baby, and they couldn't be happier, so of course, he wants to see his best friend meet the right girl, settle down. You know?"

"Yeah." Sarah laughed. He relaxed at the sound, glad he seemed to have allayed her suspicions. "Sounds just like Annie. She's worked for me since I could afford to pay her salary, and she's hounded me about finding a nice guy since before that."

"Friends are sometimes a pain in the neck."

Sarah nodded. "So no right girl for you out there?"

"If she is, I haven't met her yet." Justin smiled and looked at Sarah. *Or maybe I have,* Justin thought and almost choked on his own tongue. *Where the hell did that come from?* He recovered enough to find his voice. "What about you. Any guys out there wearing the *perfect* suit?"

"I haven't met him yet, either." Sarah drank the last of her coffee and glanced at Justin from beneath her eyelashes.

At the look, Justin felt himself flush. *Time to stop this right here.* He drained his coffee and stood up. "So let's go be prison inspectors."

*

Justin stopped the car in a visitor parking space at the Freeman Prison.

"See, that's where I read about Alabama's first governor." Sarah pointed to the historical sign.

Justin had to resist the urge to shake her. He couldn't believe she'd been standing around in a prison parking lot in the middle of the damn night. "Interesting," was all he could manage.

Hopefully it would be easy to flash their fake prison-investigator badges and be let in. Perhaps the other prison inspectors being in town would add to their success. They'd planned each step they would take once they were inside.

The men standing at the entryway just nodded after seeing their badges and let them through. Once the buzzer sounded that opened the main entrance, they requested to see the room that held all the old filing. One of the guards led Sarah down a long passageway with offices on both sides. It reminded her of a military base with all its mysterious doors.

While Justin stood outside and occupied the guard with worthless questions, Sarah found the folder listing all the names of the people who worked at the prison when her mom was there, along with the inmate names, numbers, and the cell assignments. Not wanting to waste time finding the name of her mom's cellmate, she just tucked the list at the back of her clipboard

For what they needed next, they had to go into the prison itself. Sarah had never been in a prison before. Throughout her career, she'd had a few chances, but she could never bring herself to do it. The guard at the gate pressed a button, and the large bars slid almost noiselessly aside. Sarah and Justin walked in, followed by the guard. And the bars ominously shut behind them.

As they walked farther into the building, the first thing Sarah noticed was the air. It was stagnant. It was cool but damp. It smelled like stale human flesh and bleach. The next was the noise.

In the rows of cells following the main prison corridor, women all along both sides were dressed in the same gray uniform as the next. Some of them hooted and hollered and licked at the bars as she and Justin walked by. Some cowered at the edges of their bunks, hiding their eyes with their hands. Some spoke in innuendos, but most just came right out and said what they were thinking.

"Hey, will you look at that." A woman whistled as she saw Justin.

"I bet he's a real good fuck," another hollered.

"Do you think that bitch beside him can get him off?"

"No, but I sure to hell can. Come here and I'll show you what a real fuck feels like." The last woman peeled back her shirt and stuck her breasts between the bars while menacing laughter filled her eyes.

It wasn't exactly shock that had Sarah keeping her face forward, it was misery. Misery that her mother would willingly put herself into this situation, even if it were an assignment. She could have said no.

They only needed three things. They quickly went into the

kitchen, did a believable walk-through. Sarah, this time, kept the guard busy with technical questions dealing with nutrition for the women and the choices of food they had, while Justin stayed in the kitchen to search for the hidden receiver.

When Justin came through the double doors of the kitchen to meet up with her and the guard, shaking his head, Sarah wanted to go in and look for the receiver herself, but she was afraid of what the guard would think. She mentally checked that one off her list and moved on to the bathrooms.

They had to go to all the bathrooms to make the inspection look real and found the receiver in the second one. It was right where her mom said it would be, in the third stall. The hinges on the doors had been replaced before her mom was an inmate there. The holes from the old hinges had not been filled in. Sarah took the latex gloves out of her pocket that the guard gave her upon entry and pulled them snug. It was easy for her to fit her finger into the rusty painted over hole and pull out the receiver. She tucked it in the envelope at the back of her clipboard and walked to where Justin and the guard were, leaving the stench of body fluids mixed with ammonia-based cleaners behind.

Sarah knew going to the cell was going to be the hardest task. So far, she thought she'd done unbelievably well and had noticed the look of approval on Justin's face whenever it was her turn to play her role. She'd said the right things at the right moments and even joked a little with the guards as if she were truly a prison inspector, who wouldn't be shocked by anything.

But inside Sarah was moving from fury to despair with every step she took. She felt as if she didn't get out of here soon, she'd crumble. It was impossible to know what she'd feel as she walked the same steps her mother must have taken. She had no idea how horrible and how proud she'd feel in the same second.

"We want to check some of the cells," Justin told the guard as all three of them walked in the direction of where Helen had stayed. "We need to see a few that are empty and maybe one or two that are currently occupied."

"Sure enough, Mr. Plummer." The guard nodded. "Just tell me which occupied ones you want to see, and I'll have the inmates moved."

"Let's start with this one first." Justin pointed to Helen's old cell.

Sarah glanced in Justin's direction. He was flipping through the pages on his clipboard, asking questions. The guard in his stiffly ironed shirt looked eager to answer any question he could. To be helpful or to get them gone, Sarah couldn't be sure. She shrugged her shoulders and turned her focus back to the cell.

Standing outside cell number C17 was the hardest thing Sarah had ever done. Taking a step into the cell where her mother had died was the next.

Walking across the dimly lit room, Sarah could feel the coldness of the floor, of the place, seep up into her, chilling her. It seemed to take an eternity to reach the steel bunk where her mother had slept. Her legs moved at a creeping pace. Her quick eyes, which would've normally darted about, gathering facts, paused with shock. Under her feet, the concrete floor was littered with stains. Some were small, probably spit or droplets of old dried blood. There were a few that were large, as if there had been a pool of liquid. Sarah wondered what could have made those blots. Spilled coffee? Leaky pipe? Blood? Was it her mother's?

As Sarah slumped down on the edge of the mattress, her nose filled with the musty, old scent of it. Her hands felt its thinness through her gloves and the wadded, cotton texture beneath the coarse fabric. Her eyes moved around the empty cell, trying to imagine her mother sitting here, sleeping here, living here day after day, for weeks on end.

Her mom had sat at that tiny table writing her letters, telling her how proud she was to have a daughter as brave and fast as hers was. The letters always sounded as if she'd been on vacation or something lighthearted to match her tone. But no. She'd been here. Here in this hell of a place, where a fire had taken her life.

The idea of it overpowered Sarah's senses. As she pulled in her next breath, she could smell the choking, thick smoke that would have filled the cell as the fire burned. She could almost hear her mother's screaming as the flames ate at her clothing and seared her skin.

Sarah couldn't take it anymore. She had to get out. She closed her mind against the image of her mother's form as she huddled away from the wicked fire. Leaning across the bunk, she found the loosened end cap on the steel frame, just where her mother said it would be. Using her thumbnail, she pried off the cap. With shaking hands, she pulled the last receiver from the dark hole, blinking against the stinging in the back of her eyes.

"I have to go," Sarah whispered when she got to Justin's side. She felt as if she were suffocating and would have been glad for it, so powerful was the pain in her heart.

The deep misery evident in Sarah's eyes tore at him. He wanted to pull her into his arms, but they had a pretext to keep up. "Okay."

Sarah nodded, but she didn't say anything else.

"Well, I think that's all for today." Justin flipped through the clipboard in his hand and then looked at his watch. "We needed to see the warden today, but—"

"I can see if he's free to see you before you go," the guard said.

"No problem. I'll try to come back tomorrow and finish, but if not, I'll send another team in."

*

Justin had whispered all the nice words he could think of on the way to the car. He'd talked about rainbows and horses and fluffy clouds and chocolate, but nothing had penetrated the set look on Sarah's face. He'd helped her shaking body into the car and driven as fast as he could to the hotel.

Now Justin sat on the bed inside the hotel room, holding Sarah. "Sweetheart, come on. We're done. I know you're probably hungry." His heart ached as he looked at her. The woman he'd known was missing. The one curled up on his lap needed him, and he could do nothing for her. "Come on, baby. Stop crying," Justin begged. He didn't know how much more of this he was going to be able to endure. He didn't know what to do.

"I'm cold." Sarah shuddered.

"Let's take a hot shower." Justin stood, fully prepared to do whatever needed to be done.

"No," Sarah whispered. "Kiss me, Justin."

Justin's heart throbbed. "Shh, let's just go take a shower."

"Please," Sarah cried and him toward her.

Justin didn't say a word. He just laid Sarah on the bed and wrapped his body with hers. He closed his eyes and took a deep breath, breathing in the scent of her. He relaxed against her warmth and he kissed her. Not the kiss of last night. This was light and gentle. He kissed and whispered to her until her steady breathing told him she was asleep.

Cursing his luck, he caressed the warm spot on Sarah's neck and rolled over to look out at the streetlight for another night.

*

Becket Larson stared at a piece of paper he'd found on his living room floor. Words had been hastily scribbled in blue ink. *You should have listened.*

He didn't have time to feel fear. He didn't have time to turn around and see a gloved hand pull the trigger twice in quick succession. There was no noise. Not when the gun fired. Not when Becket slipped lifelessly to the floor.

CHAPTER 9

Sarah woke up with a pounding headache and the bright light of the sun shining in her eyes. Shading her face, she looked across the muggy hotel room at Justin. He was sitting at the table going through the list they'd gotten from the prison yesterday. His goblet of ice water was sweating; beads of moisture dripped down the stem.

"It's hot," Sarah said in a first-thing-in-the-morning voice.

Justin looked over at her. "William said the air conditioner broke for this end of the hotel sometime last night. I woke up about six and went to get breakfast. But I don't know how good it'll be."

"I'll try it out." Sarah sat up and brushed the hair out of her eyes. She had no idea how she'd gotten here, how long she'd slept, or even what time it was. The only thing she knew was that Justin had taken care of her. She could briefly remember him telling her about a huge chocolate bunny he'd gotten for Easter one year and about the pony he'd had as a kid, but beyond that, she couldn't remember anything, except the pain she'd felt. She was ashamed that she'd let it consume her the way it did.

Sarah sighed as she looked at him. His shirt was clinging to his body and his shoes were kicked off underneath the table. He looked hot and totally engrossed in what he was doing. She felt a little flip in her stomach but didn't try to explain it away this time. She knew what it meant. She was falling in love with him.

"Justin," Sarah said and smiled when he looked up. "Thanks for what you did."

Justin stood and walked to the edge of the bed. "You sure look better today than you did yesterday." Justin traced his fingers along curve of her face. She felt a warm easy feeling seep through her body. The same warmth shone from his eyes as he smiled at her. "Does your thumb hurt?"

Sarah looked at the thumb on her right hand. She squinted at the two neat bandages wrapped around it. "What happened?"

"I think when you took the receiver out of the bunk, you tore your nail. It only bled a little."

"Oh." Sarah looked at it and tried to remember but couldn't. All she could remember were the tears. "You probably think all I do is cry, but that's really not true." In fact, Sarah couldn't remember the last time, beyond that day in Oregon, when she'd cried about anything. "I never break down, especially while I'm working."

"This isn't just work. It's your mom. I understand that." Justin's voice was gruff, and he looked back at what he was doing.

What's that about, Sarah wondered. Maybe tired? Maybe something else. She didn't want to think about it now. She was feeling better and wanted to stay that way. Any hidden emotion could just stay hidden as far as she was concerned. At least for today.

"What'd you find in that folder?" Sarah asked after she was dressed and had a chance to eat a couple bites of warm, butter-soggy toast. Her headache was gone, thankfully, and she was ready to see what else they could find.

"First I found out that your mom's cellmate was named Sheryl Ames. So that gives us a start on who Sherry might be."

"Good." Sarah walked to stand beside Justin and look over his shoulder. "What else?"

"I found that Becket Larson resigned shortly after . . . shortly after . . . "

"My mom died. You can say it, Justin."

"I know. I just—never mind. It doesn't give a forwarding address, but he used to live twenty-two Jackson Street, here in town."

"It's a small enough town. Why don't we ask William and see if Larson still lives here."

Justin reached down and began lacing his athletic shoes. "We can ask him about that. Then I think we ought to get going. Staying even last night here was risky."

"Hopefully our luck will hold, and we'll be long gone by the time the real inspectors get to the prison."

"Then we have a few choices. We can go to that hotel in Atlanta or we can go to Texas."

Sarah gathered the papers on the table and put them back in her bag. "I asked Annie to get some info on the Confederate Regency. I'll call her and see what she found out. But my vote is we drive to Atlanta, see what we can dig up at the hotel and then hop a plane to Texas."

"Sounds great, I'll take care of the travel arrangements," Justin said.

"But Annie can—"

"I'll take care of it." Justin walked over to his duffle to finish packing.

"Okay, but I want at least one layover," Sarah teased, feeling much better.

Justin rolled his eyes and smiled. "Okay."

*

"Thanks for staying, folks." William handed their receipt to Justin. "Sorry for the inconvenience with the air-conditioning. I wanted to have it replaced last summer, but the committee voted for this year. It will all be up and running day after tomorrow."

"We had a nice time." Sarah smiled, slow and sweet. "Oh, we wanted to see an old friend of the family before we left town. The phone number I have for him is disconnected, and I didn't bring my address book. Do you think you might know him?"

Her charm obviously worked. William's face turned a nice shade of red. "Well, ma'am, I might. Who are you looking for?" William asked as he leaned across the counter separating them.

"Becket Larson."

William stood up. "Oh. Well, he owns a little bar across town. Not the best of places, if you know what I mean. But he still lives in his mama's place, God rest her soul, over on Jackson. I don't know the number, but it's the only two-story one on the second block."

Sarah widened her smile. "Thanks William. And if we ever come back this way, we'll stay here again."

"That was despicable," Justin said as he shut the door on the car and started the engine. "I can't believe it. He was like putty."

Sarah laughed a low chuckle. "I know. It was fun."

"Do you do that often?"

"Well, we do what we can." Sarah grinned secretively and laughed at Justin's appalled look.

They found the house easily. Justin pulled the car alongside a dented mailbox with the name Larson printed in faded blue letters.

"Maybe he's home." Sarah pointed at the two-tone green Ford truck.

Justin nodded and looked behind him down the block. He felt off, as if something was wrong or somebody was watching them, but didn't see a soul out in the stifling heat.

Sarah pinned a smile on her face and knocked on the big, oak door. There was really no way to know how the person who answered the door would react. She knocked again and waited. The porch she stood on didn't look well cared for, but it didn't look run-down either. The sidewalk looked like it had been swept clean recently, and there were only a few weeds in the rose bed beside the steps. She felt more comfortable, thinking that Becket might be a guy who wouldn't waste their time.

"He might be around back." Justin started to step off the porch, but Sarah grabbed hold of his arm.

"Justin, look," she whispered and pointed to the window to the left of the door. A large sofa filled a good part of the living room. A chandelier hung from the ceiling, with the light still on. There was a long bookcase covering one wall, and beyond was the dining room table. It looked like a well-furnished, cared-for house. But that wasn't what had caught Sarah's attention. At the end of the sofa, a hand was visible in what looked like a comfortable position. Any onlooker would assume that the person had sunk into a deep sleep on the couch and the hand had fallen off sometime during the night. But the hand wasn't what caught Sarah's attention. Blood was what had her stopping Justin from walking off the porch.

Justin looked at Sarah. He knew what she was going to say. But disturbing what seemed to be a homicide scene for private gain was against his personal moral code, much less the Bureau. "We're not going in," Justin said.

"I have to go in there," Sarah said.

"No." Justin said firmly.

"This is what I do. This is my job." Sarah pointed to the house. "You're a reporter. You don't know what to do or not to do in a situation like this."

"Maybe you should just call the police. It's their job, too."

"But I'm here now, and he may need help. It would take too long for them to get here if he does."

"You're not going in there." Justin felt fear at what might be beyond the door, and he didn't want Sarah to see it. Didn't want her to be exposed to that horror. "Besides, maybe he hit his head and just needs help. And even if I'm a reporter, I can still help a fellow citizen in need."

"No. I can't let you go in there."

"Well, either I go with you, or we both just leave." Justin took a hold of her arms. "How 'bout that?"

Sarah squinted at him. "No."

"I will pick you up and throw you in that car." Justin's voice ground out in quiet anger. "Because you are not going in there alone."

"Fine. But you stay behind me, and if I tell you to get out, you have to go."

"Fine." Justin tired the door and silently swore when it opened and walked in—in front of her.

It was blinding. The smell. It wasn't the normal smell of a house that got too hot. It wasn't the left over whiff of food cooked that morning or burnt coffee from the pot being left on all night. It was a stench. It reeked of rancid rot.

Justin knew Becket just didn't hit his head and knock himself out. He knew Becket was dead. And as he walked around the edge of the couch, he saw the proof.

Becket's frame was laid out along the base of the couch. He lay on his stomach, which was starting to bloat, making an arch in his back. His head was tilted to one side, his eyes staring into nothing. Two, neat bullet holes penetrated the shirt he wore.

There was so much blood. It had seeped into the very fiber of the tan carpet, making a huge pool.

Justin had known the second he opened the door what had happened. He barely looked at the body and the blood. He wanted a clue as to who might have done this, and then he wanted out as quickly as possible. He wanted to get Sarah out even faster. His eyes scanned the area for signs of a struggle, or even a door or window having been forced open, but saw none. Damn.

"Sarah, go outside." Justin turned to look at her and swore when he saw her pale face and wide eyes. "Sarah, go outside," he said louder. "I'll be there in a minute."

But she didn't budge.

"Ah, hell," he muttered to himself, knowing that he'd just have to go. But then he saw it. A crumpled piece of paper near Becket's hand. Justin leaned down, read the words, and committed the handwriting to memory. "Let's go, Sarah." Justin turned and pulled her out the door. He took a moment to wipe the doorknob with his T-shirt tail, knowing that the hit inside the room had been done neatly and that whoever had done it wouldn't be stupid enough to leave prints on the door handle. And he didn't want himself or Sarah connected to this at all.

As soon as the fresh air hit Sarah, she was thinking again. "I'm fine. I need to go back inside and look for who did this. What if it's something to do with my mom's death? Becket Larson might have known something. We need to find it."

"No you don't." Justin pulled Sarah toward the car.

"Yes, I do." She yanked her arm back. "Now let go."

Justin didn't let go. "Now you listen to me. This is not Portland, Oregon. This is Freeman City, Alabama and you don't do things here like you do in Portland. The cops around here will see you as some big-city hotshot coming in here doing their job. Do you think they have any use for you?" Justin asked at her blank look.

"Of course they have use for me. I'm good at what I do. This is important," Sarah said through clenched teeth.

"You are not going back in there. You are going to go and get in that car or I'm gonna put you there. Do I make myself clear?"

"Perfectly." Sarah stomped away down the walk.

CHAPTER 10

Justin drove northeast out of Freeman City toward Atlanta, Georgia, listening to Sarah fume. The heat rose off the ground in silver waves, and the idea of mirages was very believable. Trying out the radio, Justin found everything from a Baptist minister speaking his mind to hard-rock, screaming voices. Settling on a channel that had fiddle music pouring out, Justin leaned back in his seat and prepared for the several-hours' drive ahead of them, wishing for his motorcycle.

When Sarah's phone rang, she pulled it out of her bag to answer it.

"Hey, Annie."

"I found out some information on that hotel."

"Just a second." Sarah dug around and found a notebook and pen. "All right, go ahead."

"You're in luck. The hotel's for sale, and I have you guys down as perspective buyers. I figured the only way for you to get a tour was to do that. Oh, and I sent you a package to the hotel."

"A package? What for?"

"Just some things you'll need."

Sarah took notes on all the details that Annie gave. "Thanks, Annie. Sounds great. How's my father doing? Is he driving you crazy, yet?"

"No. He comes in every couple of days to see how things are going. The guys get a kick out of him. He's off to have lunch with your aunt today."

"Good. Tell him he can always file if he gets in the way. That'll make him be quiet."

Annie laughed. "Oh, wait. I forgot one thing. The hotel manager said that the sellers weren't interested in anyone corporate purchasing the hotel, so I told them that they didn't need to worry about that because my clients were man and wife."

"What! Annie! Couldn't you think of something better to say?"

"Sorry. It just slipped out." Annie had her fingers tightly crossed and behind her back.

"Well, did you get us separate rooms?"

"I couldn't. It would've looked funny. You're registered under Bobby and Candi Porter."

"Oh, Annie." Sarah's voice fell. "Well, thanks for everything. I'll check in pretty soon. Tell Dad and Aunt Lainey hi." After Sarah ended the call, she could practically see Annie dancing around her office, laughing.

Justin turned the radio off. "What's the package for?"

"She didn't say. Only that it's stuff we'll need."

"Hmm," Justin said. "What else?"

"Just that the hotel's for sale and that we have an appointment for a tour—and that because the sellers don't want to sell to any corporate firm, we have to pose as man and wife. We're the Porters. I'm Candi and you're Bobby."

"How does Annie think these names up?"

"The bigger question is how are we going to act like man and wife?"

"Easy, we just act like we're in love."

"I've never been in love before so how would I know what to do?" Sarah looked over at Justin. Oh, he could make her so mad— so pushy, so bossy! And here she thought she was falling in love with him. What a mess this was.

"We'll just do what the people in movies do."

Sarah shook her head. "That's acting."

"Can't you act?"

"Of course I can!" Sarah scowled, determined to do a better job at this than she'd done in Larson's living room.

"See? There you go. And besides it's not like we have to do it for months. It's only a couple of days at the most."

"Fine." Sarah folded her arms and looked out the window. "But I still think we should see if we could stay someplace else."

They zipped along the wide freeway of Atlanta at breakneck speed. Justin handled the car with ease as he followed the exit that would lead them to the Confederate Regency.

Sarah didn't know what to expect of the hotel. Drawing from the idea that someone from a prison had one of the business cards, she had the impression that it wouldn't be a top-notch sort of place. As they drove the streets of Atlanta, Sarah saw all the signs it was Friday night. Bars had their neon lights flashing, young people in cars had their music blaring, and all up and down the streets were people going somewhere. There were couples holding hands, probably on their way to the movies. A few blocks down, there were people dressed up in gowns and tuxes, *maybe on their way to a wedding,* Sarah thought.

Cracking her window, Sarah pulled in the aroma of outside. Damp water from the gutter, hotdogs on the corner, somebody's expensive perfume, cigarette smoke, and exhaust, all mixed together to say, "welcome to the city." She could hear the wail of a siren, someone's high-pitched laugh, and the backfire of a car. She couldn't help but feel excitement start racing through her veins. All around her were the reasons she lived in the city herself, and right in the middle of it all was the grandest hotel she'd ever seen.

Justin gave a low whistle as he pulled up to the valet.

Several wrought-iron benches bordered the wide cobblestone walk leading to the wide pillars guarding the main entrance of the hotel. A tall, dimly lit lamp stood at each bench, like candles on a bed stand at midnight, giving off the same ambiance of romance. The white building shone like marble in the soft light.

Stepping out of the car, Sarah could smell the sweet fragrance of the beautiful ivory flowers, which filled the massive pots scattered about. Heat radiated from the pavement, mixing with the humid air, giving the night a warm, sensual feel. Sarah was so busy absorbing the sights and sounds and smells around her that she forgot she was supposed to be someone's wife. But when she felt Justin's hand close around hers, she remembered.

"Well, sweetheart, what do you think?"

Justin's low voice turned Sarah's insides to mush. "I love it." She smiled, probably a little too enthusiastically.

"We're Mr. and Mrs. Porter, checking in," Justin said to the woman across the long, shiny, cherry wood counter. "I believe we also have a package waiting, as well."

"Okay, sir, it'll be just a moment," responded the woman.

Sarah tried to pull her hand back, but Justin didn't let go. She was surprised at the way she'd felt when he'd said *Mr. and Mrs. Porter.* It was kind of a warm, butterfly-fluttery feeling, even though the names were fake. She may be able to come to terms with the fact that she was falling in love with him, but this . . . this was too much.

So she tried to focus on her surroundings. The ceiling stretched high across the wide space. Chandeliers hung in glittering clusters, giving the room an expensive feel. *Why would a prison inmate have a business card from such a ritzy place?* She wondered. *Maybe this is all new. Maybe it's been remodeled.* But the cherry wood tables and chairs didn't look new. They looked well cared for, but used. People in suits and spectacular jewelry went about their business with ease and elegance. Only a place with a good, long-standing reputation would have men dressed in Armani suits and women wearing diamond necklaces.

"Mr. and Mrs. Porter?" called someone behind them.

"Yes?" Justin said and turned around, pulling Sarah with him.

"I'm Harold Stephens, manager of the hotel." The man was dressed in a suit and tie. He was all buttoned-up and prim looking. "I'd like to welcome you."

"Thanks," Justin said as his hand was firmly pumped up and down.

"Would you like to see the hotel tonight or would you rather wait until tomorrow?" Harold asked.

Sarah leaned her body against his, wrapped her free arm around him, and looked up into his eyes. "Honey, I really want to see it as soon as possible." Then she smiled at Harold. "Is that okay?"

"Sure," Harold said. "Right this way. I'll see to it that your bags are taken to your room." Harold picked up his concealed radio and spoke with someone, giving them directions. "And the package." He nodded to the woman behind the counter, indicating his wishes.

As they walked, Harold gave descriptions of how long a certain feature had been at the hotel and other necessary bits of information. Sarah oohed and aahed at every turn. They started in the basement and worked their way up.

The separate floors were long corridors with glossy, cherry wood doors on each side. At each one, a gold, glowing light shone. Narrow strips of thick gray-and-blue carpet covered the hallway floors. Tasteful pictures of Atlanta's skyline at different times of day and year were displayed every few doors. There were several marked plainly with small, gold, engraved signs saying Linen Closet or Storage. On the first floor, Sarah counted the number of doors as she walked. On the second, they didn't add to the same amount, and she wondered where the extra space went. When they went into several rooms on each level, Sarah noticed some of them were bigger than others and some were significantly smaller. Now, she really began to wonder.

On the top of the hotel was the fitness area. Sarah let go of Justin's hand and walked to the glass door that led into a huge room filled with exercise equipment.

"Oh, wow. A whole bunch of free weights. Look, honey, your favorite." Sarah grabbed his arm and squeezed. "Not that you need them, but—oh, and look! A playroom. Wouldn't little Tommy just love to play in there while his mommy and daddy work out?" Sarah looked at Harold. "We have a little boy who's four-and-a-half years old, and he would just love this." Sarah looked back at Justin and almost started laughing. His eyes were as wide as saucers. "Don't you think, honey?"

"Yes, sweetheart. Tommy would love it."

Sarah took off toward the pool, with poor Harold and Justin in tow. "Oh, it's beautiful." Sarah leaned down and tested the water. "It's perfect." Then she splashed the remaining water on her hand on Justin's shirt.

He grabbed her and pulled her tight against him. "Make sure you don't make promises you can't keep." He kissed her hard on the mouth.

Harold cleared his throat. "Well, that's the end of the tour, except for the lounge area and the restaurant. If you'd like, I can show you to your room, and you can look around downstairs later."

Sarah looked at him and smiled. "Sure. I'd like to freshen up." Then she looked at Justin and gave him her raised eyebrow, sly smile. "Is that okay, honey?"

"Yes."

"It was nice to meet you, Harold." Sarah smiled as he turned to walk away. "Honey, why don't you go on down to the lounge, and I'll meet you there in a few minutes. I just want to change my clothes and freshen my lipstick." Sarah eyed Harold meaningfully as he walked away.

Justin hesitated, but apparently catching Sarah's hint, he followed Harold. He pretty much had to when she shut the door in his face.

Once inside, Sarah knew they were given one of the smaller rooms. It was as if a wall had been built on one end of it. She worked her way around the room, knocking on each wall.

On one of the side walls, she had a guy knock back and tell her to quiet down. When she knocked on the wall where the closet was, it sounded very hollow. She moved pictures, pulled the dresser out, but couldn't find an entrance to the space obviously on the other side.

Frustrated, she decided to just put some of her things away and then change her clothes, as was the plan. And then she'd go down and meet Justin. Maybe he'd have an idea.

*

Justin entered the elevator right after Harold intending to follow him after they got to the lobby. Harold just went where Justin went, so he had no choice but to go to the lounge.

Deciding a nice cold beer sounded just about right, Justin strode up to the bar and sat on a stool. The lounge was about the same as most hotel lounges, except this one was busy, very busy. People were everywhere: dancing, playing pool, and drinking everything from martinis to bottled beer. If Justin were in the market to buy a hotel, he'd look into this one because of the bar business alone.

He thanked the bartender for his drink and leaned back enough to relax into the room. At first glance, the space looked like any other bar, but there were touches here and there that made a difference. The grand piano edging the shining, hardwood dance floor. There were flickering candles centered on each smooth-topped table surrounded by high-backed chairs upholstered with the same deep burgundy as the barstools. As Justin looked closer, he couldn't see any stains or spots. He whistled between his teeth. This place must make a lot of money.

It didn't take him long to figure out where the money came from. There were a lot of businessmen in fancy suits sitting with women who certainly weren't their wives, and there were a lot of women who were hoping to find such companionship. Justin shook his head and took another swig of his beer.

"Hey, sugar. You sure look like you needed one of those." A sultry voice said.

Justin could see the owner of the voice out of the corner of his eye. She was dressed in a long, form-fitting, red dress with sequins in all the right places. She could have just put a sign on her body saying, Lady of the Night and she would have been just as successful. "Sure did," Justin said.

"Do you want some company?"

"Why not?" Justin motioned to the stool next to him.

"So what are you in town for?"

"Just looking around. My name's Jeff." Justin held out his hand.

The woman looked at his hand for a second, shrugged her shoulders, and shook it. "Karen."

"Nice to meet you Karen. So what do you do?"

"I'm an accountant."

"Really?" Justin smiled real easy. "Never saw an accountant that looked like you." He wanted to see how far she'd play this out.

"What do you do?"

"I'm a doctor." Justin almost said reporter, but he figured she'd walk the other way, not wanting a story written up on her.

"So what room are you staying in Jeff the Doctor?" Karen leaned her long body against his.

"Three-forty-eight," he said and smiled.

She slipped a piece of paper in his hand, kissed his cheek, and walked away.

CHAPTER 11

"Hey, I was just coming down to meet you," Sarah said as she walked out of the bathroom.

Justin had been sitting on the bed, waiting for the shower to stop running. He hoped he'd have a chance to explain to Sarah about Karen before she actually showed up.

"I was wondering how long it would take you to 'freshen your lipstick.'" Justin smiled at the embarrassed look on Sarah's face.

"I was just acting, remember? That's what you wanted." Sarah was still angry about what had happened in Freeman City and wanted him to know it. "Are we going down to act some more, or did I just waste my time changing clothes?"

"You can go down and act all you want, but I have someone who's going to come meet me in a little while. I think you should be here."

She couldn't take it anymore. "Why are you always ordering me around?" Sarah stood with her hands on her hips. "I'm getting sick of it. First, it's the hotel, you tell that guy that we're going to stay, without asking me. Then you drag me out of the house where Becket was without letting me do my job." Sarah flung her hands out. "And here, you say, someone's coming up to meet us so we can't leave. I'm not a weakling, you know. I can handle myself."

"Mmm-hmm. How many dead bodies have you seen?" Justin asked and crossed his arms.

"One." Sarah looked at her hands.

"Including Becket?"

"Just Becket."

"Geez, Sarah, I thought you said you had training. That that was your job."

"It is my job. I know more about it than you do, Mr. Reporter from Texas. How many dead bodies have you seen?"

"Many."

"When?" Sarah stepped closer to him.

"We're not talking about me, Sarah. We're talking about you." Justin stood and faced her.

"Don't change the subject!" Sarah jammed her finger in his chest.

Justin grabbed it. "Now, listen here. You don't get to go around being mad at me unless you know all the facts. I didn't want you to go inside at Becket's house, but I knew that if I went in alone, you'd feel humiliated. I didn't want that, because I understand your pride. And neither one of us could stand there and not know what was in that house. So be mad at me if you want. But at least now you know the truth."

"Fine." Sarah tried to pull her hand from Justin's grip. The warmth of his touch was making it hard for her to concentrate. "What about the hotel in Freeman City? Why didn't you ask my opinion?"

"Because I was exhausted. You may have felt like a million bucks, but I didn't. The other hotel was over two hours away. Nothing happened, anyway, so what's the big deal?"

"Nothing." Sarah couldn't help but feel hurt. "What about now. Why do we have to stay in the room instead of trying to get the information we came for?"

"Because I thought it would be fun to act like husband and wife." Justin kissed the tips of her fingers, one by one. "So act." Justin pulled her into his arms and kissed her slow and easy, licking and begging with his tongue until he felt her sag against him. "So are you done being mad at me?"

"No. I—"

Justin's arms banded around her again, lifting her off her feet. "I can kiss for a long time."

"Fine." Sarah glared at him. "Fine. Put me down."

Justin slid her body in an exquisitely slow movement down his body and enjoyed the play of emotion on her face and the feel of her body on his. "We're not going to wait forever, you know."

"Meaning?"

"Don't give me that. You're a smart girl. You know damn well what I'm talking about." Justin pressed his lips to the base of her ear. "But just so you're certain, I plan to take you to bed, love you soft and easy, hard and fast, and then do it all over again. I plan to bury myself in you until you cry out my name." His breath was hot and sexy against her skin. He wanted to glory in the scent they created together. "Am I making myself clear?"

Sarah took a deep breath. "Perfectly." Sarah didn't think her whole body had ever tingled before, but it was now. Even her fingertips. She hurriedly changed the subject. "I opened that box from Annie. She sent you a few suits and a couple of dresses for me."

Justin walked to the box, which had been ripped open and the contents laid out on the round table near the textured wall. He crumpled his nose at the fabric of the suits. "Really. I guess these will come in handy. Everybody sure dresses nice around here."

"She sent this, too." Sarah handed Justin a ring made of gold.

"Shit," Justin said.

Sarah laughed at Justin's reaction. "It's just acting." And she wiggled the golden band on her own ring finger. "Anyway, I'm gonna change." Sarah picked up a light blue, silky dress, which would fall to the floor once it was on.

"Hell." Justin flipped out one of the suit jackets. As he did, the gold from the ring on his finger flickered. "I hate this part."

*

"She just asked you what room you were in?" Sarah asked after she'd heard the story about Karen.

Justin nodded and handed Sarah the piece of paper Karen had given him. "I don't exactly know what this means."

Sarah took the paper and her eyes flitted over Justin's form. He was wearing a suit. He didn't look like a stockbroker or a lawyer. Or even a guy who only put one on to go to the opera just for the night. He looked tall, sophisticated—perfect—with strength and mystery following his every move. *Wow, the guy in the perfect suit,* Sarah thought and cringed inside. *Just pay attention to what's going on now. Read the paper!*

"I won't come to the door." Sarah read and nodded her head. "I think I know what it means. Come here." Sarah walked to the closet and pulled back her clothes. "Look. It's a false back that slides over." Sarah slid it to the side showing a door.

"Interesting. Did you try the door?" Justin asked, but couldn't help notice how the shimmering blue dress caressed Sarah's skin.

"It's locked, but I bet you if she comes, she'll use that door."

"I wonder what's back there?"

"Who knows. Do you want to go? I bet I can pick it."

Justin chuckled. "You've never seen a dead body, but you can pick a lock. Now, just where did you learn that?"

"Our bathroom at home locked on its own half the time. I was the only one who could open it." Sarah smiled. "And I practice all the time on doors at the office. Drives our security guy nuts."

"I'll bet. But why don't we wait and see if she comes. If she does, we'll ask her. If not, we'll go back there. What do you think?" Justin replaced the false back and slid Sarah's clothes back in place.

"I guess. I'm really curious, though." Sarah sat on the bed, glad about Justin asking her opinion.

"Curious is right. I think I recognized her."

"Where would you have seen her before?"

Justin turned out the overhead lights, leaving only a lamp on beside the bed and then sat beside Sarah. "At Freeman Prison."

"What? Do you think she got out?"

"No. Let's put this together. You know your mom was asking about where some of the women went at night?"

"Yeah." Sarah squinted. "No. You don't think—"

"That's exactly what I think. I think the women were gone because someone was bringing them here to be prostitutes."

"That's outrageous, disgusting. Illegal!"

Justin smiled. One of his favorite things about Sarah was her innocent view of the world. He hoped she'd never lose it. "I know it's illegal, but people do illegal things all the time."

"Who would do it . . . ? How . . . ? Why?" Sarah shook her head.

"I don't know who or how, but I bet I know why. Money. Prostitution is a big business."

"How much money could they possibly make?"

"Depended on the number of girls."

"That's a horrible thought."

"We don't even know if that's really what's going on. Maybe she just looks like one of the women at the prison."

"This is the wildest thing I've ever heard." Sarah scooted up on the bed to lean against the wall. "You don't think the women who come are forced to, do you."

"I can't say."

"Do you think this was going on when my mom was on assignment?"

"Prostitution is as old as the world. If not, something was—think about what Sherry said to your mom about not asking questions."

"If that's what happened I bet my mom would have found out, eventually." Sarah could hope. "And if that's what's going on, I owe it to my mom to stop what she would have. Justin do you think—"

"Shh," Justin said with his finger to his lips and then motioned toward the closet.

A tiny thrill of terror shot through Sarah as she waited for whatever was coming. She heard the tumblers fall into place as the door was being unlocked. Then the muffled scuffing of wood on wood, as the false back was pushed to the side, and the scraping of hangers moving over. The seconds seemed to take forever. The first thing Sarah saw was a long leg. On the foot was a heeled shoe, high enough to make any woman cringe at the thought of having to wear it, and red fabric glinting with sequins draped the sexy form.

"Hello, Karen," Justin said.

"Hello, Dr. Jeff," the woman said as she stepped the rest of the way into the room. "Ooh! And Dr. Jeff has a friend. Does she want to play, too?"

Justin put his arm around Sarah and smiled.

"I'm just going to watch for a while. I like to watch." Sarah said.

"Gonna cost you double," Karen said.

"Maybe we'd better get the payment over with first," Justin said.

Sarah reached for her bag. "How much are we going to owe you?" She couldn't help thinking about how young the woman looked. Her eyes were aged as if they'd seen too many things, but her hair still shone with the luster of youth. Her skin was smooth and free of wrinkles. If it hadn't been for the downturned sadness of her lips, her profile would have been youthful, almost carefree.

"One thousand dollars."

Justin whistled. "Well, I guess for our anniversary, that's not too bad."

"Anniversary, huh? How long you guys been married?"

Sarah looked at Justin to quiet him. She wanted to answer because when Karen answered the money question she'd also, probably unconsciously, signed the amount with her fingers. Sarah wanted to experiment, so instead of answering with her voice she signed her answer, "Three years."

Karen answered vocally. "That's cool. My—" She stopped and looked at Sarah "—parents were married about that long before my dad split." Then she signed, "How did you know?"

Sarah responded with her hands, "I saw you sign the amount with your fingers."

"Oh," Karen signed back, and then asked Justin, "So what do you like, sugar?"

"Everything," Justin responded and waited to see what Sarah would do.

Karen stepped out of her shoes and crawled onto the bed.

Sarah stopped her from taking off her dress by signing, "We

don't want to have sex. We want to ask you some questions." And when she saw fear leap into Karen's eyes, she signed, "We will still pay you. Ok?" Sarah continued when Karen nodded. "Is there a reason you're afraid to talk to us?"

"Yes." Karen signed.

"Why?" Sarah asked with her hands.

Karen lightly touched the clip in her hair and signed, "I'm wired. Jeff and I have to talk so they don't think I'm lying."

"We can do that. Just a second," Sarah signed and then dug in her bag for a piece of paper to write down what Karen said for Justin.

"Yeah, that feels real good," Justin said after he'd read the note.

"You like that, do ya? What about this?" Karen said and then signed, "What do you want?"

"We want to help you," Sarah signed. She'd been trying to figure out how to have this girl trust her. Through her mom was the best way. "My mom was an inmate at Freeman Prison. Her name was Helen Johnson. She went there not because she committed a crime, but because she wanted to help the inmates have a better life. She died there, before she could help anyone. I want to help where she couldn't."

"I've heard of your mom," Karen signed and then said, "How you doing, baby? That feel good?"

Sarah wanted to ask her how she'd heard of her mom, but wanted to keep going forward with her own questions.

"Oh yeah," Justin returned.

"I can't talk to you," Karen signed. "They'll kill me if they find out."

"Don't talk. I don't need to know names or anything; I need to know if I'm right. Are you forced to do this?" Sarah asked with her hands.

"Yes," Karen signed. "We get out of other work at the prison because we do this, and then we get released early."

"Oh, yeah, keep it up," Justin said as he watched the Sarah and Karen's fingers communicate with each other.

"How many girls?"

"I don't know. A hundred, maybe, altogether."

"How are the girls chosen?" Sarah signed.

Karen shrugged her shoulders. "They're young, I guess."

Sarah took a moment to relay everything to Justin. He moaned a few times while he read the note, and Karen laughed. *Ask her if she and the other girls have anything in common,* Justin wrote on the paper.

Sarah made the signs to ask.

"Not really. A lot of us are about the same age. But we're from different parts of the country."

"Where are you from?" Sarah signed.

"Texas."

Texas was too much of a coincidence.

"Baby, you're doing great," Justin moaned as he kicked his feet against the wall and then read the note Sarah gave him. *Ask her why she's in prison,* Justin wrote.

Sarah signed the question.

"I was at a college party and arrested for drugs."

"Were you doing drugs?"

"No."

"No?" Sarah questioned. "Were you selling?"

"No. I was only there with a friend. I've never done drugs in my life."

Sarah could see the anger in Karen's eyes. "What were you in college for?"

"I was going to be an interpreter."

"You would have been a good one." Sarah smiled. "Maybe you can continue after you get out."

"Not likely. They don't give jobs to convicts."

Being arrested for being at a party with drugs was believable. Going to prison for it wasn't. Sarah couldn't get past it. "Was being at that party your first offense?"

"Yes."

Justin moaned and rolled over on the bed, knocking the lamp off the nightstand.

"I don't understand." Sarah signed. "How can you be in prison then?"

"The investigator said I had too much money to be just at a party and that there were remnants of coke in my purse."

Justin laughed and poked Sarah, apparently wanting to know what was going on. Sarah wrote it all down for him.

Ask if she thinks it was a set up for some of the other girls, too, Justin wrote.

Sarah asked.

"Maybe. They say it is, but everybody says they didn't do it. Some even say they don't remember being arrested or even seeing a judge. But they're probably lying or were high or something." Karen signed. "I wouldn't worry about it. There's nothing you can do, anyway."

Sarah wanted to know more, but decided that this topic was over for Karen. She could get the other information, like the college she attended, with Annie's help. She smiled and changed the subject. "Do you know a Sheryl Ames?"

"No."

"Heard of her?"

"No."

"You said you heard of my mom. What did you hear?"

Karen looked at Sarah. "Just that she burned to death in her cell. And that will happen to us if we don't do as we're told." Karen signed.

Sarah could tell Karen wasn't telling her everything. But the way Karen looked away, Sarah knew she'd get nothing more.

"Let's go again," Justin said. "My wife won't care."

"That'll cost you another five hundred," Karen said, with eyes wide.

"Fine by me. You're worth it." Justin winked. Making sure she got a lot of money was no problem for him. Perhaps her life would be a bit easier because of it.

"How often do you come to Atlanta?" Sarah signed.

"Is that where I am?" Karen asked with her hands.

"Yes."

"I didn't know." Tears fell down Karen's face. "They don't tell us where we're going."

Sarah wrapped her arms around Karen while her body shook with silent shudders. Sarah now knew why the business card was so important to her mom. She was going to get to the bottom of this, Sarah promised quietly.

CHAPTER 12

"You're pretty amazing, you know that?" Justin asked the next morning on the way to the airport.

"No. Why?" Sarah asked.

"Last night with Karen. You really gave her hope."

"I plan on giving her a whole lot more than that." Sarah looked out her window. Atlanta was a different city in the daylight. She supposed, as with everything else in the light of day, it changed. It wasn't the city's fault that this awful crime was being committed in it. Atlanta was as much a victim as the girls were. Maybe I'll end up helping more than just them, Sarah thought as their rental car whisked by the tall buildings.

"I was only able to schedule in two layovers on the way to Austin." Justin turned the wheel to park the rental.

"Austin? I thought we were going to Dallas so you could write?"

"My grandfather lives outside of Texas Hill, and maybe I can borrow his computer. But the main reason we're going is so that we can talk to my dad's college roommate, Simon Newell. And don't say I didn't ask you. I didn't have to. I can tell you want to get the answers to all your questions. Plus, it might be nice to see where your mom grew up. And I can tell Pat that I need more time. No big deal."

"Thanks, Justin." Sarah smiled. She hadn't thought of that. What would it be like to see the place where her mom grew up? She frowned, what would it be like. Looking over at Justin, she was glad he was with her. He never ceased to amaze her. Last night he was beyond generous with Karen. Sarah knew he hoped that the girls' lives could be better, too. "I really want to get to a place where we can listen to those final chips we got from the prison. I'm hoping that they'll have a lot on them to help us here."

"Grandpa's is the perfect place for that. He has a huge guesthouse that we can use." Justin smiled as he thought of the bunkhouse his grandfather had turned into a long, rambling guesthouse. It would be fun to share that space with Sarah.

"Does he have a place for me to run? I'm beginning to miss it."

"Yes. There's loads of room. In fact, he's got about a thousand acres. So you can run until your heart's content."

"Really. So is it like a ranch?"

"Yup."

"Does he have horses?"

"Of course. Do you ride?"

"Never. I grew up in the city."

"That's a crime. I'll take you, if you want to go."

"I would love it." Sarah smiled at the prospect of riding a horse for the first time.

*

"Now, we can stay in Austin or we can drive out to the ranch," Justin said after they landed. "Whatever you want."

"How far away is it?" Sarah asked as she looked at all the people wandering the Austin airport.

"Depending on traffic getting out of the city, about an hour and a half, maybe more."

"I'd like to go. I'm anxious for a bed that's not in a hotel room."

"Well, we timed this just perfect," Justin said as he pulled out of the rental-car parking lot. "We get to be stuck in all the five o'clock traffic."

"I don't mind. I haven't been here since my grandma died and that was, I think, when I was nine or something."

"So you don't have any family in Texas anymore?" Justin asked.

"Nope. It's just Dad and me. And Aunt Lainey. But she's always off on a cruise or some other crazy trip."

"That sounds fun." Justin came to a complete stop behind an entire line of cars.

"Yeah, she's always sending us postcards from different ports of call."

"What did she do?"

"She was a crime scene investigator for a couple of different police departments. I know she worked in Texas, and Oklahoma even."

"How can she afford all her trips?"

"She married a really rich guy. But he died a few years afterward in a car accident. It was really horrible, I guess. But I don't even remember him."

"She didn't remarry?" Justin sighed at the traffic as it pulled ahead only a few hundred feet.

"No. I think she really likes her freedom." Sarah looked over at Justin. "But what about you? What about your family?"

"It's just Grandpa and me now. I think I might have a great-aunt on my Grandma's side, but that's it."

"Has he always been a rancher?"

Justin shook his head and changed lanes. Traffic was finally moving at speed-limit rate, and he was glad to get out of the city. "No. He was a judge here in Austin forever."

"He was?"

"He married pretty late in life, and by the time Dad was born, he only worked on special cases."

"Your dad was a judge here in Austin, too, wasn't he?"

Justin smiled and looked over at Sarah. "Are you just making conversation? I thought you would've looked all this up in your research on me."

"I did. But it's nicer to hear the story from you. I do the same with all my clients. It's always interesting what they sugarcoat."

"Is that what I am to you, a client?"

"No. Of course not. I just thought we could get to know each other better. But we don't have to talk if you don't want to." Sarah crossed her arms and looked out the window.

Justin smiled. *What a pair we make,* he thought. "Yes. My dad was a judge here. I was born here, too, but you already knew that."

"So tell me something I don't know."

"I like chocolate cake and scrambled eggs."

"Together?"

Justin laughed. "No. Those are just foods I like."

"Oh." Sarah laughed, too. It was good to hear their laughter mix together. "I like grilled chicken and apple pie. And I wouldn't mind eating them together."

"Grandpa likes to brag that his cook is the best this side of the Mississippi. So I'm sure we won't starve."

It was full dark by the time they reached the ranch and Sarah had fallen asleep. Justin couldn't help feeling disappointed. He wanted Sarah to see one of the most beautiful spots in the world, as far as he was concerned. *But we'll just wait until morning,* he told himself as he pulled under the tall, wide ranch entrance, carved with the single word, *Breslow.*

He didn't have to see it to know it was there. Knowing it was like knowing that his heart beat. It had stood for generations. His own kids would see it rising high into the Texas skyline, and for some reason that made Justin as proud as anything he'd ever done or would do. Kids, Justin startled at the thought. He always wished in the back of his mind that he'd have a few. Have a wife, a family, a home. But, he'd always avoided it. Never was ready to look much less plan. Yet, seeing Sarah here in the world that built him into the man he was, he felt drawn to the idea. Maybe he could start that looking.

Justin turned the car off and got out. It was good to be here. Nothing ever really changes. It was home, a place he'd been away from for too long. He opened Sarah's door and leaned down close to her. In the dim light from the car's interior, he could see her sleeping eyes and her full mouth. A swift shot of feeling raced through his body as he looked at her. The warmth had nothing to do with lust and everything to do with another emotion he wasn't ready to face, even if he had just been thinking about kids and a family. That was thinking. This was feeling. Way different.

Ignoring it, he whispered, "Sweetheart, you want to wake up?" He brushed his fingertips across her face.

"Hmm." Sarah moved in her seat and stretched.

Justin clenched his teeth at the sound. Maybe lust wasn't as far removed as he'd thought.

Sarah opened her eyes. "Are we there already? How long did I sleep."

Forever. Justin had barely been able to stand her soft, warm body sleeping next to him in the car. "Not too long. But Grandpa's expecting us. I called him right after you fell asleep to tell him to have chicken and chocolate cake ready."

"What?" Sarah sat the rest of the way up.

"You think you deserve chicken *and* pie? Well forget it. I want my cake." Justin smiled and unlatched Sarah's seat belt.

"No. I meant he didn't have to do that. I can just eat whatever."

"He's not doing it. Stella is." Justin pulled Sarah out of the car.

"You know what I mean. Now knock it off." Sarah laughed as Justin coaxed her toward the house. He was different, she noticed right away. He wasn't edgy or watchful. *He's comfortable here*, she thought, and was transported into Justin's world.

"Oh, honey. Why didn't you call sooner? You know I would've had a huge pot of chili waiting for you," Her Cajun voice crooned.

Sarah's eyes grew as she watched a perfectly round woman with a perfectly round bun hug and kiss Justin as if he were seven.

"Ah, Stella, you know me. I can't live without your fussing over me."

"Ain't that the truth," Stella said as she turned to look at Sarah. "Now, who's this you brought in? Land sakes, she's beautiful. What are you doing with a beautiful girl?" Stella curled Sarah into her arms, her black eyes shining.

"Stella, you're the beauty. You know that." Justin pulled on her apron string.

He remembered the first time he'd seen that beauty. She was

sitting pretty as anything atop an old sorrel mare. The sun was blazing down on her hair, making it shine like a raven's wing. Her eyes stared back at his, making his breath hitch. Her skin looked smooth and sweet like butter-whipped molasses. His ten-year-old heart melted for the beautiful black-haired girl in the picture in his hand. She'd razzed him about mooning over a girl in a picture until he'd looked closer and realized it was her.

Justin looked at her now. Her hair was almost all gray, but her eyes were still bright and her skin still smooth. "So what'd you make for me to eat?"

"You? And what about this girl?" Stella still had her arms around Sarah. "What's your name anyway, honey? Since you were brought home by a heathen who doesn't know one decent manner from the next?"

"I'm Sarah." Sarah couldn't believe the teasing, flirty way Justin was being. It was definitely a side of him she liked.

"Well, Sarah, let's go see if we can find the old man." Stella walked off in the direction she'd come. "You can bring the heathen."

"So, heathen, want to go?" Sarah smiled. She almost reached over and kissed him, so fun was her mood, but she stopped herself. She didn't think it would be a very sensible thing to do.

"Let's go." Justin grabbed her hand and walked after Stella, calling for his grandpa.

"Hello boy," Justin Thomas Breslow said from the doorway of the dining room. "I was wondering what became of you." J.T. smiled as he looked at his grandson.

Sarah looked at the owner of the voice so similar to Justin's. He stood very straight and strong. The gray in his hair only made him more wise and distinguished looking. The pipe in his hand seemed to be an act of habit rather than need. He was an older replica of Justin or Justin was a younger one of him. His blue eyes were the same searching blue. His mouth set in the same almost nonchalant manner.

"Hello, Grandpa." Justin walked forward and shook his hand

but smiled when he was pulled into a bear of a hug. "This is Sarah Johnson."

"Nice to meet you, Judge Breslow." Sarah reached out her hand.

J.T. pulled her forward, too. "You must be the reason for the spring in his walk and the smile in his eye. The last time I saw Justin, I starting worrying that the fun-loving boy would disappear for good. Glad to see my worrying was for nothing."

Justin cleared his throat.

"Well, you can call me Judge Breslow if you want, and be a stranger. Or you can join my friends and call me Judge."

Sarah smiled, feeling very welcomed. "Okay, Judge." Sarah looked at Justin, wondering about that fun-loving boy the Judge was talking about.

"Thatta girl." J.T. looked at Justin. "I suppose you're hungry. I know there's barbequed chicken and we have some leftover apple pie from yesterday."

Justin started at Sarah's laugh as it pealed through the house. But he joined her when she said, "I get chicken *and* pie."

CHAPTER 13

Long, rolling hills stretched out on both sides of the hidden path that Sarah had chosen to follow on her morning run. The sky was such a deep blue that it almost hurt to look at it. But she did, anyway. She was amazed at the clouds. They were massive wads of cotton candy, seeming very much like huge, feather beds, drifting in the sky. She even caught herself wondering what it would be like to sleep on a cloud. The air, though beginning to warm to the heat of the day, was pungent with a sweet aroma that Sarah couldn't name. And the green all around her was a marvel. She was used to green, because she lived in Oregon. But the green here wasn't the too-wet green. It was a green that had to work for it. The plants had to pull from the soil all the moisture they could and not depend on rain. It was like the land was used to hard work and long days. That was something Sarah could relate to, even if she hardly knew a cow from a horse.

As she continued, she stopped once in a while to look at a flower, tempted to pick it. But she decided against it because she wouldn't know how to keep it alive until she returned to the bunkhouse turned guesthouse.

Sarah liked the easy sound her feet made as they hit the dirt, taking her farther and farther along the winding path, leaving dust puffs behind. It was a calming sound. A sound she'd missed in the last week or so. She enjoyed how her lungs expanded to fill with air and the tight warmth in her legs when she demanded more from them. She forced all other thoughts from her brain. She needed this time to recuperate and even meditate. But when she rounded the next curve, she was met with a sight she hadn't expected to see.

She stopped and stared. When she thought of Texas, she thought of tumbleweeds and dust, and oil wells. But what she saw could have been a piece of paradise. It was breathtaking.

Between a gap in the trees, Sarah saw a tall waterfall splashing waves of silver mist into the sparkling pool below. Shining foam moved and tumbled with the falling water. The rushing sound lured Sarah. She wound her way through the brush that guarded such a secret place until she reached its edge. She laughed as she kicked off her shoes and socks and stuck her feet in the water. She couldn't help herself. It looked so cool and inviting. Relaxing back on the cushion of grass beneath her, Sarah felt peaceful, exhilarated. *This is just what I need,* she thought as she looked up into the billowing trees that danced in a breeze only they could feel. She closed her eyes.

It was the laugh that caught his attention. He'd been looking for her and had seen her footprints on a cow path leading to the south pasture. Following them, he was beginning to think he wouldn't catch up. But when he heard the laugh, he knew he'd found her. It only took him a moment to see where she'd gone. A long, lazy smile crossed his face as he walked down the hill to her. He was glad he knew the way. His steps were quiet on the grass as he crossed the distance and knelt down.

"I brought you some flowers." Justin held out a handful of wildflowers and looked at her relaxed form. Her arms were at her sides. She'd taken the band out of her hair, so the flaxen waves spread over the grass. When she opened her eyes, her pupils adjusted to the light, giving him more view of the gray in them. "You're beautiful," he whispered.

"What? Sorry. I was daydreaming." Sarah sat up and saw the flowers. "Are those for me?"

Justin nodded and sat down with one knee cocked up so his arm holding the flowers could rest on it. "I picked them as I followed your footprints on the cow trail."

"The what?"

"The path you ran on." Justin smiled.

"Oh." Sarah took the flowers he offered and filled her nose with them. They emitted the scent she'd been unable to name. "Thank you. They smell wonderful."

"You're welcome." Justin looked at her as she looked at the flowers. Her eyes were bright—glowing, in fact. A sure sign she didn't get flowers often. "You could kiss me. That's a good thank-you."

"You could kiss me. And I already said thank you."

"I just might." Justin thought about it. That's pretty much all he'd been thinking of. There was hardly a second that he didn't physically feel a pull in her direction.

When he woke up this morning, he'd felt fear that she was gone and maybe in danger. It had taken him a few minutes to remember that she'd probably gone for a run. But the fear hadn't gone away completely until he'd seen her. In his experience, there was only one cure for what was ailing him. He had to have her. Maybe then all the jumbled emotions he was feeling about her would cease.

"Did you need something?" Sarah asked when she looked up from the bouquet.

"This," Justin said as he cupped her face in his hands and pulled her to him. "Just this."

Sarah smiled against his lips. She'd been lying there with her eyes closed, thinking of him, of this.

He kissed her as if he had all of his life to spend doing it. His mouth caressed hers with soft need. His lips were warm against hers and she melted into them.

"I want you, Sarah," he whispered.

Sarah nodded her head and pulled him with her as she eased back on the grass.

His hands were patient. He couldn't believe it. All he wanted was to rip away her clothes and take his fill. But his hands slowed as they touched her body. They skimmed her waist and were light as air as they pulled her shirt over her head.

He kissed the dip in her shoulder and felt need shoot through him when she sighed. He saw her hair pooled around her face. The blossoms he'd brought her had made a blanket beneath them. The sight was lovely, achingly so.

Her fingers tangled in his hair, urging him to do more.

Wanting to feel his skin against hers, he unlatched the tiny hooks that fastened her sports bra.

Feeling the same urgency as Justin, Sarah reached to pull his shirt from his frame.

"Go slow sweetheart. We've waited so long; let's make this last."

Sarah changed her speed and looked into Justin's eyes. They were boiling with anticipation. She squinted, wondering why he didn't just leap when it was so obvious he wanted to.

There wasn't time to ask. Justin trailed his fingers at a leisurely pace down her throat and up the rise of her breast.

She arched to meet his mouth as it closed over where his fingers had been.

He lingered. He feasted on one nipple, then the other. Filling himself, he went back to sample her mouth.

His body was strong against her skin. His flesh quivered beneath her fingers. His arms tensed with slow, deliberate movements. She slid her palms along those arms, delighting in the effect she had on him.

He knew where he wanted her. He'd known the moment he'd seen her. He wanted her here, not at the water's edge, but beneath the ripples.

Shedding the rest of his clothes, he lingered on hers. He was unwrapping a beautiful gift. He wanted to treasure it.

She felt cherished as his eyes gazed at her with longing. She felt beautiful as his hands followed his eyes and then when his lips followed them.

Her skin was burning with need.

He knew a spot in the water that was perfect for his height and perfect for her body. He scooped her up and drew her legs around him. He kissed her until her body pleaded with his for release. Then he stepped in the water.

It was warm as it covered them. It was like the punch of desire he'd felt the first moment he saw her was flowing over his skin, enveloping him.

The first touch of water Sarah felt was shocking but wonderful. It was freeing and intriguing to be in such a secret spot.

With their bodies saturated with the water, their sweat, their longing, they moved in the primal fashion that had been known since the dawn of time.

She took where he gave. She begged. He withheld. Twining their arms and legs, they sailed into a paradise of sensation. His tongue aroused her to the point of surrender.

"Justin, please," She pleaded.

"Not yet."

His hand worked its way lower to find her slick with need. He just touched her, and her body erupted.

He'd knew he wanted that, craved it even, but he hadn't known he needed it.

He kissed her face and called her name over and over until she went slack against him.

Sarah felt as if she was floating. She felt hazy and expended. When she opened her eyes, Justin saw they were dark and heavy.

He couldn't wait any longer. Moving her hips to align with his, he immersed himself in the gray eyes he knew, knowing he'd never be through with them, and slid deep inside her.

Drawing all of him in, she arched so far that her hair brushed the water. Then raising back up, she threw her arms around him and matched his rhythm beat for beat.

Thrusting and accepting, they built pleasure on top of pleasure until reckless with desperation.

He linked her fingers with his and took her as he plunged.

Tremors followed the earthquake. Sarah kept her eyes closed until she knew she could see when she opened them. When she did, she saw that she was still in Justin's arms and that their bodies were submersed up to their shoulders.

"Sweetheart." Justin brushed his fingers along her spine, enjoying the shivers they caused.

"Hmmm." Sarah looked up and into Justin's eyes. She saw the leftover passion fade, but something else remained. "What is it?"

"Nothing," Justin said. He'd done what he'd intended to. Hell, even what he wanted to. He just didn't expect to feel the guilt that instantly started prodding him. He kissed the tip of her nose and felt himself want her again. He almost swore. "I just remembered why I came down here."

"It wasn't for this?" Sarah smiled.

"No." Justin grinned. "Grandpa says there's a summerfest in town tonight, and I just wondered, since we've been so busy, if you wanted to go?"

"So. Like. There'll be cotton candy and popcorn?"

Justin winked at the excitement shining in Sarah's eyes. "I suppose."

"Will you buy me some?"

"Of course."

"Will you kiss me again?" Sarah asked.

"Of course." Justin felt himself go hard inside her.

"Will you kiss me again, now?"

He didn't answer, he plundered. Before where he'd been soft, he was harsh. Before where he'd been patient, he was intolerant. He pushed her harder and harder until she screamed his name and raced over the edge with him once more.

CHAPTER 14

Sarah laughed and laughed at the three-legged races. She ate cotton candy, candied apples, and grilled corn on the cob. She hugged tight the little furry horse Justin had won for her. Growing up in the city, this is what she'd missed. She'd never known anyone could eat so much watermelon, but the crowds of people around her devoured the sweet, red fruit with relish. She knew she'd never seen grown men push lemons with their noses or a bathtub race, for God's sake. She couldn't have described what she'd expected from a bathtub on wheels flying down Main Street even if she'd been asked. She held her breath as boys and girls of all sizes tried their hand at riding a mechanical bull. And she cheered and yelled as loud as she could when Justin walked up and said he'd show 'em how it was done. The goofy-looking machine, which didn't look at all like a bull, bucked and twisted and turned. Justin held on tight with one hand, had the other high in the air for balance, and spurred with only his athletic shoes. When he was finished, she wiped the tears from her eyes and kissed him hard.

"Geez, sweetheart. I didn't mean to make you cry," he said as he kissed her back.

"It was just so funny. I never would've imagined you riding a bull." Sarah was still laughing.

"Well, I've been to a couple rodeos in my day." Justin laughed with her. "And it's not as easy as it looks. You want to try?"

"No way. I'm not getting on that thing." Sarah pointed at the bucking machine. "But I'll ride the Tilt-A-Whirl with you—whatever that is." She'd heard some teenagers talking about it and it sounded sort of fun.

"You don't know what a Tilt-A-Whirl is?" Justin asked, astonished. "Come on then." He pulled her away to the football field where all the carnival rides were.

The main street was filled with vendors selling everything from fresh-squeezed lemonade to huge corndogs on a stick. Twinkling lights were strung from one lamppost to another, shining like swinging fireflies in the night. All around people laughed and chatted and got caught up on all the births and deaths and weddings.

Gossip doesn't sound that different in small towns than it does in big ones, Sarah thought to herself as she held Justin's hand while they waited in line for their turn on the whirling, twirling ride. She didn't quite know what it felt like to be seventeen and in love on a hot summer night, but she thought she could imagine it, especially when Justin leaned over and kissed her full on the lips.

She knew she was closer to feeling it as the ride spun and dipped and made her scream. She'd been on huge roller-coasters that flipped the riders upside down, but she didn't think she'd ever again find a ride that was as fun as the red contraption she was riding in this small town in Texas.

Pretty soon, the little kids who had run all day were droopy-eyed and tired. Some of the parents were ragged, too, and went home to tuck themselves and their kids into bed. But those who stayed were there for one reason, the dance. At the opposite end of Main Street from the football field, a band had set up. Sarah listened to them while Justin ordered each of them a lemonade.

Sipping their sugary drinks, they walked to the edge of what looked to be the dance floor. There were chairs and benches of all sorts forming a huge oval. Intermixed were torches stuck in planters, letting off a citrus-smelling smoke. Sarah leaned easy against Justin as the band tuned their instruments to a song that talked about a cowboy making 'it to Amarillo in the morning. She'd never heard it before, but the fiddle was so sweet and sullen it made her wish she knew if the cowboy made it.

"Well that's a Breslow if I ever saw one." A booming voice sounded behind them.

Justin turned and smiled as he shook the man's hand. "Hello, Mr. Mayor."

"Hello, Justin. Long time no see."

"Yeah. I've been out digging up stories," Justin said, hoping he wouldn't blow it.

The man took the hint and smiled at Sarah. "It looks like you've been out digging up beautiful women." He winked at Justin. "Tell me where you got her, and I'll take my shovel."

"Nah, she's a one of a kind." Justin hugged Sarah to him. "Sarah, this old goat is Gregg C. Vaines. He's mayor of this one-horse town. Mayor, this is Sarah Johnson."

"Nice to meet you, Mr. Mayor." Sarah smiled and shook his hand. His voice didn't go with his body. He was a short, round man with round glasses, a cigar, and snow-white hair. He looked like a train conductor in his black suit, with eyes to match.

"You sure remind me of someone, or rather a couple someones, I used to know." He thought for a second. "Oh, well. What are you doing here?"

"We're just visiting Grandpa, and I thought I'd show Sarah the town her mom grew up in."

"Oh, yeah. Who'd that be?"

"My mom's name was Helen Prescott. Her parents lived on West Avenue, I think, and she worked for the *Texas Hill Gazette*." Sarah tried to imagine her mom growing up here. She'd always looked as if she'd been born right beside her father.

"I'll be damned! Helen's your mom? Must be almost forty years since I last saw her. Good gracious, everyone loved her. Even me, mostly likely, that's why I recognized you. I was sorry to hear about her."

"Thanks." Sarah bowed her head. With everything that had been going on, her death seemed just days ago. She appreciated Justin's tightening his hold, supporting her.

"It was just horrible. I remember when Lainey told me about it, I cried." Gregg sniffed back the tears that threatened.

"I didn't know Aunt Lainey came down here anymore."

"Oh, she hasn't been, not for years. But she just happened to be passing through, and I saw her. As for Helen, the last time I saw your mom was the summer she turned eighteen. I think." He rubbed his jaw. "Yup. Her mom was in buying plates and ice cream for their party. She and Lainey were out in the street having a water-balloon fight with some of the local ranch boys." He looked at Justin. "I think your dad was one of 'em."

"Really?" Sarah laughed. She was trying to visualize her mom throwing water at a bunch of guys in cowboy hats.

"Yes, siree. I remember it like it was yesterday. Those two long-legged girls eyeing those boys. Their blond hair waving in the breeze, their arms linked. They were inseparable, those two." His eyes teared up a little.

"I'm sorry. I didn't mean to make you sad." Sarah reached for his hand.

"Don't worry, doll. I ain't sad. It does my heart good to remember those tan legs and laughing eyes. Makes me feel young again." He smiled as he walked away, his mind probably off in another decade.

"I just can't imagine my mom having a water-balloon fight," Sarah said.

"Why?"

"Because she was always so refined." Sarah shook her head. "I mean, she always tried to run around the backyard with me, playing catch and tag."

"That doesn't sound too refined."

"No, it doesn't. She was always so elegant. And the reason she goofed around throwing Frisbee with me is because she felt bad, I think."

"Why would she feel bad?" Justin asked and leaned closer to Sarah.

"Because I was always asking for a baby sister. I would've loved a baby brother, too, but a sister is what I wanted. She and Lainey were so close. I wanted to have someone to play with."

"Oh." Justin said. "Why didn't she just have another baby?"

"They tried for years. But when she turned forty, she stopped taking all the medicine the doctors gave her for infertility and they pretty much gave up. And just a few months after that, she died."

"That's sad." Justin held her face in his hands.

Sarah nodded. "That's why Dad and I made the pact we did."

"What pact?"

"That we'd always take care of each other." Sarah laughed. "And that he'd try to live forever." A tear slipped down her cheek.

Justin wiped the tear away. "Why did he say that?"

"Because when he dies, I'd be all alone." She tried to smile, but remembered crying in his arms about how scared she was. It had been a lot for a sixteen-year-old to deal with. It was a lot for anyone to deal with.

"Sweetheart, as long as I'm around, you won't be alone."

"Thanks, Justin." Sarah smiled through a teary sniff. "You mean you'll heat up my TV dinner in the microwave and wrap my feet in blankets when I'm old?"

"Of course, I will." He smiled too. He felt his heart move. The idea of holding her when she was cold, when time had faded her hair to white, didn't seem too bad of an idea. Even though it wasn't bad, it scared the hell out of him.

Sarah turned and looked at the dance floor. Couples were entwined, moving in a graceful movement around the oval. They looked sweet, she thought. It looked like the kind of dance she wouldn't mind doing.

"Do you want to dance?" Justin asked, picking up on her thoughts.

"I don't know how." Sarah looked at him.

"It's easy."

"What's it called?"

"Well, around here we're egotistical enough to call it the Texas Two-Step. But most places just call it the two-step."

Sarah looked back at the dance floor, feeling doubtful.

"I'll teach you." Justin pulled at her.

"Okay."

As Justin showed her the steps, she noticed they were getting quite a few funny looks. *Well, I must look funny,* she thought. *I'm a city girl trying to learn something they do in the country. Of course, they're looking at me funny.*

"Look, you're doing great." Justin smiled and tilted her face up to his. "But don't look at your feet."

"But you said, look." Sarah giggled.

"I didn't mean that, and you know it."

"I wish they'd play a slower one."

"This is as slow as it goes," Justin said as he twirled her around and let her fall into a slow dip. "You're beautiful," he whispered.

Sarah felt her face get red. "Everyone keeps saying that."

"It's true. The lights shining in your eyes. Your hair, how it waves around your face." Justin combed it through his fingers. "Your face, when it blushes. And your lips. Mmm, those lips. I could kiss them forever." Justin pulled her closer and matched his lips with hers and kissed her. Long and easy, he wound his tongue with hers.

Her body felt warm and needed against his. When Justin lifted his head, they were still dancing. Sarah had no idea how. And people were smiling.

Later, after she and Justin had gone for a walk in the moonlight, danced a few more steps on the kitchen floor, laughed and made love in the big bed with candles shining all around, Sarah thought about those people smiling. Maybe she could believe that her mom had grown up in such a town. Maybe she could believe that she was welcomed by that same place. She smiled to herself as she went to sleep, feeling closer to her mom than she had in years.

*

Across the sparsely lit yard, J.T. was sitting on the porch. His pipe smoke was carried away by the night wind. As he took his last puff of the day, he thought about the conversation he'd had earlier with the mayor.

"It sure is good to see that fate finally decided to play her hand." The mayor had sucked on his cigar.

"Fate. Hmm. I don't know if it was fate, Gregg."

"Well, I don't know what else you'd call it. It was no secret that son of yours was in love with that girl's mama."

"Yeah. And look where it got him." J.T. still felt sadness and anger over his son's death.

"Maybe this will set all the wrongs right. Maybe love will find her justice."

"It won't bring my son back." *No matter what I do. Nothing will do that.*

CHAPTER 15

"That was Annie." Sarah flipped her cell phone closed. "She found Sheryl Ames, but she's still working on the information for Karen." Sarah walked across the hardwood floor of the guesthouse living room.

Lariats were coiled and hung in various places on the walls, almost as if they'd never been moved from when the bunkhouse had been a place for cowboys to sleep when they weren't out riding the range. Beside them were pictures of those cowboys doing what cowboys do, sitting tall in the saddle, riding a bucking bronco, teaching a freckle-faced kid how to rope, and saving a newborn calf from a spring blizzard. The pictures had fascinated Sarah. When she thought of a cowboy, she thought of the guy who did cigarette commercials. She supposed the image was good. But looking at the photographs of real-life men, who seemed to live their lives on the back of a horse, was different. Their faces looked weathered from the sun, but their eyes looked quick to laugh and easy to love.

While the pictures were intriguing, there were other parts of the décor that had taken some getting used to. Above the fireplace was a massive set of Texas Longhorns and at the foot of it was a red-and-white cowhide, which adorned a huge chunk of floor. The chairs that were scattered about the long space were covered in the same-colored hide. The cushy couch where Justin sat held a beautifully woven green-and-white saddle blanket along its back. But the horns and cowhide hadn't taken as long to get used to as she'd thought they would. Because they were part of Justin, part of what they had together.

Sarah knew that when she had to go back to the life she'd had before Justin, she would think of this bunkhouse, nestled in the rolling hills of Texas, with fondness. In it, she'd fallen utterly in love with a man who had eyes that were quick to laugh and were very easy for her to love. She was trying to get used to thinking that thought without having fingers of uneasiness clutch her heart. There was so much to be uneasy about. So much. But she couldn't deal with that now.

"You'll never guess where she lives."

Justin looked up from the notebook in his hand. He'd been trying for the past hour to come up with something to write on Helen Johnson. He needed to get something down. He didn't want Sarah to think he couldn't write, although he really couldn't. But that was beside the point. "Somewhere in Oklahoma?" Justin smiled.

"No. She lives here." Sarah sat next to him and tapped her notebook with her pen.

"Here?"

"Yup." Sarah couldn't help but smile at her use of such a western word. "Except her name isn't Sheryl Ames anymore. It's Caroline Bennett. I guess she and her sister run a floral shop in town."

"Really? She was probably there last night."

"That's exactly what I thought. Annie called her and told her that a couple of reporters were doing a piece on siblings in business together. So we can go see her this afternoon."

"Is Annie sure this Caroline was your mom's cell mate?"

"Not really, since she changed her name, but at least it's a step in the right direction."

"I agree."

"So do you want to make up some quick questions we can ask her?"

"Sure." Justin flipped a page in his notebook. "Do you want to do that now or listen to those chips we got from the prison?"

"We can do that when we come back." Sarah began writing on her own paper.

"Sarah."

She looked up. "What?"

"We have to listen to them sometime."

"I know." Sarah's shoulders slumped.

"What is it?"

"Nothing."

Justin pulled her onto his lap. "Come on. What?"

"It's just that I know my mom is dead, but hearing her die . . . I don't know if I can do that."

"God. That's right." Justin wrapped his arms around her. "I'm sorry. I didn't even think of that. I'm sorry." Justin kissed her hair. "Do you want me to listen to them?"

"No. Yes." Sarah tucked her head beneath his chin. "I don't know."

"Well, let's worry about that later. Maybe this Caroline if it is her can tell us all we need to know about the women being used as prostitutes."

"Maybe."

"And then we won't even need to listen to them."

*

"Did I tell you that Annie said Sheryl Ames was born in Boston to a very wealthy family?" Sarah asked as Justin turned down a shaded side street.

"No." Justin signaled to pull over in front of a small, blue house set away from the road. "Wait a minute. *The* Ames from Boston? Senator Ames? My God. I remember hearing about their daughter running away?"

"You do?"

"Yeah. We learned about it at the—in college. I took some criminal psychology classes—you know, for my journalism degree."

"So did my mom." Sarah unfastened her seat belt, wondering why Justin had faltered. "So what's the story?"

"Basically, this high-society couple didn't have proper supervision for their teenage daughter, and she ran off."

"That's horrible."

Sarah walked up to the front door and knocked. Then smiled when a when a woman in her late forties welcomed them in.

"Caroline Bennett?"

"No. I'm her sister, Jackie."

"Oh, nice to meet you. I'm Sarah and this is Justin. We're here for the interview. I think the paper called you."

"Yes." Jackie shook her hand. "Caroline's in the back. You can go on in. She's on the phone but expecting you. I have to run to the shop. So I won't be here for the questions. But you can call me tomorrow if you want."

"Thanks." Sarah smiled and watched the woman get in her sporty little car and drive away. Sarah was beginning to have serious doubts that Caroline was Sheryl. Because if she was anything like Jackie, she'd never been any one's cell mate, much less been in prison.

"Well, let's go." Justin held the door for Sarah.

Justin and Sarah walked toward the sound of a very pleasant, woman's voice, speaking French. Around them, her house was welcoming, plush, and very expensively decorated. When Sarah saw the woman, tall and elegant, she knew this woman wouldn't have known her mom, not the one in a prison cell, anyway. Her long, peach silk pantsuit and manicured fingernails were just window dressing, but the way she held herself was what would have never fit in.

Caroline's eyes flitted briefly over the pair. "Thanks for coming," Caroline said as she hung up the phone. "Let's sit. You ask." She pointed to a long couch.

Sarah raised her eyebrow at the quality of language. She'd been expecting the voice that had talked to her mom and was glad when Justin began his questioning, after they all were seated.

"How long have you been in business?"

"Five years," Caroline responded.

"Are there any other family members involved in the business, besides your sister?" Justin asked when the conversation paused.

"No. Just Jackie."

"Why did you decide to move here?"

"I knew someone once who said this was a great place to live. So here I am." Caroline was seated on a high-backed chair and seemed to really look at Justin and Sarah for the first time. Her eyes locked with Sarah's. "Helen?" She whispered.

"No. I'm Sarah . . . Helen's daughter." She knew her voice sounded just as surprised.

Every bit of color drained from Caroline's immaculate face. "Oh God."

"Sherry?"

"Nobody's called me that for years," Caroline said. "I'm Caroline now. Sherry's dead."

Sarah nodded. "So you did know my mother?"

"Yes." Caroline stood and walked to shut the door. She flicked her fingernails all the way there and back. "What do you want?" Caroline asked as she fiddled with a pack of cigarettes.

"We ran across some evidence that there are girls at the Freeman Prison who are forced to be prostitutes. We wanted to know if you knew anything about it." Sarah didn't exactly know what to say, but she hoped this didn't scare her so she'd refuse to talk about it.

"What do you care?"

"My mom died there." Sarah squared her shoulders. "And I care about the treatment of the women there."

Justin sat forward on the couch, taking hold of Sarah's hand.

"Why? They're just convicts, crooks." Caroline took a long drag on her cigarette.

"My mom wasn't."

"That's what they all say. What the hell was she there for if she didn't commit some crime?"

"She was an investigative reporter. During her career, she changed the workings of many prisons. She wanted to improve Freeman Prison but died before she could."

Caroline raised her eyebrows at that. "Reporter, huh?" She shook her head. "I guess that's why she asked so many damn questions."

"Will you help us find out who was involved in the prostitution?"

"Why should I?"

"I'm helping Justin, who is a reporter for the *Dallas Herald*, do a story, sort of a dedication, on my mom." Sarah paused. "And I want to stop the prostitution from happening."

Caroline shrugged her shoulders and narrowed her eyes at Justin.

Sarah frowned, seeing that Justin couldn't seem to meet Caroline's gaze. *Why*, she wondered.

"We've been to the hotel in Atlanta," Sarah added.

Caroline's eyes got big. "Really. So it's still going on there? How'd you find out about that?"

"My mom smuggled a business card from there out to my father. We only found it a week or so ago."

"After all these years. I remember it like it was yesterday. So that's where it went." Caroline smiled. "I was working on a way to blow the whole operation and that card was a key element. But when I couldn't find it, I had to wait until I could get another one. But I never did."

"Who's doing it?" Justin asked.

"I don't know. Might not even be the same person now. None of us ever saw him."

"The girl we spoke to didn't seem to have enough of a record to be in prison," Sarah said. "It seemed like she was set up."

"Yeah, who wasn't?"

"What do you know?"

"Nothing. I just did my time and got the hell out." Caroline stubbed out her cigarette and lit another after a long pause. "But there is something I might be able to help you with, if you promise not to tell anyone I helped you. I still have a connection on the inside. Do you have a way I can get a hold of you?"

"Yeah." Sarah dug in her bag and pulled out one of her business cards and handed it to Caroline.

She looked at the fancy card, its fancy lettering saying, Sarah J. Johnson. "Damn," Caroline said. "It is *that* Helen. Helen Johnson was *my* cellmate. Everyone knew who she was. Everyone who'd ever been in prison knew her, respected her, mourned her."

"Thanks, Caroline," Sarah said.

"I'm not doing this for you." Carline flicked the ashes from her cigarette into the tray on the end table. "I'm doing it for Helen. I owe her one."

CHAPTER 16

"What's the J stand for?" Justin asked when he and Sarah were finished eating dinner.

"What?" Sarah asked as she filled the sink with water.

"Sarah J. Johnson. What's the J stand for?" Justin finished clearing the table.

"It's just a J. That's why people call me S.J." Sarah began washing their plates in her sudsy water.

"Oh, come on." Justin pulled her away from the sink and into his arms. "There's got to be more than that." He kissed her nose.

"Nope." Sarah kissed him back. "Not a thing more."

"Does Annie know?"

"Justin," Sarah said in her best whiney voice and rolled her eyes. "Yes. Annie knows."

"Maybe I'll call her." Justin turned to find the phone.

Sarah pulled him back to her. "Fine. It's Juliet."

"As in Romeo and Juliet?" Justin smiled.

"Yes." Sarah swiped soapsuds across his face.

"Is that why you're such a good actress?"

Sarah squinted at him.

"You know, like in Atlanta."

"No." Sarah laughed.

"Then why are you?"

"I mean, no I'm not a good actress. I was in a few plays in high school. Dad liked them. But believe me, I was a much better runner." Sarah turned back to washing dishes.

Justin kept his arms around her waist and rested his head on her shoulder. "You know, we have a dishwasher."

"I know. I just like doing this. It's calming, and there aren't very many."

And it takes longer, Justin thought. *So you don't have to listen to those voice chips.* "Do you think Romeo and Juliet ever danced?" Justin asked and pulled Sarah out onto the kitchen floor.

"Sure." Sarah smiled as she wound her wet, soapy hands around Justin's shoulders.

"Do you think they ever did this?" He kissed her cheek. Her eyes. Her lips. There, he lingered.

Sarah felt the tingling of warmth travel up her spine. She leaned her body closer to his, enjoying the dizzying feel of dancing and kissing.

"Do you think they ever did dishes?" Justin asked, laughing.

"Who knows. Next time I see Shakespeare, I'll ask him."

Justin's feet moved slow, making shuffling noises on the floor. "It's just weird you know."

"What?" Sarah frowned at the dark look on his face.

"That people would kill themselves for love."

"I guess."

"Would you?" Justin asked.

"I've never loved anyone, not anyone outside my family. Least of all enough to kill myself for them. Have you ever loved a woman like that?"

"No." Justin didn't understand the feeling of disappointment he felt. Why would it matter that Sarah had never loved anyone? "My father did," he said without thinking.

"Your father?"

"Nothing." Justin started to pull away.

"No." Sarah put her hands on his face. "Tell me. I want to know." She kissed him. "Please, I'd like to know this."

"I never talk about it."

"Well, maybe you should."

"You sound like Pat."

"See? Pat and I are smart people." Sarah wove her hands through his hair. "If you don't want to tell me, that's okay. But it might help to talk to someone."

Justin closed his eyes. He didn't know if he could tell it. Didn't know if he could keep the hatred for her mother from his voice. He knew she was waiting, patiently with her bright eyes and understanding smile. But, he wanted to tell her. Wanted to share the pain he'd carried all these years with someone he cared about. Someone he knew he could love.

Instantly, he was taken back to that day in his father's study. He'd seen his father's arms sprawled out and his head down. He'd looked as if he was sleeping. But Justin had known he wasn't. He'd known it the second he opened the door. "I was sixteen. He'd just won a big case. We were so happy. We were going to celebrate that night. We had dinner reservations and everything."

Sarah smiled.

"He was watching the news like he did every night and said there was something he wanted to finish seeing and that he wanted to call Grandpa and thank him for the gift. So, he told us to go on to the restaurant. And that he'd meet us there, after he made the call.

"Only, he didn't." Justin stopped dancing and scratched his head. "Mom got worried. He'd been having car trouble with the vehicle he drove so she sent me home. I drove the way I thought he would come but didn't see anything. I figured he was still on the phone talking to Grandpa." Justin smiled at that. "They sure could talk a lot."

"What did your grandpa give him?" Sarah asked.

"An engraved Colt .45 Peacemaker."

"What was engraved on it?" Sarah asked.

"Uh." Justin took a deep breath. "'To be a true peacemaker, you must judge thyself first.'"

"That's nice."

"It's what he shot himself with." Justin remembered pulling the gun from his father's hand.

"Oh, God. Justin. Tears fell from Sarah's eyes. She wrapped her arms around him, I'm sorry."

"I never told him, my grandpa. Never told anyone. I just cleaned it and put it back in its case on the wall."

Sarah wiped the tear that fell from Justin's eye.

"I didn't know what to do. So I made it look like he was cleaning one of his other handguns while he was on the phone. And, I hid the note that apologized to my mother and me." And to two other people he hadn't known when he'd read it but knew now. Their names were Eric and Sarah.

"Did the note say why he did it?" Sarah whispered.

"No, but I know why. It was on the news that night. There was a story about a fire in a prison."

"What do you mean, Justin?" Sarah asked. She could feel the blood in her face heat. "I mean, the woman my father killed himself for was your mother." Justin stepped back and leaned against the counter.

"You can't know that."

"Sure I can. He told me."

"What? That's impossible."

"You didn't know my father. He was always prepared. I always knew he'd had things he wanted to tell me, but thought I should be older. So he wrote it all down in this journal and had his lawyer keep it in a safety deposit box. After my mom died, I was to get it."

"What'd the journal say?"

"That he loved your mother. And that if I ever found a girl I could love as he'd loved her, to not let her get away." Justin walked to the door. He was having a hard time getting a handle on his anger.

"Well, you can't be sure that he was talking about my mother." Sarah stepped toward him.

"What other Helen Prescott Johnson do you know who died in a prison fire on March 27th?"

"March 27th?"

"Yeah. It was my parents' annniversary." Justin ripped open the door. "I'm going for a walk."

*

When he came back in the house, Justin felt like a jerk. First he'd been angry. About everything. About his father's death, how he'd had to fix it, and about how it had affected his mother. He'd dealt with those old, familiar wounds while he chopped and stacked some wood and checked on the horses. As he looked at their beautiful, sleek, summer coats, he thought of Sarah. He couldn't imagine never having ridden one. He couldn't imagine growing up in the city, never knowing all the things he'd grown up with. Sure, he chose to live in the hustle of Dallas, but he never felt alone. Hearing Sarah say that she'd never loved anyone deeply had hurt his feelings, which he didn't understand, but what she didn't say concerned him more. He knew, probably more than most, that parents grow old and die or just fade away.

Trying to look at Sarah's life from her point of view was something he'd never done. Petting the smooth nose of a horse made him realize that. She'd lost her mom when she was still just a girl. All she had in life was her dad and aunt. Granted, his parents were dead and all he had left was his grandpa. But he had so much more than that. He had the Breslow name and along with that came the tradition of generations working the land and finding success.

God, it was a mess. It was a mess because he made it a mess. He was mad. Mad that the young boy he had been had to deal with so much. He was mad that his father died and cheated him out of years of knowing him. But, he couldn't find a way to blame Helen even when there were so many reasons to. He couldn't because every time he thought of Helen, he thought of Sarah. Sarah was the only light his dark, dreary life had seen in a long time. The drive he'd felt over the last few months was now deflated. What now?

Giving a small handful of sweet mix to the bay in the end stall, he'd decided to pack his duffle and leave. With a determined stride, he made it to the porch before realizing that was the last thing he wanted to do. And besides, Breslows don't leave, they stick. Which was precisely what he was going to do, what he wanted to do.

But he still felt like a jerk. He knew he needed to apologize for leaving her alone in the middle of the kitchen floor as if she'd been gut punched. To delay the inevitable a little longer, he kicked off his shoes and filled a glass with water. As he drank it, he could hear the radio playing in the other room, and he noticed the kitchen was clean. He felt worse.

Thinking she was in the living room working, he walked in and turned off the stereo. Then he heard another noise. Sarah was crying.

"Hell," he whispered, thinking he couldn't feel any lower. But he did. When he walked into her room, she was curled around a pillow; her whole body shook. "Sweetheart. Shhh, Come here." He pulled her to him.

Sarah pushed against him. "No. Justin, just go away."

"I'm sorry." He brushed the tears from her cheeks. "Listen, I know I shouldn't have left you alone. I'm sorry for getting angry. I sorry mostly for hurting you."

"Just go, please." Sarah rolled back over to her pillow. "You can't help me with this."

Justin frowned. There was something he was missing. In his mind, he backtracked through the house. The kitchen, the living room. Then he nodded. On the dining room table there were all her notes and the playing device and the chips. She'd listened to them. "What'd you hear?" Justin pulled her back to him. "Was there more about the girls? What happened?"

"She was going to have a baby," Sarah sobbed.

"What?"

"A baby. My mom was pregnant."

"How do you know?" Justin grabbed her arms.

"She told Dad on the recording." Sarah wiped her face but couldn't control the tears. "She was so happy. I was going to be a sister." Sarah punched the pillow beneath her and let her agony pour into it. "Why?" Sarah asked no one. "Why did she have to die?"

"I don't know." Justin had a hard time controlling his own confusion. "It was just a terrible accident."

Sarah nodded. She felt so empty, so tired. She had nothing left in her, but black misery.

Justin stepped into the bathroom, filled a glass with water, and got a few painkillers. "Here, take these." He pulled her onto his lap. "There you go. This'll help."

"I'm sorry about your dad," Sarah said in a quaking voice after she'd swallowed the pills.

"I'm sorry about your mom." Justin said. He kissed her gently on the lips. Lying her back down on the bed, he angled his body along hers, holding her to him, not letting her pull away.

He held her until her steady, even breathing told him that exhaustion had finally taken over. Then he went to the dining room to hear to the recordings himself. He was confused at first when he began listening to the bathroom chip, but soon he realized what was going on.

"What the hell are you doing in here? Are you sick?" Sherry's voice.

"No. Now get the hell outta here." Helen's voice.

"Shit, no. You asked for extra ketchup for your damn chicken. Who eats ketchup on chicken?"

"I do."

"Bullshit."

"Fine. I'm getting old, and sometimes I skip a month or two, and I don't want the guards to find out."

"But you're not one of the girls."

"Just get me the damn ketchup!"

"Fine!" The door of the bathroom banged shut as Sherry left.

Why would the guards care? Justin wondered. And before the thought was fully formed, he had the answer. Because the girls who were prostitutes couldn't get pregnant. How would they explain that one? Justin shook his head and went back to listening. He didn't have to wait very long for the next recording.

"Eric, I know I'll get to tell you before you even hear this." Helen's voice said in an excited whisper. *"But you're going to be a daddy again. You get to spend your retirement years changing diapers."* Helen laughed.

Justin squeezed his eyes shut and pressed Stop on the player. He'd just heard a laugh that was Sarah's. Sarah's sounded just like her mom's, and in that moment, no matter how hard he tried to hold on to the hate he felt for Helen Johnson, he couldn't. All he wondered was, who was she, really?

He fingered the last chip. The one from Helen's cell. He didn't know if he should listen to it. Didn't know if Sarah would want him to without her, but he felt as if he needed to. The investigator part of him was urging him to listen, to know what was on it. It was almost as if this chip held an answer, to what, he didn't know.

He put it in the player and turned the volume down. He pressed Play.

"We're in the dark again." Sherry's voice.

"Yeah so?"

"So they should fix that light."

"I like it. I don't have to look at you that way."

"Bitch. So did you get all your shit figured out?" Sherry's voice.

"What the hell do you care?" Helen returned.

"I just wanna know when you'll be gone so I can get ready for the next bitch who's gonna stink up the joint. Maybe then whoever's in charge of fixing shit will fix our light."

"I doubt it, but you only have about five more days of me."

"That's a long damn time."

"Listen, I wanted to say thank you for, you know, from before."

"What the hell do I care that you're an old damn woman, huh?"

Justin blew out a breath. He already knew all of this. But Sherry and Helen sounded almost friendly this time. *What's going on?* He wondered.

"You ask too many damn questions, you know that, you bitch?" A voice Justin had never heard before sounded from the player.

"What do you mean?" Helen asked.

"Don't play dumb with me," The new voice again. *"You know exactly what I mean. But the judge'll take care of you. It'll just be a matter of time."*

"Stop being in a pissy mood and get the hell outta here." Justin recognized Sherry's voice. Then he heard a click and Sherry saying, *"Hey look! The—"*

Then there was a loud pop, almost like a balloon popping.

Then all he heard was screaming. The final words Helen spoke were on the recording.

"Eric, God. I love you. I'm so sorry. Sarah, oh, honey. My baby, my baby. No. No."

The final no was barely more than a whimper.

"Son of a—" Justin buried his head in his hands and was surprised to feel tears on his cheeks.

CHAPTER 17

"Justin?" Sarah called.

Justin lifted his head from his hands and looked across to where she stood in the doorway. It was long past midnight, and the only glow in the house was from the yard light outside. It illuminated her pale face, making her features look drawn and tired. If his heart could have felt any worse at that moment, it would have.

"Yeah, sweetheart?"

"Are you okay?"

"Sure." He scrubbed his face. "Do you need something?"

"I was just wondering. You know, since . . . " Sarah looked at her feet.

Justin walked to her and lifted her hands to his. "What?"

Sarah sucked in a breath. "I want to be with you. I need you."

Justin felt long spikes of heat roll through his system.

"Then, will you kiss me?" Sarah wound her arms around his neck and rose up on her toes. The tears she'd worked so hard to get rid of, stung the back of her eyes.

Justin looked at her trembling lip and almost turned away. He couldn't take advantage of her like this. But he needed her right now as much as she needed him. He didn't say anything. He just picked her up tight against him, cradling her and walked to his room.

He laid her on the smooth quilt and knelt at her side.

"It won't stop with kissing, Sarah," he said, searching her face for any doubts.

"I know." She moved to unbutton her shirt. "I don't want it to."

He stopped her hands. "Then, let me do this."

With his legs straddling her, he pulled her up to meet his mouth. His kiss started at the warm hollow of her neck and worked its way slowly down the length of her body. He reveled in all the sensations he made her feel. Her muscles bunched and bowed toward him as he moved.

Traveling back up he pulled at her breast with his lips and could feel her harden against the shirt she wore. He knew her body now. He knew the warm spot on the back of her neck that made her shiver, and he wanted to take his time. Make her forget, as well as himself.

Sarah was tucked into Justin's arms where she felt warm and needed. The scents of wood chips and horse filled her nose. It felt sweet and warm. She filled her hands with his curling hair and pulled him closer to her.

He moved his hands along her body, aching to feel her skin. Freeing each pearly button down the front of her shirt, he was closer to what he wanted. When the last one was loose, his fingers slipped into the opening and revealed what he'd wished for. Seeing the simple bit of lace, he felt himself go hard. He didn't take time to wonder why a bra could make a man forget himself. He was too busy brushing his tongue along Sarah's skin.

She wanted to feel his body against hers. Feel the warmth, his heart beating. She needed to remember why she was alive and what the reasons were for going on each day. She reached to pull his shirt over his head.

He slowed her hands. "Just wait. I want to see all of you first." With his whispered words, he removed the rest of her clothes.

She didn't feel cool in the house, lit with midnight. She felt hot, flushed with need.

She trembled beneath his hands as they caressed her, taking her to the edge and then drawing back. His lips and tongue followed the same path. He moved and lapped until she cried out his name, pleading for him.

Only then did he kick out of his clothes and join her. Side by side, lips a breath apart, he found her wet and wanting.

She arched against his hand, begging for more.

Moving slowly at the very brink of pleasure, he waited for what he needed. He was connected to her. He'd felt it the minute he found himself drowning in her eyes. He knew it now as her body went beyond her control and into his. He took that like a precious gift and sent her over the edge.

She trembled and bucked and collapsed in his arms.

He held her tight until the trembling subsided. Looking in to her eyes, he saw the passion swimming there. He moved to be with her. Rolling with her beneath him, he angled his body.

"I want you," he whispered.

"I want you more." Her mouth ground against his. She locked her legs around him and pulled him beneath her.

He felt his eyes grow wide.

She rose over him, heat filling her own. Tangling her hands with his, she took him in slowly. So very slowly, he knew he'd never breathe a normal breath again. When there was no more to pull in, she slid off and then back again. Slower this time than the first.

"Sarah." Justin grabbed her hips. He was crazy with wanting; he slammed up into her, making her scream with pleasure.

Every nerve ending was raw. He felt as if liquid silver flowed over their skin, burning and possessing them as it went.

She took it all in, demanding more. She needed this. She felt alive. She was a woman, strong and sure. She stretched high above him, lifting her arms to the ceiling. She rode with him, pushing him.

Spots of light and dark flashed in his vision. He could see her above him, her golden, sweat-slicked body driving him to madness.

They pumped in the same glorified rhythm.

He felt her tense, just as he reached the unbearable. He could wait no more; he matched her breath for breath as she arched and he plunged.

Afterward, Justin waited a long time before saying anything. Her body had stopped shaking, and her breath was back to even. But still she didn't move. Not that he wanted her to. Having her body entwined with his was not something he wanted to change.

Except that he wanted to see her face, look into her eyes.

"Sweetheart." Justin scooped up her hair. "How you doing?"

"Good." Sarah sat up and smiled.

Her cheeks glistened with tears. He sat up with her and pulled her tight against him. "Oh, no." He rocked her back and forth. "I'm sorry."

Sarah's body shook, but not from sadness, from laughter. "For what?"

Justin looked at her when he heard her giggles. "Didn't . . . did I hurt you?"

"No." Sarah wiped her face. "I've never felt like that in my life, but I know it wasn't pain."

Justin's grin cocked to one side. "Oh."

"'Oh' is right. Do you think you can do it again?" Sarah laughed at the stricken look on Justin's face.

"I can hardly breathe right now, but if you want to try again, I bet I can help out." Justin smiled long and slow. "Do you think you can keep up?"

"Hah! I'm so fit. I could run miles around you, you know."

"Let's see about that." Justin flipped over, pinning her back against the mattress. He knew a place right at the base of her hip that was ticklish. He used it. And laughed with her as she rolled and kicked.

"I love your laugh." Justin spoke without realizing.

His lips met hers with such fierce possession that Sarah had to concentrate to keep up. She'd focus on what he'd said later. Much later. She was on a ship, being tossed by a violent, but fantastic storm.

*

Justin felt as if he'd been looking at the notebook in his hand for months rather than the two days he had been. The lines weaved in and out of his vision as the yellow paper stared back at him, mocking him. He'd written what he considered a few good paragraphs and had even gone so far as to type them on his grandfather's computer. But, now he was just waiting for the time to pass. They were scheduled to meet with Simon Newell, the previous director of Freeman Prison, in a couple hours.

Sarah, meanwhile, was going back through her notes on the prostitution activity at the prison. She had lists of people who'd worked there, anyone who was associated with it, and multiple names of people from the hotel in Atlanta. There were several names that showed up on all three lists, but had said there was one name in particular that had caught her eye. She was just waiting for a fax from Annie telling her the facts.

The fax machine hummed. He gratefully abandoned his article to go fetch the message.

"Who's Evan Peterson?" Justin asked as he brought the fax paper over to Sarah, who was sitting at the dining room table.

"Don't know, but he shows up on all my lists." Sarah handed Justin the pile of papers she'd been looking at and took the fax from his hand.

"Hmm." Justin put his stockinged feet up on the edge of the table. He chewed on his pen as he looked over the names Sarah had highlighted in yellow. "Evan *Elvis* Peterson?" Justin tapped the pen on the paper. "Hey, isn't that the name of the guy who used to—"

"He was my mom's contact for her surveillance equipment." Sarah looked at Justin, and he saw her eyes soften. She looked back at the fax. "Yeah. And this is why. He's an ex-Navy SEAL. Skilled in counter-intelligence, espionage. My God. Here." Sarah handed the paper to Justin.

"Geez. He sounds like the kind of guy who could go out, shoot twenty people, and pass a lie detector test, saying he'd been in church all night."

"No kidding."

"Do you think he's the same guy?"

"Who knows? But Elvis isn't really that common."

"What's he got to do with the prostitution?"

"I don't know, but it says on one of those papers that he visited the prison a few days before the fire and that he frequented the Atlanta hotel a lot. Seems sort of fishy to me."

"What do you want to do?"

"I'd like to find him and ask him a few questions." Sarah stood and walked to the kitchen to fill her glass with water. "But you're working on the story. We have to go see Newell." She rubbed her forehead with her hand. "And I've got to go see Dad. I have to tell him about the baby. He'd want to know."

"Yeah. I guess."

"But I really feel like I have to finish this. Mom would want me to. I want to. Plus, I think there's more to this than what we know. I think it goes deeper."

"I can hold off on the story for a while. I'm sure Pat will understand."

"That'd be great. I feel like we're getting closer."

"Do you think we can find Peterson?"

"I already asked Annie to do some digging. If anyone can find this guy, she can. That's her." Sarah reached across Justin for her phone, put it on speaker. "Hey Annie. I've got you on speaker. Justin is here, too. What'd you find?"

"Well, I got a birth date, maybe. If it's the same guy. The government sure covers its tracks well."

"What is it?" Sarah wrote down the information as Annie talked. "What else?"

"It's pretty weird. There's all sorts of information on his travels, assignments. Up until about thirty years ago. Then it's like he drops off the face of the planet."

"But I've got sign-in lists for the prison, and he's on them."

"Maybe it's not the same guy?" Justin said.

"I know it is. It has to be." Sarah blew out a breath.

"I'll keep looking." Annie said. "I have a friend in the Navy who might be able to come up with something."

"Thanks." Sarah hung up with a frown. "I hate being this close, only to have a roadblock thrown up." Sarah looked at her watch. "I guess it's time to go. I just wish we could find him. I bet he could answer who's in charge of the prostitution."

"Maybe he's the one who is," Justin said. *And maybe he knows why your mother was murdered.* Justin shook his head. He still had no idea how to tell Sarah what he'd heard on that last recording. But he knew he had to find a way.

CHAPTER 18

"Hello, Mr. Newell. I'm Justin and this is Sarah." Justin held out his hand to the man he remembered from his childhood. He'd grown older, wiser, maybe a little sadder, but his eyes still shone with good humor.

"Sonny. I remember you." Simon pulled Justin and Sarah into the house. "Man, the last time I saw you, you were off to Quantico, Virginia. How'd that go?"

Justin gritted his teeth. "I never went. I decided I'd be better at walking a different beat."

"What the hell did you do?" Simon's eyes searched Justin's face. "Become a lawyer?" His eyebrows wiggled as he laughed.

"A reporter."

"What? Dear God. What's the world coming to? A Breslow as a reporter!"

"I still investigate things." Justin smiled, trying to defend himself.

"Well, I'm still proud of you, sonny." Simon looked at Sarah. "Now, who's this again?"

"This is Sarah Johnson. We're working on a case together."

Simon raised his eyebrow at Justin's choice of words.

"A story." Justin corrected.

"Well, now. This is the prettiest reporter I've ever met." Simon's faded blue eyes were tucked beneath aging lids, but they still examined her with all the thoroughness of the police officer he used to be.

Sarah smiled. "It's nice to meet you. But I'm not a reporter. I'm a profiler, a psychologist. I own a private investigation firm in Portland."

"Got yourself a first-class sort of gal from the looks of her. My wife dabbled a bit in cheating husbands and missing poodles herself."

"Interesting." Was all Sarah could manage. She didn't know if he was teasing about the wife or the poodles.

"Let's go sit." Simon motioned toward an ancient, over-stuffed couch.

Sarah's eyes flitted momentarily around the room and she thought she could accurately describe Simon Newell. He liked to read. Books were strewn here and there, lining every shelf and lying within easy reach of any chair. He liked music, too, old music. Records of jazz musicians Sarah had never heard of were scattered near his stereo system. She could still smell the heated-vinyl scent that records emit while being played.

"Would you like something to drink?" Simon asked before he sat. "I've got water and even a beer or two, I think."

"Water'd be fine," Justin offered.

"Yeah. That's great." Sarah sat next to Justin on the couch. His hand absently brushed through her hair, as Sarah continued her perusal of the house.

The carpet was well-worn but clean. The walls needed a little wash down, as did the pictures that hung on it. She recognized Simon in many of them. In some, he was younger and laughing with a pretty, brown-haired woman. In others, he was alone with a floppy-eared, golden dog. There were a few with him and people Sarah assumed might be friends or relatives.

"So to what do I owe this visit?" Simon asked when he came back with their glasses of ice water.

"We have some questions concerning the time you were director of Freeman Prison," Justin said.

"Oh. Ok." Simon sat down in his chair and pulled up the footrest. "Your daddy got me that job after twenty years on the force." He nodded to Justin.

"Really?"

"Yup. I enjoyed it but was glad to move out of that heat."

And into this heat, Sarah thought. She was barely used to the hot breeze that blew during her sunrise runs.

"So what are the questions?" Simon asked.

"My mom was there for a time while you were the director. She came across some information leading to some criminal activity. And we were wondering if you knew anything about it," Sarah said.

"Criminal activity in the prison?" Simon took a drink of his water and shook his head. "No. But I was hardly ever in the prison itself. My office was in downtown Freeman City. What do you think she found?"

"We don't think. We know. We've verified the activity through several sources." Sarah tapped a finger on the notebook she'd gotten out of her bag. "The inmates were taken to Atlanta and were forced to be prostitutes."

Simon sat forward in his chair. "Are you sure?"

"Yes," Justin said.

"My God." Simon stood and walked to one of the pictures hanging on the wall. "How long has this been going on?"

"We don't know. We're not sure when it began, but we know it's still happening."

"How do you know?" Simon turned back to them, holding the picture in his hand.

"We chatted with one of the girls almost two weeks ago," Justin added.

"Where?"

"At the Confederate Regency in Atlanta. She came to our room."

"What'd she say?" Simon sat down again.

"She was afraid, and she didn't know who was in charge of the operation, either," Sarah said.

Simon frowned. "You know the only person who would have the power to allow such a thing to happen is the warden." Simon looked up quickly. "Did you talk to a Becket Larson?"

"We tried," Justin said. "But we heard he'd been shot."

Simon frowned again. "That doesn't surprise me. He was an asshole." He looked at Sarah. "Pardon."

"No problem. Can you think of anyone else who might be able to help us?" Sarah asked.

"Did you try the current warden?"

"Not really. We were acting as prison inspectors when we talked to him. So we couldn't really ask those kinds of questions," Justin said.

"Probably wouldn't be of any help anyway. He's a lot like Larson."

"The girl we talked to in Atlanta seemed to think that she was set up and put in prison on purpose," Sarah said. "Do you think that's possible?"

"Depends on the judge or the arresting officer. If the evidence was strong enough one way, any judge and jury could easily convict someone," Simon said.

"Even if the evidence was planted or circumstantial?" Sarah asked.

Simon looked dismayed. "How many people do you know of who have actually committed a crime and who walk away free?"

"Probably a lot," Sarah said, "depending on their lawyer and the evidence."

"It's the same with people who didn't commit a crime, too. Many are wrongly convicted. Some very convincing evidence can be created," Simon said.

"That's horrible." Sarah looked at Justin.

"It is." He nodded. "But it happens."

"Why? Why would someone put a young girl in prison who hasn't done anything wrong?" Sarah was furious at the idea.

"I think you found your answer with what those girls were doing in Atlanta." Simon smiled sadly as he looked at Sarah and Justin.

Sarah couldn't believe it. She couldn't believe that there could be anyone in the world who would be so cruel, so mean, all for money. She was all the more determined to find out who was in charge and to stop them. "Do you know an Evan Peterson or anyone with the nickname of Elvis?" Sarah questioned, leaning forward. Her voice was no longer pleasant. It now held an edge.

"No. Who are they?" Simon asked.

"We think they're the same guy, and that he might be in charge or at least involved in the operation," Sarah answered.

"I don't even know who I could ask." Simon sipped the rest of his water. The ice clattered when he set the glass down. "But there is something I should tell you." Simon got up and walked from the room.

"Well, this is hopeless." Sarah slumped back against the couch. "How can it be that no one knows anything?"

"Someone knows." Justin patted her leg. "We just have to find them."

Simon came back into the room. All of the previous cheer was gone from his features. When he sat down, he somberly looked directly at Justin. "Your dad was my best friend. Still would be, I'm sure, were he alive. I loved him like a brother. There wasn't anything we didn't know about each other. Save this. Only because he died before I *could* tell him." Simon wiped his face. "But I'm telling you this because I think it might help you."

"Okay." Justin smiled. He was remembering all the stories his dad had told him about Simon. He sort of figured he and Pat had the same bond. "I know he thought of you as a brother, too."

"After you hear this, you'll probably think less of me. But sometimes men do stupid things. And that's just what this was. A stupid thing."

"I'm sure you're still a good man," Sarah prompted.

Justin understood she wanted to hear what Simon had to say and was afraid the more he talked of being stupid, the more chance there was of him talking himself out of telling them.

"I think you remember my Betty Sue?" Simon handed them the picture he'd been holding.

"Yeah. I always thought she had the funniest jokes." Justin pointed to the brown-headed woman in the picture.

"Soon after we moved to Alabama, she got pretty sick. Cancer. We didn't catch it soon enough." Simon's face grew anguished. "She held on years, when the doc said she'd have only a few months. She went through everything the medical profession could throw at her, but she didn't get better. In the middle of all of it, I had a new job I wanted to be good at, great at. And she wanted the same thing. She kept trying to move out, but she was too sick to be on her own. She wanted to file for divorce, but I wouldn't let her." Simon paused and swore under his breath. "There was only one thing that would keep her from going. She said she wanted me to find someone else. She told me I was young and deserved to feel the body of a young woman, not some dying one." Simon slammed his hand down on the arms of the chair. "She even went so far as to get a list of names together for me."

"What happened?" Justin asked.

"There was only one stipulation. I couldn't tell her if I did it or not. I had to pretend that I was completely faithful, until the end. I gave up and said fine. But I could only do it once. I was sick for days. Physically sick. I even went to the doctor hoping I was dying." He shook his head. "It was just guilt. Well, not long after, she took a turn for the worse, and I spent every spare hour I had with her. Sometimes I'd go into the office in the middle of the night when she was sleeping to try to catch up on work.

"On one of those nights, I had a visitor. It was a man in a long overcoat and hat. He gave me all these instructions, but I never heard his voice. He wrote them all on a little black notebook he kept in the pocket of that coat. He told me I was to give an order to have one of the inmates at the prison killed, but that it had to look like an accident. I, of course, said no." Simon got up and wandered to the stereo and put on some low, bluesy music. "But he had pictures of me with that girl. He threatened to show them to my wife. We tore that office up, fighting. But, then he pulled a gun on me. So I said I'd give the order. He made me type it up right then, told me I had three days to deliver the order and have it carried out." Simon held up a small, gold pin. "I pulled this off his sleeve." He handed it to Justin.

Justin turned it over in his palm. The pin was a slim gavel. Engraved on it were the words, The Judge. When he turned it over, he saw the initials, TJB, were engraved on the back. Justin felt as if the wind had just been knocked out him.

"This was my father's."

"I know."

"Was that man my father?"

"No. I'd know that better than anyone." Simon returned to his chair. "Anyway, I took the order home with me. I was conflicted, to say the least. I didn't want my wife to see the photographs that guy had, but I didn't want to be responsible for some woman dying."

"What'd you do?" Sarah asked. Justin looked at her; she'd gone white. He knew she needed the answer to this question. So did he.

"Nothing. Betty Sue died the next day. I had no reason to send the order. And I didn't care anymore if that man came back and shot me or not. " He handed the envelope he'd gotten from the other room to them.

"It's still sealed," Sarah said.

"I had no reason to open it."

Sarah ripped the envelope and read the letter aloud. "'Please arrange to have inmate, 59240, disposed of. Note: It must appear to be accidental.'" Sarah's eyes went hot. "She was my mother! How could you do it?" In an instant, she was across the space that separated her from Simon. She grabbed the front of his shirt with both hands and pulled him out of his chair. "How, damn you?"

"Jesus. Sarah, sweetheart. He didn't send the order. He didn't send it." Justin pried her hands free. "That's why we have it."

Simon remained standing. Tears clouded his eyes. "I had specific instructions on how to give the order and then what to do with the letter. You might want to know about that."

"What?" Justin asked and coaxed Sarah to sit back down.

"I was to show the letter to Becket, then find a place to burn it. Then I was to destroy the ashes."

Sarah had a tight grip on her chair arms. "That's strange. Why would you have to destroy the ashes?"

"Because they can be salvaged and treated and the print can still be read," Justin said.

Simon raised his eyebrow at Justin. "Maybe you should've been a cop and not a reporter. That is something somebody with special training would know."

"What about an ex-navy SEAL?" Sarah asked.

"Maybe," Simon answered. "I was going to tell all of this to your father. I even called him, but the funeral arrangements for Betty were taking all of my time. Then there was a fire at the prison I had to deal with. And then your dad died. I barely made it through the week." Simon looked at Sarah. "I'm so sorry about all this. Grief had me crazy back then."

"You might not have killed her, but you knew someone was trying to." Sarah glared at Simon. "She was an investigative reporter trying to help the people at the prison." Sarah wiped the angry tears away. "And she was pregnant when she died in that fire."

"She was the one who died?" Simon asked with a stricken look on his face.

"You typed her number yourself!" Sarah yelled and shook the letter in his face.

"I didn't connect that with the fire. The fire was just a horrible accident."

"It was no accident." Sarah walked toward the door.

Justin stood up. He could see she was trying to hold it together. But, by the time he got to her side, her whole body was shaking.

"Let's go, Justin. I want to find the man who wanted my mother dead." She walked out of the house toward the car.

Shit, Justin thought as he followed. *I should have told her. I should have found a way for her to know so she wouldn't have to hear it this way.*

"Justin," Simon called after them. "You can keep that pin."

Justin paused for just a moment. "I was going to." He nodded as he looked at the pin he held in his hand. He felt sick somehow. Did his dad have anything to do with this? Is that why he killed himself? Because he couldn't stand the thought of murdering another human being. "But, I don't know where he got it."

"I do," Simon said.

"Where?"

"A woman he'd been in love with when he was a kid gave it to him." Justin shook his head. He knew the name Simon would say.

"Helen Prescott."

"Son of a bitch," Justin swore.

"What?"

"That was Sarah's mom."

CHAPTER 19

"Why do you think the man in the overcoat wanted my mom dead?" Sarah asked while she and Justin spent some time with the horses, something that had become a daily ritual.

"I don't know. Maybe she found something that connected him to the prostitution. Or maybe she stumbled on to something else that doesn't have anything to do with it."

"Do you think he rigged the fire?" Sarah patted the smooth neck of a pretty bay mare.

"Maybe. I think somebody did." Justin reached for her hand.

"What? Why?" She braced herself, knowing from his expression it was probably bad.

"I listened to that last chip. I know you probably didn't want me to, but I needed to know what happened."

"I've been thinking about it and decided I'd just have you listen to it. I didn't know if I could." Sarah looked at the sun setting beyond the hills, which were turning purple in the changing light. They looked peaceful. She wished she could just walk toward them and keep on walking. Maybe even to the edge of the world. She felt so many things, all things. She was mad and sad and confused. Nothing made sense. She shook her head. "No, I don't think I can."

"I'm sorry if I overstepped my bounds." Justin squeezed her hand.

"It's okay." She looked up into his eyes. They were warm and sad. "What'd it say?"

"She talked about you and your dad and the baby in the end," Justin said. "She said she loved all of you, and that she was sorry." Sarah felt the tears well. She dropped her face in her hands as Justin wrapped his arms around her shaking shoulders. "I'm so sorry," Justin whispered and held her until the world was dim with dusk.

Sarah could feel anger welling up inside her. "Of course, she said she was sorry," Sarah nearly yelled. "It's what she did. She was always responsible. Always felt responsible for things she couldn't even control. That's why she was there in the first place. Being responsible for somebody else's mistakes. Somebody else's conscience problems."

Justin stepped back.

"Damn it, Mom," Sarah cried. "I'll find who was responsible for your death, and you can be sure they'll be sorry."

"We'll find them." Justin said.

Sarah looked at Justin and smiled for the first time in what felt like days. She felt certain they could do this. "What else happened on the recording?"

"At the beginning of the recording, Sherry asked how long Helen had left and . . . " Justin told Sarah about what he'd heard.

"I wonder who that other woman was?" Sarah asked.

"We could call Caroline and see if she remembers."

"Let's." Sarah turned and in a few long strides, she was at the house.

When Sarah walked across the dining room to her bag, her phone started ringing. Looking at the caller ID, she saw it was Caroline. Tersely, she answered.

"Hello."

"I was calling because I have some more information for you." Caroline's said.

"Yeah? Justin and I were wondering what you were doing tonight or tomorrow."

"I've got time tonight. Jackie's out of town, so I'm free."

"Would it be too much trouble for us to come over now?" Sarah asked.

"No. I'll see you in a few minutes."

"Excellent," Sarah said and hung up, feeling that they might get some answers tonight.

*

After she'd disconnected from Sarah, Caroline turned to face the figure clothed in a dark hat and long coat. "How's that? Is that soon enough for you?"

The figure nodded.

"Now what? Do we just wait for them so you can blow them to smithereens?" Caroline dipped her head toward the gun in the figure's hand. She closed her eyes briefly and heard the clicking of the hammer as it was pulled back. "You better hope you kill me, you fucking bastard."

"I will," the figure whispered.

Two quick shots whistled silently through the air. They punctured the skin as they entered Caroline's body a few inches apart. She jerked when the first hot bullet slammed into her chest, and fell with the second. A raging roar filled her ears. She could hear each pounding beat of her heart.

There should have been pain, but she felt none. She felt sleepy. Letting her head roll to the side, she saw a pad of paper. She focused on it. If she could get it, she could tell Sarah and Justin who shot her. But her body wouldn't move. Blackness came. Silence followed.

*

"I wonder if Caroline will remember." Sarah raised her hand to knock on the door.

"Wait!" Justin commanded and walked in front of Sarah.

"What?" Sarah stopped.

"The screen door isn't latched, and the door isn't closed." Justin pointed.

"Oh." Sarah's alarm turned on. "She seems like the kind of person who would check something like that."

Justin's gaze searched the walkway and the flowerbed on both sides. His glance ranged over the windows, but nothing seemed out of place. "Knock and call her name."

Sarah rapped hard on the doorframe. "Caroline!" Then she

looked at Justin when there wasn't an answer.

"Again," he whispered. *Just protocol,* he thought. He knew what they'd find inside. "Open the door and call inside."

Sarah pulled the screen door open and pushed on the door. "Caroline! It's Justin and—" Sarah didn't finish. "Oh. God."

Justin pulled Sarah out of the doorway. "I know first aid. You call an ambulance." Justin was in the house before Sarah could respond.

*

Hearing Sarah speaking to a dispatcher outside, Justin knelt beside Caroline, but he knew there was nothing he could do for her. She'd bled out. His eyes scanned over her still form to see if there were any clues as to who had done this. He had a pretty good idea, but still he looked. A small discoloration near her temple caught his eye. It didn't look like a bruise. Leaning closer, he saw that it was a scar, maybe from a burn. He squinted, wondering where she'd gotten it. In Helen's cell, most likely, he nodded to himself. Is that what Caroline meant by Helen saving her life?

"Is she alive?" Sarah asked. She'd come inside and stood on the carpet near the edge of the couch.

"No. We were too late."

"Damn it," Sarah stormed and turned around. He thought she planned on walking out to the sidewalk to wait for the cops, but he saw her pause. She walked over to a lit computer screen. "Justin." Sarah pointed to the monitor. "Look."

Justin joined her. He read the message on the screen, "Stop asking questions or you'll be next."

"He just left," Sarah said.

"How do you know?"

"The screen saver wasn't on."

"True. Do you have a pencil or pen or something similar in that bag of yours?"

"Yeah." Sarah dug and found a yellow wooden pencil. "Why?"

"Because the cops can't see this. If they do, they'll keep us from continuing our search." *And I'll have to prove who I am.* "Because we're only reporters."

Sarah handed Justin the pencil. "Right. We don't have any identification here and ready to use. Can we use yours from the *Dallas Herald?*"

"Maybe." Justin moved the pencil eraser around on the keyboard until he'd closed the document, making sure to not save the changes. Then he figured if the cops realized the computer screen saver wasn't on, they'd investigate the reason why. So he just shut the computer down. If, by chance, they felt it to see if it was warm, he hoped they'd assume Caroline had just been working on it. "Let's go outside and wait for them." Justin motioned.

*

As they sat and waited, Sarah thought about how different this had been than the last person she'd seen dead. Caroline still looked peaceful, as if she were sleeping. Time hadn't taken over and turned her body into a stiff resemblance of her former self. The smell was an acrid iron smell, which was very different from the stench in Becket Larson's house, but not so different that it didn't make her stomach turn. But the blood was the same. It seemed as if gallons of it had just poured out. She closed her eyes, trying to block out the images, but all it did was make it worse.

"Stop thinking about it, Sarah." Justin cupped his arm around her shoulders. "It just makes it worse."

"It is worse. I didn't even cry, and I knew her, sort of." Sarah closed her eyes again. "Why didn't I?"

"Nobody can answer why we react to certain things, certain ways. But I'd say you knew more of what to expect this time."

Feeling confused, Sarah looked at him..

"I guess it's kind of like going deep-sea diving for the first time. No matter how many times you think about breathing that far underwater, you still panic when you get there. But after you done it once, you know what to expect."

"I guess." Sarah nodded, thankful Justin had gotten her thinking about bright salt-water fish and coral when she'd been focusing on things that were much worse.

They got to their feet as sirens sounded and the first squad car pulled up to the curb. The cops separated them and started their interrogation.

It seemed to Sarah that each cop asked the same damn question. But everything really started to mellow out as soon as Justin showed his ID from the paper. Actually, the questioning was pretty much finished after that. They got to drive away long before the coroner showed up.

"Do you want some dinner?" Justin asked after they arrived back at the guesthouse. He and Sarah sat at the kitchen table. "We haven't eaten since . . . breakfast."

"Sure. Do you think we could have waffles? I like your waffles." Sarah smiled, hoping that thinking of something cheery would actually make her feel that way. She remembered the last time they'd eaten them. It seemed like years ago rather than the month it was.

"I think I can dig out the waffle iron. If not, I'll go ask Stella." Justin moved around the kitchen gathering everything he needed to prepare their midnight snack. "Can you get me a couple eggs?"

Sarah opened the door of the fridge and grabbed a few. "When do you think the funeral will be?"

Justin pulled the eggs from her hands. Kissing her on the lips, he said, "Let's not talk about it tonight. We can face real life tomorrow."

"Okay." Sarah nodded. "Then let me stir." She grabbed the wooden spoon and stood near the mixing bowl, waiting for Justin to measure in the ingredients.

Later, after the dishes were done and Sarah sat on the couch to look through her notes but fell asleep instead, Justin went for a walk. Stepping out into the night air, he filled his lungs with the scent of tamarack and the sweet river. He needed to stretch his legs and clear his mind. Maybe then the answers would come.

He walked to the edge of the waterfall where he and Sarah had been on their first day here. But standing at the pool's edge didn't help. All it did was distract him from the problem at hand. So he walked on. Not that he didn't like remembering the way the water fell over Sarah's smooth, naked skin. It was just that he needed to focus.

The note on the computer screen kept haunting him. When he'd seen it, he hadn't been frightened, not for himself or even Sarah. But after he'd answered all the questions the cops had and showed them his FBI identification, he felt, honestly, terrified. It was as if holding the small ID in its leather pouch had driven home the fact that all of this was real and not some dream.

He'd somehow or another worked it out in his head that this wasn't a real case. After all, he wasn't talking to his usual contacts or even reporting to his boss. His mind had just decided that they weren't in any danger, and that all the people involved had long ago worked out their issues and had buried their ghosts.

But that wasn't true. They were in danger. And with him having really no idea who could've possibly killed Caroline, he had no way of knowing who to protect them from. But as he looked at the stars winking in the dawn, there were two things he was certain of. One, Sarah would never be in any position where a gun would even so much as be pointed in her direction. And two, the same person who killed Becket Larson had also killed Caroline Bennett. And he was going to find him.

CHAPTER 20

"Are you sure?" Justin asked into his phone.

"Pretty sure," answered Pat.

"When do I have to be there?"

"The proceedings start the day after tomorrow. I tried to stall it, but they're not going for it."

"How the hell am I supposed to do that?" Justin kicked at the dirt.

"Don't know, but you better figure it out. Judge Holt's on the stand." Pat paused. "But it seems like it'll be cut and dried, once it gets going."

"Nothing's ever easy with Holt. I'll be there." Justin slammed his phone closed. "Damn it," he swore as he looked across the yard to Sarah. *How the hell can I go to Dallas tomorrow when I'm supposed to go to Portland with Sarah?*

Justin walked toward the rental car where Sarah was. He forced his walk to be easily paced, so she wouldn't think something was wrong. She'd probably notice anyway. They'd had a lot of time in the last few weeks to get to know each other, while they waited for the coroner to release Caroline's body for burial.

"I'm ready," Sarah said when he got closer.

"Me too." *God, she's beautiful,* he thought as he looked at her. Even for a sad day, she was. The ankle-length dress she'd chosen to wear flitted in the warm breeze. Her hair was curled on top her head and had black ribbons lacing through it to match the dress. "You look really nice."

"Thanks. You, too." Sarah nodded her head. They'd decided to go shopping rather than wear the clothes Annie had sent them in Atlanta, figuring they'd draw less attention to themselves. He'd chosen a pair of black slacks, a navy shirt, and he'd even traded in his white athletic shoes for a pair of black ones. When she'd raised her eyebrow at him in the store, he'd simply said, "You can't run in fancy dress shoes."

"Too bad we're going to a funeral." Sarah opened the door of the car and got in.

"Yeah. Too bad." *We should be going to a nice, quiet dinner somewhere.* "I've got something to tell you." Justin shut the door and started the car. Figuring he might as well tell her now, before she started asking questions.

*

Sarah had expected it to be raining. At her mother's funeral the sky had poured. But standing in the wide cemetery with dipping hills, the air was blazing hot. The priest, with his pristine white collar, had beads of sweat rolling down his face. The mourners blotted their eyes, as well as their foreheads, with their well-used handkerchiefs. The various perfumes the women wore mixed with the faded scent of wilting roses, giving an added sadness to the day. Faintly, she could hear the soft weeping of the people behind her and the voice of the priest as he said the final prayer.

At her mom's funeral, there had been only her, Aunt Lainey, and her dad. Dad had made sure no one else came. It was to be a family affair only. He was kind enough to allow a public graveside service later, but none of the family had attended. Sarah was glad of that now as she watched Jackie hug and smile at people who could be perfect strangers to her.

Sarah's mind kept backtracking to her mom. She couldn't help it. Hers was the only other funeral she'd been to. It was odd to Sarah that her second funeral was for a woman who had been with her mom when she'd died. They seemed to have been allies of sorts when they were alive. Would they be friends in death? Sarah wondered.

"Thanks for coming," Jackie said to Justin and Sarah. They were the last ones there.

Justin shook her hand and Sarah kissed her cheek, saying the worthless words people say at funerals. Jackie smiled only slightly at them.

"I don't know what your plans are," Justin said. "But we sure would like to ask you a few questions, when you have time."

"Is this about the article?" Jackie asked.

"No. We aren't going to run the article," Justin said. "Out of respect for your family."

"Thanks." Jackie smiled, briefly.

"Through the course of the interview, we learned that my mother had something in common with Caroline." Sarah looked at Jackie. The face Sarah had seen before now seemed aged and tired, not excited for life as it had been the other day.

"What was that?" Jackie asked.

"Do you think we could sit for a moment?" Justin pointed to a park bench beneath a weeping willow.

"Yes." Sarah nodded. "What I have to tell you might require sitting."

"Okay?" Jackie's skeptical look stayed on her face until she and Sarah were seated and Justin was standing beside them.

"Caroline was with my mother when she died." Sarah clasped her hands in her lap, trying to decide how much to tell her.

"When did you and your sister become acquainted?" Justin asked.

"What do you mean?" Jackie stared at Justin.

"I read she was an only child." Justin paused.

"And this isn't going into any newspaper?" Jackie questioned looking at both Sarah and Justin.

They both shook their heads.

"I can personally guarantee no one else knows this." Justin dipped his head toward Sarah. "But us."

"I wouldn't bet on that."

"How come?" Sarah asked.

"My father knows."

"I thought Sheryl was his only daughter, only child," Justin said.

"By his wife, yes, that's true. I'm Sheryl's half-sister. My mother was the housekeeper for the Ames household."

"Hmm." Sarah frowned. "Did you guys know each other, growing up?"

"Oh, yeah. We were the best of friends. But one day Sheryl caught my mother with our father and figured out the whole thing." Jackie looked at her feet. "That's why she ran away. I tried to stop her, but she wouldn't listen to me."

"Where'd she go?" Justin asked.

"I don't know." Jackie looked up and let the slight breeze that started to blow sift through her hair. "Sometimes I'd get a letter in the mail with no return address. Only the postmark was a clue. But they were always different, New York, California, Alabama, and here."

"What do you know about her time in Alabama?" Sarah turned to face Jackie.

"She didn't talk about it much. She got in touch with me soon after she moved here, inviting me to visit. I stayed for a long time. I'm still here." Jackie smiled. "But when I first came, she was pretty messed up. She had burns all along the right side of her body. She'd get really mad at me if I tried to help her." Jackie twisted the smooth, cotton gloves she'd brought, but hadn't put on. "And she had nightmares."

"About what?" Justin asked.

"I don't know. She never would tell me. Once I heard her yell our father's name. So I figured she was dreaming about him. I'd never seen anyone hate another person as much as he hated her."

"Why'd he hate her?" Sarah asked.

"I guess because she found out he wasn't as perfect as he always pretended to be." Jackie looked at Justin. Tears swam in her eyes. She wiped them away. "He beat her. The day she found them together. I thought she was going to die. She left as soon as she was able." She shook her head, eyes distant as she remembered her sister.

"Yes, she was always waking me, calling out his name in those nightmares. 'Judge! Judge!' Everybody always, even my mother, called him Judge. That's the name Sheryl used, too."

"Isn't he a senator?" Sarah asked.

Jackie nodded. "But he wasn't always." She looked at Sarah. "You said she and your mom had things in common. What were they?"

"My mom was an investigative reporter doing a story on a prison in Alabama. She was undercover as an inmate and Sheryl was her cellmate."

"What?" Jackie stood up. "She never said anything about being in prison. Are you certain it was her?"

"Yes." Sarah stood up too and placed a hand on Jackie's arm. "I know where Sheryl got those burns."

"Where?"

"From the fire my mom died in."

Jackie looked up at the sky, peered through the swaying branches. "I can't believe she never said anything."

"We think the fire was set on purpose." Justin stepped forward.

"Murdered? Did someone have a reason to kill your mom?" Jackie asked.

Sarah shook her head. "No, not that I know of."

"So do you think maybe killing your mom was a mistake, and that they just missed my sister?"

"Maybe," Justin said. "We never looked at it like that."

"Do you know anyone who might want Sheryl dead?" Sarah asked. *A mistake?* She didn't know if that made her mom's death easier or harder to accept.

"Not here, everyone here loved her. All of my life, anyone who knew her loved her, except one person."

"Who?" Justin prompted.

"My father, the Judge."

*

"You said you had something to tell me," Sarah mentioned as they were packing their bags that night for their trip.

Justin threw a pair of socks in his duffle. "Yeah. My editor needs me to go back and do a follow-up on a previous story. I wouldn't have to do it, except that I did the last one."

"Oh. Well, that's okay." Sarah felt the seeping edge of fear and sadness work its way across her heart. "Do you want me to go with you?"

"No." Justin stopped. "I mean, I know you want to go see your dad and I . . . " Justin scratched his fingers through his hair. "I think this is really the perfect time for me to go." He reached for her hands. "Telling your dad about what we've learned should be something that is between the two of you for a little while."

Sarah worked to close her heart. Tried to keep the pain from taking over. "Sounds good." Is this how he's going to end it? She wondered and turned back to her suitcase. She'd never had a broken heart before, but she could feel it splitting.

"It should only take a few days, and then I'll fly out there."

"Don't worry if it takes longer. I'll be fine and can continue this on my own," Sarah said with a who-cares, defiant tone.

Justin spun around toward her. "Is that what you want?" He asked.

"I have packing to do." She began stuffing her clothes in any open space.

"I'm gonna take a walk." Justin stalked from the room, slamming the door behind him.

"Fine." Sarah yelled into the empty house. "Just fine." She flung herself on the bed and curled her legs underneath her. She gripped a pillow to her face to scream, but it was drowned by her misery. She could smell him on the pillow. She could even smell him on the clothes she wore. It's as if they'd meshed, to make one person. Scents and time and space. She knew she'd never be through with him. She'd never fall asleep without his name being the last on her lips. She'd never wake without his face being the first she'd see. The tears came. She let them fall down her cheek, drip across her lips and run down her neck, hoping that she could purge her body of the love she felt for him.

Justin walked across the horse pasture, twirling one of the last blooming Firewheels between his fingers. The flower had so many different facets with its petals and colors. It reminded him of Sarah. The red of the flower was the red of her passion. It burned hot and fierce. The yellow was her mellow, understanding side, the side that warmed his heart and made him feel things he'd never known existed. The petals layered and lined and twirled together, the red and yellow in the pattern of a never-ending circle, giving the illusion of order. They were the essence of Sarah. Even though she seemed orderly and neat on the surface, she couldn't fool him. He'd seen the drama of her passion, the fire and the warmth. And the tears. He'd felt them, all of her emotions, with her.

When he walked back in the house, the moon was just rising. All the lights were on, so he called for her, but she didn't answer. Wandering through each room, turning the lights off as he went, he found her. She was asleep on the bed they'd shared, with a pile of his folded shirts beneath her head. He smiled as he crossed the bed to her, until he saw the streaks left by drying tears.

"Damn, Sarah. I'm sorry." He pulled her into his arms and kissed her awake. He loved her until sleep pulled them under her spell, and the stars winked out.

CHAPTER 21

"She's gone, boy," J.T. said. He was fiddling with a tractor wishing it would make it one more season. The wishing turned to swearing when he realized it wouldn't. "She had me take her to the airport first thing this morning."

Justin stepped off the porch. He walked gingerly across the graveled yard on his bare feet to where his grandpa stood with wrench in hand. His hair was mussed and his jeans unbuttoned at the top. "Damn. Her flight didn't leave till this afternoon."

"Guess she's not too good at good-byes."

"Did she say anything?" Justin asked.

"You mean, about you?"

"Shit, Grandpa, I don't know."

"Nah. But she hid her face a lot, not wanting me to see her cry."

"I *gotta* go to Dallas. I'd have gone with her otherwise."

"Does she know who you are?" J.T. pointed the greasy wrench in Justin's direction.

"No."

"Don't you think you ought to tell her?"

"I think it'll ruin everything we have." Justin flicked a stone with his big toe.

"You don't have nothing, if you don't tell her."

"Son of a bitch," Justin mouthed as he went back to the house. "I have to go to Dallas."

Grandpa chuckled softly when he heard the door slam. "It's hell being in love. Especially when you don't know it."

*

Sarah had stopped crying hours ago, which she was glad of when she walked into S.J. Investigations. It didn't matter that she'd been held in Justin's arms all night. It didn't matter that she'd still been in them this morning when she woke up. All that did matter was that she was here and he wasn't.

Hearing the soft swish of the glass door closing behind her and the feeling the press of her shoe on her own pale carpet made Sarah feel better. Grounded, at least, with the wish of things going back to normal.

She didn't make it three steps without being pulled into a warm embrace accompanied by giddy laughter.

"Sarah! What are you doing here?" Annie laughed and twirled around with Sarah in tow.

"I work here." Sarah chuckled. "I think."

"I know. But you weren't supposed to be back for days."

"I came back early." Sarah walked into her office to find it neat and tidy, just as she'd left it.

"I only dusted." Annie pointed to the lush, green plant on the file cabinet. "And watered that thing."

"You didn't dust." Sarah winked. "But thanks for watering my philodendron."

"Whatever." Annie rolled her eyes and sat down in one of the chairs reserved for clients. "So how'd it go?"

"Good." Sarah shrugged her shoulders. "Bad. I wish I'd never gone." *No, I don't,* she thought. *I wish it wasn't over.*

"What happened?" Annie leaned forward, eyes compassionate.

"Where's my Dad?"

"He went home. I think there was some baseball game or something he wanted to watch and he wanted to mow the lawn. But he said he'd be back the day after tomorrow."

"I need to talk to him," Sarah said.

*

The air in Justin's apartment smelled stale and old. And very unwelcoming. He'd rather be anywhere else. But he resigned himself to the need to be here, checked his messages, and almost called Sarah. What would he say? How do you say you're sorry on the phone? So he poured himself a drink, instead. Thinking a nice two fingers' worth of Macallan on ice would do the trick; he sat down in his oldest chair and took a sip. Sadly, it didn't help. Even though it felt good to sit with his shirt unbuttoned and his shoes kicked off, he still felt lonely and worried. As far as he was concerned, he was too many miles away from Oregon and the person who might be needing him. Swearing, he took another drink. He normally enjoyed the smoky-tasting liquid, but today it seemed to scorch his throat as it flowed down to heat his blood.

In the dim room, lit only by the security system light and the bright city of Dallas at night, he looked over at the box of things his grandpa had sent with him. He thought about digging through it. But he didn't quite feel like looking at old notes and keepsakes his father had collected. Besides, he needed to be in court early tomorrow morning, so he swigged the rest of his scotch and tried to prepare for his first night without Sarah.

*

She didn't think she'd actually be able to sleep. But Sarah forced herself to try for a few hours. Really, it was good to be home. Her apartment was as she'd left it, as well, except for the odd magazine on fishing or cooking her dad had left here and there. It was obvious he'd slept in her spare bedroom, as there was a whole mound of magazines on the nightstand in there. His touch was other places. Her fridge was stocked with all the foods he liked and she didn't. There were three eggplants piled on the top shelf next to the milk. She'd never buy eggplant, much less three of them. Her kitchen was sparkling, but there were things put away in the wrong places and the cutting board was still out on the counter, as if he intended to use it right away, to make an omelet or something. She'd smiled at that.

It had felt good to come home to a place that looked as if it had been lived in while she was gone. It didn't hold as much loneliness that way. She'd wandered around, putting her things away and starting the laundry from her trip. The hours had gone by very slowly. And night had finally come, but she couldn't sleep. She'd had a shower and even drank a small glass of wine, hoping that would help.

She was flat on her back, looking up at the ceiling. A thin blanket was covering her. Resting beneath her head was her most comfortable pillow, but her eyes wouldn't stay closed. She had a wonderful bed, and usually she could sleep perfectly and wake up refreshed and re-energized. Tonight, she had a headache and didn't feel like taking anything for it. She didn't have the will to cry. She'd done enough in the last month to fill her quota for years.

"Aww!" Sarah threw back the covers. "This is worthless."

She flicked on the lights and glared at the clock on her DVD player. She hated being awake at four o'clock in the morning. It wasn't quite morning and it wasn't quite night. It was the worst time of the day as far as she was concerned.

"Might as well do something with my life," she moaned as she walked across the carpet of her living room.

She had a report to type. She needed to make it accurate and clear, without any of her personal feelings clouding the wording. But first she needed to get organized. The table in the dining room would be an excellent place to work. In the middle of it was a candle arrangement from her Aunt Lainey that was supposed to give the room a Feng Shui appeal and a pile of her running magazines.

"Well, Aunt Lainey, I'm not Feng Shui today." Sarah smiled as she moved the items to the side and began laying out her notes.

She grabbed her laptop from her study and booted it up on one of the table's edges. After she typed the heading, which included her name, the date, and the title of the case, she sat and looked at the blinking cursor. *How to begin?* she wondered.

"Hey Sarah, open up!" Annie's voice hollered from the hall as she banged on the door.

The noise made Sarah jump in her seat. And then she grinned, realizing who it was.

"What are you doing here?" Sarah asked as she pulled the door open to her frizzy-haired friend.

"Ben said your lights were on." Annie dumped her purse on the cabinet inside the door and walked to the kitchen carrying a large grocery bag. "I brought sugar!"

"Why was your husband out driving around this time of night?" Sarah asked as she followed Annie.

"He had to get some fever medicine for Jason."

"Is he all right?" Sarah asked, concerned for their youngest son.

Annie nodded. "And as soon as we got him back into bed, I came over. Here." She handed Sarah a bowl and a spoon.

Sarah frowned at the ice cream in the dish. "I can't eat rocky-road ice cream at four in the morning."

"It's almost five." Annie pointed at the ice cream with her spoon. "Now, eat."

"Annie!" Sarah shook her head and took a bite.

"I brought bagels and coffee, too. I didn't know if you'd have any worth drinking." Annie moved around the kitchen, measuring the coffee and pouring water into the maker.

Sarah smiled. "What are you really here for?"

Annie turned to look at Sarah after she'd pressed the on button to the coffeemaker. "I've known you a long damn time." Annie picked up her bowl of ice cream. "I can see the dark circles under your eyes and the sad frown around your mouth. But more than that I can see the regret and misery you're trying like hell to hide. So I know that you never come right out and say what you're thinking. You need somebody to prod you along and make you tell." She took a big bite of rocky road. "I'm that somebody."

"There's nothing to tell." Sarah perched on the edge of the counter.

"Yeah, right."

"Really. Justin and I had a nice time together, but now we have to get back to real life."

Annie did a jig in her seat. "You're not talking about the case. So what did you and Justin do?"

"You know very well what we did," Sarah huffed and set down her bowl and jumped off the counter.

Annie followed Sarah to the living room and sat next to her on the couch. "No, I don't. I may have arranged flight plans and hotel rooms, but I have no idea what you did."

"Sorry." Sarah wiped her face with her hands. "I'm just tired, I guess."

"So is he good in bed?" Annie laughed at the look of horror on Sarah's face.

"Annie! My God. I can't believe you."

"Of course you can. I'll never change."

Sarah laughed for the first time in days. "I know."

"So is he?" Her eyes were full of mischief.

Sarah looked down and her clenched hands. "I don't know what to do."

Annie stopped laughing and leaned toward Sarah. "What do you mean?"

"I mean, I think he's through with me."

"Is that what he said?"

"No. It's just that—"

"It's just what? What did he say?"

"He said he had to go to Dallas to do a follow-up on a story and that he didn't want me to go with him." Sarah slapped her knees, feeling more like a young child having a tantrum than a grown woman with a broken heart.

"Did he say why he didn't want you to go?" Annie finished her ice cream and set the bowl on the lamp stand beside the couch.

"He said now would be a perfect time to talk with dad. That we needed some alone time."

"Well, that sounds nice to me."

"Do you think he really meant it? I mean, really. Or do you think it was just a ploy to get rid of me?" Sarah looked at Annie.

"Does Justin strike you as the kind of guy who brushes women off? Does he seem like a coward to you? Or that he's the type of guy who needs a ploy?"

"No." Sarah shook her head. "Not at all."

"So then maybe he's just being nice."

"I know it seems that way. But this isn't one of your romance novels, where I can count on a happy ending. This is for real, involving real lives." *My life.*

"You're right. We can't just flip to the end and see how it turns out. You're going to have to see this one through. Unless he's not worth it."

Sarah squinted. "I think he is."

"Then I think you should go for it."

"There's nothing to go for when he's halfway across the United States." Sarah shrugged her shoulders.

"Then make him come here."

"How?"

"I'll tell you."

They spent the next half hour going over ways to get Justin to Oregon. Sarah didn't think a nude video of her would quite do the trick. And calling him sounded too teenager-ish. But a nice letter might be a step in the right direction.

"Oh, hey. I almost forgot," Annie said as she picked up her purse. "I found this outside the door."

"Deliver to Sarah J. Johnson," Sarah mumbled. "I wonder who it could be from?"

"Maybe it's from Justin." Annie giggled on her way out the door. "By the way, you never answered my question."

Sarah looked at Annie's face poking around the entryway.

"What?"

"Is he good in bed?"

Sarah grabbed the handle out of Annie's hand. "Yes. Now go away." She slammed the door, laughing as she heard Annie's exclamation of "Yes!" from the hallway.

Turning the envelope over in her hand, she had a fleeting thought that it might be from Justin. But that changed when she saw the contents. There was a single picture and a single note. The note was typewritten and said, "If you want him to live, you'll do nothing with the information you've found." The picture was one of Justin, in a place she'd never seen. He was lounging back in an old recliner, holding a drink to his lips. His shirt was unbuttoned, and he had a scowl on his face. The scowl was the only thing she recognized.

"You're not going to scare me." Sarah jammed the contents back in the envelope and got to work on her report.

*

"Son of a bitch." Justin slammed his door behind him as he walked into his apartment. He'd gotten up early. Or rather he'd just stayed up, getting ready to go to court. He went through his notes from the case, paying close attention to detail. He knew Judge Holt would want obscure facts. He'd shaved, changed, and left.

It was in the hallway that he'd found the note. After he'd berated himself for thinking that it might be from Sarah, he'd opened it. There was a picture and a note. The note said, "If you want her to live, you'll do nothing with the information you've found." The picture was of Sarah in a T-shirt and a pair of sweats. She was holding candles in her hand. She was smiling.

"Son of a bitch," he said again, just for the hell of it. He punched the code on his safe, threw the envelope with its contents inside, and left. He had responsibilities to take care of, and then he was getting out of Texas as soon as possible.

CHAPTER 22

"Yes, Justin. I'm fine." Sarah had been saying the same thing to him for the past four days, each time he called. "I dropped the report off with my contact at the police station. He's been doing some checking, so we should see some action happen pretty soon."

"Why didn't you wait until I could be there?" Justin spoke into his cell phone as he walked along the sidewalk to the courthouse.

"What are you going to do? Keep the guy from killing me with your pen?"

"Sarah, damn it. You take this seriously!"

"I am. I live in a secure building, and I've told the manager to watch for anyone who might be lurking. Aunt Lainey and Dad come by the office all the time. Dad's in fact due here in about 15 minutes. Annie never leaves me alone. And the guys here are always checking up on me. I barely am alone long enough to go to sleep by myself." *Not that I've been sleeping.* He could hear Sarah tapping her pencil on her desk.

"Stop tapping your pencil like you're impatient and listen," Justin scolded.

"Fine." Sarah threw it down.

"I only have one more day on this story, and then I should be able to fly out there. You keep yourself safe and don't go anywhere without someone either going with you or unless it's someplace very public. You got it?"

"I got it. And you be careful too" Sarah hung up.

Justin shook his head as he flipped his phone closed. Judge Holt had better get her act together, he thought as he walked. He needed to be gone tomorrow. Looking at his watch, he noted that he had half an hour before he had to be in court. Maybe he'd stop in and see how Sarah's belated birthday present was coming along.

*

"Hi, Daddy." Sarah hugged him. "Where have you been? I thought you were going to come by for dinner last night. Your eggplant is missing you."

"Hi, sugarplum." Eric kissed his daughter's cheek. "I've been watering the lawn, watching reruns, and playing catch with Nathan. Plus, I figured you'd want your privacy and didn't want your old man hanging around."

"Of course I want you hanging around." Sarah smiled and kissed him back. "How are Nathan and Carla?"

"Good. They've been missing you."

"Maybe I can come out in a weekend or two and catch one of Nathan's games."

"He'd like that." Her dad smiled. "Well, what are you working on this week?" He asked as he sat down on the small couch along one wall in Sarah's office.

"Just gathering some new facts on an insurance-fraud case." Sarah sat next to him. "It's all paperwork, mostly. What are you doing besides watching last winter's shows over again?"

"Watching you. Have I told you lately how beautiful my daughter is? I'm very proud of you." He looked closely at her face. "But there's something wrong. What is it?"

Sarah blew out a breath. She didn't want to get to it so fast.

"Does it have anything to do with that Justin character who was mooning over you at your birthday party?"

God, what a long time ago that was, Sarah thought. "No. It's something different."

"Tell me about him first, so I can quit worrying." He crossed his ankle over his knee and leaned back. "I am a father, you know. I need to know these things."

"Really, it's nothing."

"Do I need to get my baseball bat?"

Sarah laughed at that. He'd always threatened to beat up any guy who didn't meet his standards. "He's a good guy, Daddy. He works hard and is nice to me."

"So why's he making you sad?"

"It's just because he's not here. And I miss him."

"Should I be worried that this guy's going to take my little girl away?"

"No. It's not like that."

"So you don't love him?" Her dad sat forward.

Sarah took a deep breath. "I didn't say that."

"So you do?" He grinned.

"I didn't say that, either."

"What are you saying then?"

"I don't know. I guess it's too soon to tell."

"Tell who?" He tickled her chin. "You sure grew up too fast."

"Really? I didn't think I'd ever grow up." Sarah flicked her hair out of her face. "Sometimes I don't think I'm grown up now." *Now or never, Sarah.* She gave herself her small version of a pep talk. "Dad, there's something I need to tell you."

"Okay." Her dad frowned, probably at the apprehension on her face. "What is it?"

"It's about Mom."

He swallowed hard. "This has to do with her last assignment, doesn't it?"

"Not really. It doesn't have anything to do with the assignment itself." Sarah looked around her office. What a terrible place to tell someone something awful. "Maybe you should come over to dinner tonight, and we can talk about it."

"No. You should tell me now." He pulled her hands into his.

"We went to the prison, pretended we were inspectors, and tried to get the last three recordings. But we were only able to get the one from the bathroom and her cell."

"You did? Why . . . why would you do that?"

"Because Mom found out something that needs to be stopped."

"What'd she find?"

Sarah nodded. Of course, he'd want to know what she'd found. He was as much a part of this as she was, as her Mom had been. "She found out that some of the girls were taken to Atlanta and forced to be prostitutes there."

"Good Lord. Is that on those recordings?"

"Not much of it. But Justin and I were lucky enough to interview a current inmate who was in Atlanta."

"How did you manage that?" He shook his head. "This is unbelievable."

"I know. I've reported it downtown, so there should be something happening with that soon."

"That's good."

"But that's not what I needed to tell you." Sarah gripped her dad's hand and looked into his eyes. "Mom was going to have a baby."

"What?" His hand trembled. "What did you just say?"

"Mom was pregnant."

"How do you know that?"

"On one of the recordings, she was in the bathroom. She told you about the baby. She was so excited."

He held Sarah's arms tight.

Sarah saw anger—true, red hatred—in her dad's eyes for the first time in her life. She nodded. "She was laughing about you changing diapers during your retirement years."

He bowed his head into his hands.

Tears fell down Sarah's face. "Dad, I'm sorry." She wrapped her arms around his shaking shoulders.

"Damn you, Helen," he whispered. "Why'd you have to go?" He looked up and pulled Sarah into a hug. They wept again as they'd done the day they'd found out she'd died.

Sarah didn't have the heart to tell him the other thing she'd intended to say. She couldn't tell him that her mother had been murdered, even if by mistake.

*

"Your dad looked pretty torn up when he left." Annie sat on one of the chairs at the edge of Sarah's desk.

"Yeah. Telling him about the baby was terrible."

"Did you tell him the other?"

"No." Sarah shook her head. "I couldn't. I'll tell him when I learn more. If I ever do."

"Somebody knows." Annie took a drink from her ever-present water bottle. "Maybe even someone you've talked to already."

"The only person who's left is Simon Newell, and I don't think he knows anything more than what he told Justin and me."

"Don't be too sure. Sometimes people know more than what they let on. And sometimes they know something even if they don't think they do. You just have to ask the right questions."

"I know." Sarah began to sort her mail. "Is this all current?"

"Yeah. Pretty much. There were a few things that I kept in a crate under my desk. Things that looked like advertisements and credit card applications. But other than that, it's all today's or yesterday's."

Sarah held up a white box about the shape of a middle-sized book. "When did this come?"

"It's been here a while. It looked like an advertisement video or something."

"It's from Alabama."

At that, Annie rose and walked around Sarah's desk. "We'd better open it."

Sarah slid her letter opener along the tape that fastened the box. A letter and a videotape fell out. Sarah unfolded the typed letter.

Sarah, Sherry told me to send this to you. It's a copy of a video that the guards show the inmates at Freeman Prison. They use it to scare us so we'll behave. I don't know why you need this, but if there is a God, may He help you use this . . . to save us.

"Who wrote it?" Annie asked.

"It's not signed." Sarah looked inside the box for further clues, but there were none.

"Let's watch it." Annie pulled the shades on Sarah's office and turned on the television.

Sarah nodded. There was no writing on the outside of the tape giving a hint as to what was on it. "I hope there's really something here."

"I'll be a son of . . . " Annie pointed to the television.

"What? Is your team losing again?" Sarah asked without looking up.

"Sarah, look!"

Sarah glanced at the screen. She realized what she was looking at, then glared. "Wasn't he doing a story at a racetrack? That doesn't look like a racetrack to me. Does it look like one to you?" Justin stood, big as life, on the outside of a courtroom. He was holding a notebook in one hand and a pen in the other.

"Damn, no it doesn't."

"What the hell is he doing there when he's supposed to be reporting on racehorses?" Sarah stood up and jammed her finger in his direction.

"Maybe he got another assignment." Annie hoped for his sake he did.

"Maybe. But, if he was finished, why didn't he come like he said he was going to?"

"Let's turn it up and see what's going on." Annie pressed the volume button on the remote only to hear the final lines of the report. "Damn local news."

Sarah picked up the videotape fighting against the hurt and disappointment edging across her heart. "I don't have time for that, anyway. We've got to see what's on this thing."

"Okay." Annie turned the channel to three and stuck the tape in the VCR.

Faded, gray images grew clear as the tape played. The scene was a cell with two people standing in it. Sarah recognized who she thought might be Sherry. The other person, she was sure, was her mother. There was no sound. But the angle of the camera showed four other feet outside the cell.

"What are they doing?" Annie asked.

"I don't know." Sarah pointed to the figure on the left. "That's my mom and the other woman is Sherry, her cellmate."

"Who are these other people?" Annie pointed to feet at the edge of the screen.

"Don't know." Sarah watched Sherry stick her hand in their direction and her mom pull her toward her bunk. She could imagine her telling her not to worry. But Sherry was insistent. She pushed against her mom, but she pushed back.

Then a bright flash lit the screen. The light bulb above them burst. Chunks of burning matter exploded into the cell. Her mom reacted in a second. She pushed Sherry under the bunk and hunched over. Her shirt was on fire, her pants. All of her. Then the screen went black.

Sarah stood shocked. Time didn't pass. She could hear the ticking of the clock behind her. She could hear herself breathing and smell the cold coffee on her desk. Her fingers throbbed as blood pumped through them. Her eyes stung from not blinking. The headache she'd had for the past week dulled her vision.

"Is that the end of the tape?" Sarah asked in a whispered voice.

"Yes." Annie took the tape out. Walked to Sarah and wrapped her arms around her. "Oh, no. I'm sorry. I'm sorry."

Sarah squeezed her eyes shut and took a deep breath. "Oh, God. Oh God." Sarah repeated over and over and over. She didn't feel like she could breath. She stumbled to her chair. She buried her face in her hands and rocked back and forth. Breath. Rock. Breath. Rock. She told herself. She kept up the rhythm until she felt like she could get air without panicking. Until she could think. Until she could talk.

"Who was outside her cell? Someone knows. We should watch it again." Sarah pointed toward the television.

"Oh no, we aren't. Not today. Not ever if I have anything to say about it." Annie put it back in the box on her desk.

"Why not?" Sarah asked.

"You're going to have an awful time getting those images out of your head. You can't live with something like that stuck in there. Besides that, we aren't even going to say we saw anything like this. Because of that note you got. The one with Justin's picture. The person who sent it to you can't know you've looked at this or even that it exists, until we can find him."

CHAPTER 23

After he parked his bike, Justin walked the winding sidewalk to Pat's door. It was still strange to him to see where his friend lived. The hard-eyed man he worked with was completely different from the family man who was currently grilling something in the backyard. As soon as he'd driven onto the block, he'd been able to smell the smoke of a charcoal. He smiled as he knocked on the door of the homey, two-story house. He could hear Pat saying, "Real men cook with real charcoal." *Yeah*, Justin thought, *even if we have to wait an extra hour. Then what we do eat is either cold and raw or burnt to a cinder.*

"Hey Marcy." Justin smiled into the eyes of a little sprite of a woman who opened the door. Her curling, auburn hair haloed her face and her sea-blue eyes smiled out from beneath her lashes.

"Justin!" Marcy laughed. "Look Becky, it's Uncle Justin." Marcy bounced the tiny mirror image of herself on her hip.

"Little Becky, you look like you're almost ready for high school." Justin squeezed one of the baby's toes and smiled when she gazed intently up at him.

"Lord help us there. Pat's already going crazy with the rules on boys and dates." Marcy kissed Becky's head. "And she's only six months old."

"Well, tell him I'll bring my shotgun anytime he needs it."

"Oh, yeah. That's just what I need, two wild men running around after some poor helpless boy."

"We're harmless. You know that." Justin leaned down and kissed her cheek. "It's good to see you."

"You, too." She smiled.

"You leave my wife alone and go get your own." Pat's voice carried across the living room. "You're early." Pat reached out and shook Justin's hand, pulling him into the house, welcoming him just as he'd always done. "From the looks of the mess in the kitchen, we'll be ready to eat in a while." Pat winked at Marcy.

"You boys go on back and check the charring meat and leave the real cooking to us women." Marcy pushed at Justin's back, moving him toward the double-glass doors. "I made a cherry pie, and you'll get some if you're good. Now scoot."

"Sounds great." Justin smiled as he shut the doors behind him and Pat.

"Grab a beer out of that cooler there." Pat pointed with his melted spatula handle.

Justin's eyes roamed the backyard as he opened his can. The trees were nicely trimmed, the lawn mowed, and the few flowers lining the fence were weeded and watered. "Sure looks good." Justin felt a tug of guilt as he walked across the wood planks that made up the deck to where Pat was standing at his smoking grill. "This ended up being real nice."

Pat nodded. He understood what was going on in his friend's mind. "I sure couldn't have done it without your help."

"I should have been here to help finish it."

"If you're feeling bad about it, you could always put on the last coat of weather seal." Pat peered through the pouring smoke and turned the burgers.

"How many did you put on?"

"Only two."

"You should put on at least three if you want it to last. You know the heat around here is pretty rough on wood."

"The job's yours if you want it." Pat shuffled the burgers on the plate in his hand.

Justin smiled. "They look good. Looks like you learned how to cook."

"Sure enough." Pat grinned, proud, as the smoke from the grill billowed around him. "You get done in court today?"

Justin nodded and took a swig of beer.

"So how long is it gonna take you to ask me?"

Justin looked up. "Ask you what?"

"Don't give me that shit. I've known you too long."

"Fine." Justin laughed. "Do you think you could work it out to come to Portland? I think I'm going to need you for a few days."

"I'll need three or four days to get things squared away here, but I think I can."

"Good. Also, do you think you could do some checking on a few people before you come? I wanted to do it myself, but I've been tied up in court."

"Sure. Who are they?" Pat's features changed from family man to serious FBI agent.

Justin dug in his hip pocket and pulled out a folded piece of paper. "I wrote it all down for you."

"Knew I'd do it, did you?"

"Well, I knew you'd do this part at least." Justin smiled and handed him the paper.

Pat whistled. "Senator Ames? That's a tall order."

"I need to know where he was on those dates listed there." Justin pointed to the paper. "And I'd really like to find out who this Evan Elvis Peterson is. Sarah found out some info, but the facts are very well hidden."

"You think he's the guy?"

"Don't know. I think one of them might be." Justin shrugged his shoulders and took a drink. "Do you think you could figure out a way to get the information you find to Annie at Sarah's office so it looks like it came in another way instead of from me?"

"Sure. Why not? You want me to walk on water while I'm at it?"

"Don't be a smart-ass." Justin laughed and punched Pat on the shoulder.

"Did you find out anything more on the inmates being framed?" Pat asked.

"No. That's why I'm hoping you'll come up with something."

"I will." Pat nodded. "So you leaving tomorrow?"

"Yup."

"Get anymore notes?"

Justin shook his head.

"That's good."

"That's what worries me."

"You'll be there soon enough, and I'll be right behind you. Don't worry too much." Pat smacked Justin on the back. "Let's eat these puppies before they get cold."

*

Sarah sighed as she got off the elevator leading to her apartment. It had been a long day. First, her father, then the tape and the conversation with Annie had been exhausting. She was also wondering why Justin hadn't told her he'd had another assignment. She'd like to shrug it off, except she couldn't quite manage it. But she was too tired to really do anything about it now. All she was really interested in was putting her aching feet up and resting her head. She was looking forward to a nice glass of wine and a hot bath.

She closed her door behind her, feeling relieved to be able to slouch her shoulders and put on some comfy sweats. Not three steps into the living room, she heard a knock on the door.

"Daddy?" Sarah stepped back to let him in. *So much for resting,* she thought, then felt bad as she watched her father walk through the door. His normally strong frame was hunched, and his expression carried a defeated look. "Did you come for dinner?"

"I'm not really hungry." He smiled blankly and looked at Sarah. "But from the looks of things, I need to fix you something." Eric pulled her to the couch. "Sit here and I'll make you a sandwich.

And tell you what I've been doing." He shuffled to the kitchen.

"Okay." Sarah didn't argue. She felt as if she were living the misery of her sixteenth year again as she slumped onto the soft cushions and leaned her head on one of the sofa's pillows. The mood she felt being with her father felt the same as it had then: complete sadness.

"You want ham and cheese or peanut butter and honey?" Eric called from the kitchen as he rattled the drawers, searching for everything he needed.

Sarah smiled through the foggy fatigue. Those sandwiches were the comfort food he'd made for her as a child. She had to fight with the tears that threatened as she answered, "Peanut butter."

"Want milk?"

"Yeah." Sarah thought about letting a few tears fall. She was entitled after all.

"Here you go, sugarplum." Eric handed her the sandwich and a tall glass of milk.

Looking at the neatly stacked bread and the four, triangle-cut pieces, she smiled and wished that they would cure her woes now as well as they had once cured a skinned knee. "Thanks." She took a few bites and a couple sips of milk. Even though she was hungry, when the food hit her stomach, it churned. She set the plate and glass of milk away from her on the coffee table. "It's good." She smiled, meekly. "But what did you do today?"

"I went to the cemetery and picked up some brochures for headstones."

Sarah looked up.

"For the baby." Eric added.

"That's a wonderful idea." Sarah rubbed her head. The headache was getting worse. "Do you want me to help you pick out a stone?"

"That's why I came, but we can do it another time. You're really tired." Eric stood up and pulled off her shoes. "Why don't you lie down here, and I'll get you a blanket so you can take a quick nap."

Sarah nodded and did as he said. She barely felt the soft fleece blanket being tucked around her. His whispered good-bye and *I love you* wasn't heard at all. She'd already drifted to a comfortable sleep.

*

Justin swore he'd never have to eat again. The food that was piled before him on Pat and Marcy's table had been enough for a small army, and he'd done his best to make it disappear. And then there was the cherry pie and homemade ice cream he had to make room for. He smiled and patted his full stomach. Marcy made the best pie he'd ever eaten, and he knew why Pat was always saying, "That's why I married her. That and her marksmanship."

Sitting at their table tonight, listening to them chatter about everyday-life matters was enough to remind him why he'd taken so long to come back here after his mother's death. Why he hadn't helped finish the deck. Why he'd always found some reason not to go or some excuse to stay away. Because even though he laughed at their silly, clean jokes and tried to follow all the neighborhood gossip tonight, he'd still felt the pang of longing and pain. He'd had all that closeness with his own family.

After his father's death, one of the only comforts he'd found was the fact that while he'd been alive, he and his parents had had as near to perfect a family as possible. Justin had always enjoyed Pat and Marcy's family get-togethers and had attended them as often as he could. But after he'd learned that his father had loved another woman, however briefly it was, and that he'd taken his own life because of her, the comfort he'd found at Pat and Marcy's had turned to grief.

Tonight was a little different. He'd found in the sadness a bit of hope for the future. He had no idea what it would hold, but he did know that if he ever found anyone he could love, he would make sure she knew it every day. That his children would never have to walk into his study and find their father bent over his desk in death.

That there would be no secrets and no past worth dying over.

His mind drifted to Sarah, and he wondered if she'd ever find it in her heart to forgive him for lying to her once she knew the truth. For coming to her under the pretext of an investigative reporter doing a story on her mother. As far as he was concerned, there wasn't anything worse that could be done to a person. Issues of love had killed both his parents. One had loved deeply enough that he took his own life. The other had faded from reality and eventually just quit breathing because of it.

He was sorry now for what he'd done to Sarah. "I'll tell her as soon as I get the chance," Justin vowed to the silent apartment after he'd packed his duffle for his flight the next day.

He leaned back in his chair, pulling the footrest up with it. It was too early to go to bed, especially with his full stomach. His thoughts momentarily drifted around the idea of having a drink, but he decided against it. Stretching, he let his hands fall off the edge of the armrest. One brushed against the box his grandfather had given him.

"I can't avoid it forever," he mumbled and pulled it onto his lap.

There were a few trophies Justin could remember his father bragging about winning. Other ribbons and certificates Justin could imagine hanging in his father's teenage room were in the box, as well, along with a faded poster of a pretty girl leaning against a pickup truck.

"Some things never change." Justin smiled as he thought of the pretty blond holding a football he'd had hanging on his wall when he was seventeen. He placed the items on the floor and dug back in the box.

There were a few more things, cards for birthdays and graduation from high school. He went through them quickly, but slowed when he spotted a faded journal. He pulled it out. His father had never mentioned having one as a kid, but since he'd always had one as an adult, it wasn't that much of a surprise. The journal was brown leather, heavily worn, and filled with the letters and notes sticking out from between the pages. A thick rubber band held the journal closed.

Pulling the band off, being careful not to disturb the loose contents, Justin began reading the first page. He smiled at his father's easily recognizable voice, his word choice. Even as a kid, he'd had a way with words. As he read through the book, the entries moved from daily-life activities to dreams for the future. It was soothing to Justin to read that his father hadn't really known what he'd wanted to be, not any more than Justin had at his age.

His eyes skimmed through dances and meetings at the library with various school friends. But when he came across an excitedly scrawled entry, he slowed down and reread.

I met the most beautiful girl today. She was captivating in a way no one has ever been. She works at the newspaper in town. She's got long legs and the grayest eyes I've ever seen. I thought they'd be blue because of her long, waving blond hair. I think I fumbled over my words when she got out of her little car and walked up to me. It was her smile I noticed right off. It was as carefree and easy as the walk that carried her across the yard to the beat-up tractor I was sitting on.

"I know a girl like that." Justin rubbed his hand across his chin.

She was doing a story on local ranchers and their children for the paper. She wants to interview me. I could've answered her questions then, but I wanted to be cleaned up and out of that greasy shirt. We'll meet on Friday, only three days away! Three days until I get to sit across from the most beautiful girl in the world. Too bad The Pizza Parlor is the nicest place in town. A girl like Helen Prescott deserves much more.

"Damn," Justin swore. "Of all the damn women in the world, why the hell did we get sucked in by those same damn gray eyes?"

Justin read on. He read about the interview, their first date, their second, a water-balloon fight in town, their four-month anniversary. Justin could feel his father's sadness when she went away to college. But the happiness returned when he described her secret trips back to town just to see him. Justin rolled his eyes when he read about his dad trying to decide how and when to tell her he loved her.

He turned the page and a neatly folded letter fell on to his lap. He earmarked the page in the journal and opened the letter. It was from Helen. She was describing college life and her classes. She talked about her love for him and the life she wanted them to have. It all sounded wonderful and perfect, except one thing. Justin recognized the handwriting. He'd seen it before and not very long ago.

"Son of a bitch!" Justin put the journal back in the box and walked to his phone.

While he waited for the travel agent to give him an earlier ticket, his mind played the scene in his head. *You should have listened,* had been written on a small, crumpled piece of paper located near the hand of Beckett Larson's body in his house in Freeman City. The handwriting was the same. So either the person who had written that note had an identical writing style or Helen Prescott Johnson was still alive.

CHAPTER 24

Sarah stirred in her dreamless sleep. Her head was pounding again. She moaned and turned over, but the noise in her head wouldn't go away. She forced her tired arms up to cover her face. Maybe a drink of water, she thought.

"Sarah!" Justin called through the door. "Open up."

"Justin?" Sarah sat up and listened. Sure enough, it was his voice. "I'm coming," She answered. In the process of getting up too fast and forgetting where she was, she tripped over the edge of the coffee table and fell against the lamp stand, knocking it to the ground.

"Sarah?" Justin yelled this time. He didn't wait for an answer. Locked door or not he was getting in the apartment. He kicked right below the doorknob and went in running. His heart stopped when he saw her crumpled over the fallen table and broken lamp. Without thinking of his medical training, he scooped her up into his arms. "Sweetheart. Oh, damn it." He laid her on the couch and turned the lamp on at the other end. "Sweetheart?" He kissed her cheeks and waited.

Her eyes fluttered open. "Justin?"

"I'm here."

Sarah struggled to sit up.

"Just lie still."

"I'm fine. I just tripped." Sarah sat up. "I forgot I fell asleep on the couch. It took me a while to register that it was you pounding on the door. And when it finally hit me, I got up too fast and tripped."

"Looks more like you fainted to me." Justin eyed her curiously after he came back from shutting the door and sliding the chain lock in place. It was good that it hadn't been latched, otherwise there would be no way to secure the door. He'd broken it. "You haven't been sleeping have you?"

Sarah shrugged and wiped at her tired eyes. "Some. It's been pretty hard with Dad. I've only told him about the baby."

"I'm sorry I couldn't be here sooner." Justin tucked a loose hair behind her ear.

Sarah felt her body warm to his touch. She didn't exactly know what to do with the sensation; there were still questions she needed answered. So she did nothing. "What are you doing here? Why were you pounding on my door in the middle of the night?"

"I had to see you." He smiled.

"Don't give me that." Sarah poked him. "Speaking of seeing, I saw you on the television today."

Justin's eyes got big. "You did?"

"Yeah. How come you didn't tell me you had another assignment?" Sarah winced at the shrewish note in her voice. Was it really her business? Did she really need to know?

"Um. I . . . my editor . . . " Justin shook his head. "I finished the racehorse deal early and Pat sent me to cover the court story." *It's too damn easy to lie isn't it, Breslow? You have to tell her,* he chastised himself. *Not yet,* he argued. *I want to be with her a little longer before I ruin it all.*

Sarah glared at him. "You can tell me the truth, you know. I'm not going to flip out."

"I know." He kissed her nose and felt like a big horse's ass. "I was just surprised. I was only there for a little while." He hoped she hadn't watched too much of it.

"Sorry. I sound like some jealous girlfriend."

"Not a problem. If I thought it would've mattered, I would've called to tell you."

Sarah nodded, not really convinced, but decided she'd let him tell her whatever he needed to after he figured it all out. "Are you hungry?"

"No way. I ate at Pat and Marcy's tonight." Justin eyed the barely eaten sandwich on the coffee table and the almost-full glass of milk. "Are you?"

Sarah shook her head and nodded toward the food. "It's Dad's way of comforting. He went by the cemetery today to buy a headstone for the baby. But I fell asleep before I could finish eating." She rubbed her eyes and yawned. "What time is it?"

"Almost four, if your little clock over there is right." Justin motioned toward the DVD player.

"Four. Great." Sarah got up and gathered the leftover food to take to the kitchen.

"If you tell me where your broom is, we can sweep up most of the mess." Justin followed her.

"Sure. At the edge of the dining room, there's a small closet. I keep all that in there." Sarah turned on the lights and pointed in the direction she meant.

"Okay." Justin took a few steps and stopped. His eyes had scanned the room. He saw the candles and the stack of magazines that had been in the picture he'd received. "Sarah, did you do something different with those?"

"What do you mean?" Sarah walked and stood beside Justin.

"Those candles and the magazines. Did you move them?"

"The day I got back. I needed room to work on my report. Why?"

"I have that in my picture." Justin looked by the door and saw his bag where he'd thrown it when he came in. He walked to it and pulled out the picture. "Here."

Sarah looked at the window beyond the table. Could someone have actually taken the picture in the middle of the night? She felt the skin on the back of her neck prickle, and she walked over and pulled the shade.

"Do you have the one you got of me?" Justin asked as he tucked the picture back in his bag.

"Yeah." Sarah went to her room and pulled out a shoebox from beneath the bed. "I don't know where it was taken." She handed it to him.

"I do. It was the night I got back to Dallas." He tapped the picture. "I'm in my apartment."

Sarah just shook her head.

"Digital cameras and email. It's not too hard to take a picture of someone, email it, and print it all in the same hour."

"So there has to be more than one person involved." Sarah put the picture back in its box.

"And more than one somebody knows something. Annie was right."

"We just have to find them."

*

"You never did tell me why you came breaking down my door in the middle of the night," Sarah asked later that morning as she made coffee.

"Didn't I?" Justin winked at her as he leaned against the counter in her kitchen.

"No. You just said you came to see me."

"And that's the truth." Justin pulled her in his arms and kissed her. "I missed you," he said before he could tell himself not to.

Sarah smiled. "I missed you too."

"You did?"

"Of course. I missed you telling me what to do all the time, making me crazy while you patter around the house in your socks, and how you slurp your coffee."

"I don't slurp my coffee." Justin poked her in the ribs.

"Okay. Maybe I got a little carried away." She kissed him on the chin.

"Do my socks really bother you?" Justin wiggled one of his sock-covered feet.

Sarah laughed. "No."

"Good." His lips nipped at her nose.

"But you being bossy all the time does."

"Really?"

"Sort of." Sarah blew out a breath. "I just wish you'd—" *tell me the truth,* she thought, "—include me in the decisions that need to be made."

"I'm used to working alone." Justin defended himself.

"But you're not alone now."

"I know. I'll try to do better." Justin smiled and kissed her again. "I did find out some pretty interesting information I'd like to tell you about before you go into work."

"Okay." Sarah nodded. "You know, you could come with me."

"I can?"

"Sure. We've worked on this together so long, why not? I'd like for you to see something I have at the office, anyway."

"What is it?"

"I'd rather not say." Sarah frowned. "Can you just wait until we get there?"

"What are you thinking?" Justin crossed his arms, intent on listening.

"It's just something Annie said yesterday. I don't want anyone to know I have this until I show it to you. I just want to be careful."

"Good point. Maybe I'll just tell you what I learned when we get to the office."

"I don't have to be in for a couple hours. What do you want to do while we wait?" Sarah smiled, thinking of a few things she wouldn't mind.

"Hmm." Justin pulled her to him. "What about this?" His lips met hers.

He enjoyed her warm body pressing willingly into his. It was nice to know he was missed. But his guilt was beginning to make him miserable. Ignoring it for the moment, he changed the angle of his lips on hers and deepened the kiss.

Sarah had truly missed him. She'd missed all the things he did. How he filled a room with his presence. How he smiled deep in his eyes. How his arms wound tight around her making her feel safe and whole.

"I'm glad you came back," she whispered against his lips as she lifted her arms around his neck.

Justin searched her eyes. He could feel himself falling into them. He didn't fight it this time as he always had before. "Did you think I wouldn't?"

Sarah nodded.

"Why?"

"I didn't think you wanted me anymore."

"I'll never stop wanting you." Justin pulled her slim body up to his and coaxed her legs around his waist. "Never." His mouth caught hers with the violent need he felt. His heart pounded as he felt her respond with the same urgency he had.

There was a fleeting thought of taking her to her room, but that's all it was, fleeting. His hands were taking over where his mind had guided. His need for her was so great it engulfed him like a huge ocean wave. He couldn't breathe unless he had her. Couldn't live without her arms around him. Her lips on his.

He lowered them to the floor, being careful to cushion her body with his. His hands roamed the body he knew so well. He took his time on her dips and valleys. He wanted to feel her skin alive beneath his fingers. But more, he wanted her as desperate for him as he was for her.

He tore his mouth away to look at her. She was so sexy in her ancient sweats and ratty T-shirt. Her hair was hidden on top her head, wrapped with a thick, velvety hair band. Long tendrils that had refused to stay put during the night edged her face, giving it a look of hazy romance. As he tucked a few of them behind her ear, she closed her eyes and leaned her face into his hand. He felt a clicking in his heart as it shifted.

"Justin," Sarah whispered and pressed her lips to his.

"Yeah." He swallowed.

Sarah pulled her old T-shirt over her head. "Kiss me," she demanded and tugged him to her.

"Gladly." Justin dove into the ocean she offered. There were no more thoughts about where his heart was moving and what it was beginning to feel.

CHAPTER 25

Sarah held a letter, which had been neatly folded, in her hands. The blue pen on the page showed the curves and dips of her mother's handwriting.

"Are you sure the handwriting is the same as the note you saw at Becket's place?" Sarah asked Justin.

Justin sat forward on the couch in Sarah's office. The walls had been a surprise to him the first time he'd been in here. But, now that he knew Sarah, their off-white almost peach color seemed to perfectly fit Sarah's sense of optimism. It all seemed to reflect pieces of her from the sturdy plant on the file cabinet, which accented the large, floral print she had hanging on the wall behind her, reminded him of her strength. The wooden desk she was sitting at went well with the thin, wood blinds that covered the two, wide windows. Even the black-and-silver coffee cup she'd been sipping from all morning went with the mismatched frames she had scattered on one edge of the desk. To a casual observer, it might seem like a hodgepodge of items, but Justin liked it.

"I have a really good memory when it comes to things like that. So, yeah I'm pretty sure the writing is the same."

"Could it be someone who would just have similar writing?" Sarah flipped through the pages of the letter.

"I suppose, but it's so rare for anyone to have such a close match." Justin stood and walked around Sarah's desk. He knelt at the edge of her chair. "Sarah, did you actually see your mom before she was buried?"

"She can't be alive. She would have come to see me." Sarah argued. "She loved me. She loved us." Her voice rose. Emotions she couldn't name bombarded her system.

"Did you see her?"

"No. Dad didn't either. The prison said the fire was too destructive. None of us were allowed to see her." Sarah bowed her head. The idea that her mom may still be alive was too outrageous to believe. And if she was, why hadn't she contacted them? Why had she led them to believe that all these years she'd been burned to death?

"She might still be alive," Justin whispered.

"Do you think she—" Sarah's voice cracked.

"Do I what?" Justin took Sarah's hands in his.

"Do you think she still remembers me?"

"How could she not remember you?"

"Then why hasn't she come to see me? See Dad? Aunt Lainey?"

"Maybe she can't."

"What do you mean?"

"Well, maybe she was kidnapped. Strange things happen all the time. While I was in Dallas, I did some searching into prison disappearances. You know, people who don't escape or maybe do, but aren't accounted for."

"Yeah?"

"I don't think we've thought through all the uses for the hotel in Atlanta. You remember what Karen said about some of the girls not remembering seeing a judge or even being arrested?"

"Yeah."

"What if those secret passages aren't just used for girls entering the rooms?"

"They could be used for other people leaving the hotel undetected, or going in, even." Sarah squeezed Justin's hand. She was already thinking about who would want to come and go without being seen. "Do you think kidnapping a girl and taking her in through those rooms is possible?"

"Yes."

"But how would they get to the prison?"

"By van or car or however Karen got to the hotel."

"So do you really think there are women at the prison who weren't convicted of anything, but just kidnapped and are being held prisoner?" Sarah asked. "This keeps getting worse."

"I think it's a possibility." Justin frowned.

"So taking someone out of the prison would almost be easier than bringing them in." Sarah tapped the end of her pencil on her desk. "I guess. It's not hard to drug someone and, while they're sleeping, pull them through that secret passage and transport them, is it?"

"Nope."

Sarah didn't think she'd ever been as angry as she was now. This big, money-making scheme was ruining lives. Not for much longer, she vowed. "Do you think that's what happened. Maybe they drugged her after the fire at the prison and transported her out of there? Where do you think they took her?"

"Who knows? My guess would be somewhere outside the United States. If that Elvis guy is involved, I'd say he'd have contacts all over the world. And with the possibility of Senator Ames being connected, she could be anywhere."

"What if it's not them? What if their names being on lists and being mentioned are just circumstantial?" Sarah stood and walked around Justin. She needed to pace, to move. She had to think.

"If it's not them, it could really be anyone. There likely were lots of people in the prison who would have wanted her to keep quiet about what she'd learned. We haven't focused on any of the other people who frequented the hotel. Perhaps if we look at the list again, we might come up with another name or two."

"I'll tell Annie." Sarah opened her door so she could walk to Annie's office. She could've called her, but moving was what she needed. She needed a good, long run to get her thoughts straight. What if her mom was alive? What if she was in danger? She wouldn't allow herself to hope. She immediately dimmed the notion of being able to talk to her mom or smile at her or hear her laugh. She buried it so far back in the deep recesses of her mind that there was only a spark of it remaining. But it was the spark that kept her moving.

Justin had no idea what he felt about Helen possibly being alive. His father's suicide would have been for nothing. And if she was alive and he ever got to meet her, would he be able to forgive her for all the heartache she'd caused? He didn't know.

*

"I wish that would have been longer," Justin said as soon as the video Sarah had received finished.

"Me, too." Sarah frowned and squinted.

Justin searched her face for any sign of hurt. But her eyes were clear and her face focused in thought, not in pain. *Damn,* he thought, *I wish I'd never brought up the idea that Helen might still be alive.* He could tell from looking at Sarah that she was getting her hopes up. He shook his head at his own thoughtlessness. "Sarah, we have to be careful to remember that the possibility of your mom being alive is just a theory."

"But the handwriting is the same, you said." Sarah pointed at him.

"I know it is." He scrubbed his face with his hands. "I know it is."

"So what do we do now?"

"Well, we could listen to the final recording from her cell and see if there are any clues there."

"Sure." Sarah stood and removed the floral picture from the wall behind her desk. In just a few short movements, she'd entered the combination on the safe, opened it, and removed the items she needed.

"Maybe you ought to put these in there." Justin handed her his dad's journal, with the letter folded and put back in place, and the videotape.

"I'd like to show it all to my dad."

"Did you want to do that tonight?"

"I'd like to do it as soon as possible to see if he knows anything." Sarah thought of what Annie had said. "He might know something and not realize it."

"Maybe we should wait until we have more conclusive evidence. It's one thing for us to think that your mom might be alive. But it's another for your dad to think so. Don't you think?"

"I guess." Sarah put the tape in the safe, closed it, and returned the picture.

"How many people know you have that safe?"

"Just Annie and the guys. It's not even on the architecture plans. I had it put in later." Sarah sat down again. "Why?"

"Just thinking about people watching you."

"I'm always pretty careful when I use it." She dipped her head toward the closed blinds. "And I'm the only who knows the combination."

"That's good." Justin sat down again on the end of the couch. "Are you sure you're going to be okay with listening to that?"

"I think. I had a hard time watching the video the first time, but now that we're looking for clues as to whether or not Mom is alive, it's a little different." Sarah inserted the chip into the player. "So I think I'll be okay." She hoped she would. She hoped she'd be able to separate herself. She hoped that she could ignore the thoughts that kept crossing her mind. What if it were her mother who was responsible for the prostitution ring. What if it were her mother who had killed Becket and Caroline. She hoped against hope that she could ignore it. That she'd be able to listen to the voice on the tape as a private investigator and not as Helen's daughter. She put all thoughts from her mind and pressed the play button. She recognized Sherry's voice right away, and her mother's. Because of the video she'd watched, Sarah could easily visualize what was happening. She knew when she heard the loud pop that it was the light bulb exploding. And when she heard the shuffling she knew that her mom was pushing Sherry under the bunk. Sarah turned up the volume so she could hear her mother's final words.

Eric, God. I love you. I'm so sorry. Sarah, oh honey. My baby, my baby. No. No.

Sarah fought with her emotions as she listened. There was nothing to show or give support to the idea that her mom might still be alive. Sarah closed her eyes, wishing that she could just disappear. Wishing that all of this would just disappear. Her emotions rocketed back and forth between hope and despair. One moment she's thinking her mother could be alive. The next she's thinking she could be involved in the criminal activity. Now, after listening to the recording, she's dead again.

"Now I don't know what to think." Sarah propped her elbows on the desk and buried her face in her hands.

"It could be just a fluke," Justin said. but felt the whole scene could have been rigged. The timing would've had to be perfect, but if there were several key people involved, it could be done. Still, there was one thing that nagged at him. Why'd the recording just stop? There should have been more to it. "You said your mom had an activator implanted in her skin."

"Yeah." Sarah looked up.

"After something like that, there would be other activity the receiver should have picked up. So why didn't it keep recording?"

"I don't know." Sarah answered, shaking her head.

Her mind worked backward through what they'd just listened to and the video they'd watched. If her mother had thought shoving Sherry under the bunk would save Sherry's life, why didn't her mother get under the other one? Why would the people outside the cell just stand there when the light bulb exploded? "How'd the light bulb explode anyway?" Sarah asked more to herself than to Justin.

"You know, I've been thinking about that. I have a buddy who knows about explosives. I'll ask him. Maybe he can help us." Justin made a mental note to talk to Pat about it.

"Hey Sarah!" Annie barged into the office. "Oh sorry," she said when she'd seen the looks on Justin and Sarah's faces.

Sarah looked over and smiled. "That's okay."

"Okay! This is going to make you smile." Annie plopped down

in the end chair next to Sarah's desk. She swiveled the chair toward Justin, too. "I was typing in the name Peterson to do a search on him again. But then the phone rang and I started thinking about what the client was saying and didn't press the enter key." Annie couldn't seem to contain a laugh.

"Annie," Sarah said in a low voice.

"Okay, okay. Anyway, when I hung up the phone I typed in your mother's name right next to Peterson's." Annie handed her a sheet of paper. "And this is what I found out."

Sarah began reading the information but paused when Annie kept talking.

"Did you know your mom had a two million-dollar life insurance policy?"

"My God." Sarah looked at the paper again. "No," she said as her eyes scanned the words in front of her.

Annie looked Justin. "The beneficiary is Evan Peterson!"

"That's a motive if I ever heard one." Justin stood and rubbed his chin.

"I can't believe this. Are you sure this is *my* mom?" Sarah tapped her finger on the paper.

"Yeah. I did some cross-referencing and everything." Annie clasped her hands below her chin and grinned. "And that's not the best part."

"This is good?" Sarah shook her head. How was this even possible? Why is everything so messed up! What the hell is going on? "Who is this guy?"

"I found an address for Peterson, an old one, but at least it's a place to start." Annie gave the address she'd printed out on another sheet of paper to Justin.

"It's in Eugene." Justin walked to stand beside Sarah, knowing that Annie would've found this information only through the help of Pat. *Good going, buddy,* Justin smiled to himself.

"We can make it there easy, in a day. We'll go tomorrow first thing." Sarah looked at her watch, wishing it was already the next day.

CHAPTER 26

"Aunt Lainey!" Sarah ran toward the woman outside her apartment door. "What are you doing sitting out here?"

"I was waiting for you." Justin watched Elaine put a book she'd been reading down and stand to gather Sarah in her arms. "I thought I'd come by here to see you instead of going to the office. You're always so busy there."

"I'm glad you did." Sarah motioned in his direction. "You remember Justin, don't you?"

"Sure." Elaine smiled and shook his hand. "Nice to see you again."

"You too." He blinked at the woman before him. The last time he'd seen her, she'd had brown hair piled high on her head. This time it was falling in long waves down her back, and it was a deep red.

"You look good." Sarah put her new key in the lock of her door. "I like the red. So are you planning any trips soon?" She asked as she walked into the apartment.

"Maybe." Elaine gathered her things and shadowed Sarah. "Come on, Justin." She winked.

Justin followed and found a space along the wall to comfortably lean against. He enjoyed watching Sarah and Elaine talk. It was as if they were two pieces of the same puzzle. Opposite but fitting.

"Where to now?" Sarah flipped on the lights and put her things down on the stand, which was now missing a lamp, near the couch.

"I was thinking of someplace close. I've never actually been to Hawaii. So maybe there." Elaine sat on Sarah's couch and put her feet up on the coffee table as if she were about to get a luxurious pedicure at a spa. "Wanna come? I can get an extra ticket pretty easy. Two even. Justin can come too." Elaine lifted her eyes to him and giggled. "You wanna?"

Justin smiled and shrugged his shoulders. "Sounds like fun."

Sarah laughed. "I don't think I can just pick up and go off on some adventure right now."

"Why not? You've never been on a real vacation with white, sandy beaches and nice, blue water."

"You haven't?" Justin asked from his spot near the wall.

"No." Sarah looked at him. "And it's really not that big a deal. I've been focusing on my business. I'll take a coconut-oil, umbrella-drink vacation sometime soon." Sarah pulled the blinds closed on the windows.

"You better do it soon, while you're still young and you look good in a bikini. Nobody wants to see an old woman with sagging body parts and hair falling out tanning on the beach."

Sarah bent over with laughter. "I promise I'll go before that starts to happen."

"Make sure of it. All you're doing now is moping around being miserable."

Elaine pointed to Sarah's face. "Your eyes have bags."

Sarah sucked in a breath dramatically. "They do?" She laughed.

"Yes. You and Justin should do something fun." Elaine crossed her arms. "Maybe a weekend at a bed-and-breakfast. Those can be really cozy."

*

"It would be fun, you know," Justin said later as he lay in bed beside Sarah with his arms wrapped around her waist.

"I know." She nodded against his shoulder. "Maybe I can spare a little time after this is over with and do something relaxing. I've always wanted to go to a bed-and-breakfast."

"I know a great one in New Zealand," Justin whispered in her ear.

Sarah looked up at him. The dim light of the room outlined his face, making it look handsome and dangerous at the same time.

"You've been to New Zealand?"

"Sure. I went after college. I needed a break." Which was exactly true. He'd done it before he went into the FBI Academy.

"Wow. I've never been anywhere like that. We took some family vacations around the country, but mostly just quick trips to the coast or weekends in Canada."

Justin found himself frowning at the idea that Sarah had never really been anywhere. It was sad that she hadn't ever been on adventures like he was so fond of, especially as much as she seemed to love to travel. Maybe he'd take her to Italy or Denmark. He knew a street corner in Copenhagen that was filled with color and people and sweet, foreign scents. She could talk and look till her heart was content. He smiled just thinking about it. "Maybe we'll go someplace when this is all done." Justin ignored the nagging in his mind. He didn't want to be reminded that he was planning ahead. This was just a nice, quick excursion, not a future.

"A cozy trip would be nice." Sarah's voice sounded wistful.

Justin nipped at her mouth with his. "I think it's pretty cozy here."

"Me, too." Sarah wrapped her arms around his neck.

Justin let himself be drawn into the warmth of his kiss and tried to ignore the feeling of regret that had settled in his stomach.

*

Sarah lay awake and watched the red, digital numbers on her clock change from four-twenty-six to four-twenty-seven. Her eyes had been open so long it seemed like she blinked only when the minute ticked by and the numbers changed. She could hear Justin's even breathing next to her in bed. Passing the time waiting for him to wake up, Sarah thought about every lead they'd had. Some had panned out, but mostly they'd turned into a dead end. She couldn't quite put two and two together. The answer never turned out to be four, because there was always something she missed.

Each time she felt as if she was a little closer to the truth, another name or another story, linking her mother with something else or someone else, would come up. It was exhausting.

If her mother was alive, why would she leave a note for Becket Larson telling him he should have listened? To what, she wondered. Didn't Simon Newell say Becket wasn't the best of characters? So what did her mom have to do with him? Did Senator Ames really kill his daughter? Who is Evan Peterson? Sarah blew out a breath and squashed her pillow beneath her head as a million other questions flew around in her thoughts. She reminded herself to ask Annie to find out where Senator Ames was on the dates of Becket's and Sherry's, or rather Caroline's, deaths. She'd send her an email asking her to do it first thing Monday but not before. Annie had been working nonstop on this case for weeks. Sarah figured she needed a break, and besides, a Saturday was not a day to go into the office.

The clock clicked to five a.m. Sarah let out another breath. She was anxious for today. They might find out who Evan Peterson was or, at least, see where he lived. She tried to visualize the address in her head, but her knowledge of Eugene was not great. She'd been there for a few seminars and, of course, a few college parties when she was in school, but that was about it.

"Why don't we just get up?" Justin asked in a groggy voice.

Sarah startled. "I'm sorry. I didn't mean to wake you."

Justin smiled sleepily. "Sure you did. You want to get this day started, and we might as well."

"Are you sure? I can go to the living room and do some work while you sleep, if you want."

"No way." Justin stretched. "I'm up now."

"Okay." Sarah smiled. "I'll be ready quick." She jumped up and her world went black. As soon as she plopped back down on the bed, her vision was clearing again.

"You all right?" Justin had grabbed her as soon as she'd started to fall.

"Yeah." Sarah rubbed her face. "I just got up too fast."

Justin frowned at her. "You need to sleep more. Are you taking your vitamins?"

"Yes. But I'll take two today." Sarah smiled at him and got up slower.

"That's not how that works." Justin frowned at her. "I'm beginning to worry about you. That's twice now you've gotten up too fast; last time you really blacked out.. You're not eating right; you eat a few bites and then spend the rest of the meal pushing the food around, and you're not exactly a small-salad-and-crouton girl. Today you're going to have a decent breakfast and have a relaxing day. Well, as relaxing as possible."

"Wow. Yessir . . . Drill Sergeant Breslow." Sarah had stared at him in amusement as he'd lectured her, but her heart was warm as she headed off to her shower. Maybe he was starting to feel something for her.

*

Sarah apparently had actually been a little hungry, so the bagel, bowl of fruit, and tall glass of milk Justin had sat in front of her and ordered her to eat was not a problem. He'd also suggested that she bring along a few pillows and a blanket so they could stop at one of Eugene's many parks and have a picnic, which she seemed to think was a good idea.

As she carried the soft throw and the few pillows to the car, he saw her yawn. Her eyes were red, undoubtedly from lack of sleep. So when he offered to drive her car, too, she gladly let him. The minute they pulled onto the freeway heading south, Sarah fell asleep.

At the first small town on the way to Eugene, Justin pulled over and tucked a pillow beneath her head and molded a blanket around her arms and legs. He whistled to himself as he got back in the car and started off again. Things were going fine today. She'd eaten well and was sleeping. It was going to be a great day, Justin decided. He ignored the little voice in his head that was asking him to examine the reasons why he was so concerned about her well-being.

Not many miles later, his cheerful mood was challenged. He'd never actually been to Eugene before, but he had faith in his map-reading abilities. The tidy one Annie had printed out for them yesterday was accurate. The streets in town were labeled and easy to see. The people waved and were friendly. The sun was shining a cool warmth. It would have been a breeze to get around, except for one thing. There was a fair lining the far reaches of downtown.

Women in long, flowing skirts, pushing baby carriages, men with braids falling down their backs, smiling behind sunglasses, kids of every shape and size, with cotton candy filling their hands, walked across in front of him. There were long red-and white roadblocks detouring them. Which was fine, but the new street took them away from the address they sought. He weaved his way back through the mess of people again. As he stopped at a stop sign, trying to figure out where to begin from again, he rolled his window down to let in the sounds of the city. The aroma from the food venders was so fantastic he almost got out and bought one of everything. He saw one guy with a basket of clam strips and wide, golden French fries. Justin's mouth watered.

Sarah stretched and sat up. "Mmm! What smells so good?"

Justin looked over at her. He smiled. Her eyes were sleepy, but she seemed rested. "It seems they're having a street fair today. People traffic is bad."

"Oh, goody!" Sarah clapped her hands together. "Let's get a corn dog."

Justin raised both his eyebrows. "Really?"

"Why not? We can't come all this way and not get one." Sarah smiled sweetly. It was the same smile she'd had on her face every time they'd had an airport layover.

He couldn't resist her any more now than he could then. "Okay. Let me just find a place to park."

"Why? Just run get something real fast." Sarah looked in the rearview mirror. "Nobody's behind us, and if somebody does come, I'll just jump into the driver's seat, go around the block, and pick you up."

"Sure?"

"Yeah. I think I want those oriental noodles, too. They look good."

Justin rolled his eyes and hopped out of the car. "I'll hurry," he called back.

*

Sarah watched him walk away. He looked easy and comfortable, easily blending in. As he disappeared into the crowd, her gaze was caught by a group of men and women dancing in circles, flipping long, baton-like sticks with round, decorated ends, and attracting a growing crowd. They looked like modern-day gypsies. Their smiles were deep and genuine, their faces painted. Their clothes, seemingly made of flowing silk, draped their bodies with bright colors. They looked so free, almost wild, in their rhythmic spinning.

Had she ever felt like that? Sarah wondered. When she was a child, she had. She remembered twirling in circles in the backyard with her mom on summer evenings as the sun set, swimming and roasting marshmallows, lying on the grass and watching the moon come up, jumping off bridges into warm, gentle rivers, and going for walks and counting the cracks in the sidewalks. But her sense of fun had died with her mother. Afterwards, she'd had to face reality and grow up fast. She hoped, if she ever had kids, life would be kinder to them, that they'd have even more years than she'd had to be carefree and not ever feel the need to mature overnight.

She rested her head back. Those childhood days had felt like magic. She wondered if these gypsies felt like that every day, if they moved wherever the spirit took them. Not that Sarah wanted to do that. She loved her job, her home. But a little fun now and then should be a priority, too. She saw Justin returning. She'd like to have that kind of fun with him.

"Hey, I got you the biggest box of noodles they had—and this." Justin held out a mountainous wad of cotton candy. "I couldn't resist. There was this little, freckled-faced kid running the machine, and he got a little carried away."

Sarah laughed.

*

To Justin's ears, Sarah's laugh was a rich, full-bodied sound, one that he'd never heard escape her lips before. A thought struck him like a thunderbolt. He loved her . . . he *loved* her! *Great,* he thought. *Here I stand, my arms full of noodles and corn dogs and enough cotton candy to rot an army of teeth, and now I realize I've gone and fallen in love—and with the sexiest, most beautiful, sleepy-eyed woman I've ever seen.*

"Justin, get in here. I'm starving." Sarah leaned over and opened his door for him.

He slid in as well as he could with all the food in his hands. He quickly passed it all to her and pulled her against him for a fierce kiss.

When he released her, she said, "Whoa. What was that for?"

"It's a beautiful day, you're a beautiful woman and I—" Justin stopped himself. He couldn't tell her, not like this. Not without her knowing the truth. "I wanted to." He smiled a toothy grin and bit into one of the giant corn dogs.

She eyed him skeptically. "Okay."

"I think I'm gonna be sick," Justin moaned twenty minutes later as he turned the corner leading them down the street they'd been looking for.

"Well, you didn't have to eat the rest of the cotton candy. We could've taken it home to Dad. He loves it." Sarah pointed out her window. "Oh, here we're in the five-hundred block; the house should be on my side." Sarah counted the numbers on the eaves of the houses as Justin drove slowly past.

"Here it is." Justin slowed the car and came to a stop behind a little, red wagon parked neatly at the curb.

Sarah looked up from her notes and studied the house. At first glance, it seemed familiar, but she couldn't say why. She'd never been here.

"Do you want to go up and ask the people living there some questions?" Justin leaned his forearms against the steering wheel.

"Not yet." The feeling of familiarity wouldn't go away. It really could have been any house, anywhere, but there was still something about it nudging her memory.

The four, white, decorative shutters hung on either side of two, large, picture windows. An arched entryway led to a dark walnut, arched door. The shrubs in the yard looked newly planted, just this spring. The narrow path of flat stones made the walk look inviting, especially with the rainbow colors of the roses that bordered it. It looked sweet, set back from the road, like a gingerbread house would be. It was like the first home a family would dream of.

"Oh, my God! That's it!" Sarah dug in her bag and pulled out her wallet. "I knew I recognized this place." She opened to pictures tucked neatly into their plastic holders and handed the one she was after to Justin.

He looked at the worn edges of the photograph and the faces of the people in it. Sure enough, the house behind their waving hand and smiling grins was this same one.

"They're my parents." Sarah pointed to the man and woman who were dressed in wedding-day clothing.

The photograph was taken to encompass the house, so the faces of the people in it weren't close enough to see distinct features. But Justin could easily tell that the man was her father. The woman looked just like Sarah. Flipping it over, Justin read, *Our First House!* penned in the same flowing handwriting as the note he'd found near Becket's hand and the letter he'd found in his father's journal.

"How old is that address Annie gave us?" Justin frowned at the face of Sarah's father. He was thinking something he hadn't before.

"Thirty or so years ago. So that places them in this house at the same time." Sarah squinted, trying to put the pieces together.

"Do you remember if, when your mom talked to her equipment contact, Elvis, your dad was home?"

"Sure he was," Sarah said immediately. Then she thought about it. "Maybe. No." She looked at Justin. "I don't know. Why?"

"How much do you really know about your dad? Before he married your mom, anyway?"

Sarah glared at him. "What the hell are you saying? That my dad is this Evan Peterson character?"

"Look where this has led. This address comes up for him, and your dad is living here at the same time. There's a two-million-dollar life insurance policy left to Evan Peterson. Why else would that be?"

"I don't know! But my dad would never murder anyone, let alone my mother, for money!"

"Money's a big motivator."

"He didn't kill her." Sarah shook her head and kept shaking it. "He wouldn't kill anyone. I can't believe it. I won't believe it. How could you even think such a thing! He loved her; he loves me. He wouldn't do it. He wouldn't—"

Belatedly, Justin realized he'd been in FBI mode and had forgotten the huge stake Sarah had in the outcome of this case. That to her, this wasn't a case at all; it was her family. "I'm sorry. You're right, it's a leap." Justin didn't believe it was that big of one, but he could understand how upset she'd be. He could have shot himself for not having more empathy. *Why did you go and have to open your big mouth and upset her,* he chastised himself. *You are only guessing at this point.* "I'm sure he just knows something about the person who lived here before, that's all. There's always mail that gets delivered by mistake, odd deliveries, stuff like that," he said, hoping, for Sarah's sake, that Evan Peterson wasn't her dad.

Sarah still looked upset with him, but at least she'd calmed down. "I'll call him." Sarah wiped her cheeks as she punched a number on her cell phone. "I'll ask him to meet us at the office. We'll show him everything we've found." Sarah looked fiercely at Justin. "And then you'll see you're completely wrong."

He sincerely hoped so.

CHAPTER 27

As Justin followed Sarah through the glass doors leading into S.J. Investigations, he felt the back of his neck prickle. It was a cold sensation that he hated but depended on. It served as a sort of warning that trouble was coming. Justin still hoped against hope that Eric Johnson wasn't involved in his wife's death, but he wasn't about to take any chances. He had a weapon stored in his duffle at Sarah's apartment, but seeing how they didn't stop there, he was unarmed. But, he wasn't helpless. When they stopped to get gas on their way back from Eugene, he'd called Pat to see if he'd made it in okay. Thankfully, he was currently sitting in his hotel room just around the corner from Sarah's office waiting for any sign that he might be needed.

The sign would come from Justin's phone. It was a regular model any customer could get at any cellular-phone dealer, but he'd made an addition to it. He'd placed a voice transmission device in its base. It didn't have to be on in order for anyone with the receiver to listen in. Justin had made sure Pat had the receiver before leaving Texas. He and Pat had tested it while Sarah had been in the restroom. Justin had smiled at Pat's, "Yeah, I hear ya, buddy."

He patted his jacket pocket, verifying the phone's presence, and felt easier. There was no way of knowing how Eric might react. No way to know if Sarah's father was guilty or innocent.

Sarah didn't bother to turn on all the lights in the entry. She flipped on only one of the single fluorescents overhead, leaving eerie shadows lurking at the edges of the office.

The feeling of foreboding followed Justin as he took each step across the dimly lit space. As he passed the chair he sat in that first day, he thought of all that had happened since then. He'd had so much anger that day. He'd had so many questions. So many plans. But what he hadn't planned on was making his own heart vulnerable. He needed to take a huge risk. He needed to tell Sarah who he was. *That* would probably break her heart and his own, as well. *I have to stop putting it off,* Justin scolded himself. After he had the answers he came for, then he'd tell her.

But first things first. Right now, he needed to focus on the job at hand.

"Sarah." His voice carried across the space separating them.

Sarah turned to face him in the doorway to the hall to her office. "What?"

"How do you want to handle this?"

"Well, I sure don't go around accusing him of things, if that's what you mean."

Justin frowned at her.

"Sorry. I just don't know what to expect." Sarah blew out a breath. "I guess I'll show him everything we've found and tell him about our suspicions and see if he knows anything we haven't thought of."

"Sounds good. Do you want to wait for him here? Let him in?"

Sarah shook her head. "I left the outer door unlocked so he won't have any trouble getting inside. Besides, I want to go in and get everything set up. I'm afraid if I don't, I won't have the nerve to go through with this once he gets here."

"Okay." Justin agreed, trailing her down the hall. He wasn't sure if telling Eric Johnson everything was such a good idea. He would have insisted on another tactic if he didn't know Pat was just around the corner.

Sarah put her key into the lock on her office. "Hmm, that's funny. It's unlocked. Maybe Annie forgot to lock it."

"Maybe." That prickle on his neck was back. He hoped Pat had heard her.

"Well, look who's decided to join me."

Justin heard the words before he saw who'd spoken. He looked over Sarah's head and saw a woman sitting on the couch at the end of Sarah's office. She was beautiful. She had long, blond hair draped over one shoulder. Her lips were painted a becoming tint of coral. Her long legs were crossed in front of her in a seductive manner. A fashionable, soft linen suit, in a color that matched her lips, covered her frame.

And in her right hand, she held a deadly slim Browning Buckmark pistol, as if it were an extension of her arm. Her gray eyes, the same gray eyes as Sarah's, were aimed in their direction. They were filled with hatred.

"Well, come on in," the woman said. "Don't just stand out there."

*

Sarah stood with her mouth half open as she stared at the woman who looked so much like her mother. Beyond the panes of the third-story window, it was just another Saturday night. She could hear the muted honking of horns and the sounds of laughter as people anticipated the night ahead. But for Sarah, tonight was a point of no return.

As they'd crossed the empty suite only moments ago, she'd known from this night on she'd never look at her childhood as she'd always seen it. It would be different. Because, even though she knew, believed, in her heart, that her father wasn't involved in killing her mother, there was something he knew that she didn't. She ached with the knowledge he hadn't shared it.

But looking at this woman—*not my mother,* she told herself fiercely. *My mother would never, ever point a gun at me*—perhaps now she'd know why.

She let her training kick in and clicked through her memories of her mom, looking for differences to refute what her eyes were telling her. The face was the same. She began to feel panic again seeping into her thoughts. She beat it back. Her eyes darted over the woman's outfit. It was exactly the thing her mother would have worn, except Helen Johnson had never liked coral. Sarah began to feel more confident. The gun was gripped in this woman's right hand. Her mother was left-handed. And while the voice had sounded similar to her mother's smooth tone, it was gruff, more like the one her mother had used while in prison.

Her knees almost buckled with relief. This woman could not possibly be her mom. But she now knew who she was, and she needed to tell Justin, who stood stock still behind her.

Sarah cleared her throat. She tried to smile; she made her voice light and cheery. "Aunt Lainey, what are you doing here? Is this some kind of joke?"

Aunt Lainey wasn't buying it. The only surprise she showed was a quick blink of her eyes. "Your dad called me and said to meet you here. He said you sounded upset. I'm sure he'll be here shortly to join the party." Elaine pointed with the gun to two empty chairs. "Sit. And shut the door."

They followed her instructions. Sarah glanced at her desk. The phone was nowhere to be seen. In fact, all the items she'd had on her desk were pushed to the floor. Her safe was hanging open, its contents set neatly on the wooden surface.

"Don't even think about using the phone. I cut the line before I came in." Elaine laughed. "Too bad for Monday morning, huh? Though I highly doubt you'll be coming in on Monday or Tuesday or any day."

"What'd you mean?" Sarah asked fear stinging the back of her throat.

"Oh, come on. And here I thought you were a smart girl." Elaine looked at Justin. "Then again, maybe not."

"What do you want, Elaine?" Justin leaned back in his chair, stretching his legs out in front of him.

"You know. You would've been my son. If everything would have worked out the way it should have."

Justin narrowed his eyes. "What are you talking about?"

Elaine got up and walked over to Sarah's desk. She picked up the journal and took out the letter. She smiled as she caressed the cover of it. "He loved me, you know." Her eyes got hard. "But he would've never admitted it. All he wanted was my bitch of a sister!" Elaine slammed the book back onto the desk and turned on her heel to walk back to the couch.

Sarah started to defend her mother, but Justin grabbed her hand and squeezed it. "Let her talk," he mouthed and kept hold of her fingers.

Elaine waved the letter in front of Justin's face as she walked by. "You don't really think Helen wrote this, do you?"

"Sure, she did." Justin tipped his chin in Elaine's direction.

"Bullshit. The only thing she ever had with him was one damn date. Then she ran off like a damn chicken shit to go to college like some goody-two-shoes." Elaine sat down on the couch again. "And I had to pick up the pieces." She smiled as she drew the folded letter between her fingers. "But I'm good at picking up the pieces."

"It sure looks like Helen wrote it to my dad," Justin said.

"Ha! Why? Because it looks like her handwriting and because her name's signed at the end? We used to do it as a game when we were kids. Copying a lefty is pretty hard, but I'm smart." Elaine tapped her head with the tip of her finger.

"So why should I have been your son?"

"Everything was going great between Tom and me. He was in love with me. And I was in love with him. But, only thing is, he thought I was Helen. I thought about telling him the truth. Making him fall in love with *me*. But then I got pregnant. He found out because I didn't throw out the trash from the pregnancy test before he came over. That was stupid of me. But don't worry, I'm smarter now. I always get rid of the trash." Elaine flipped her hair over her other shoulder. "Anyway, he was so excited. He wanted to get married right away. But see we couldn't, because I wasn't Helen. So I left him. Sent him this letter, and a few months later, I lost the baby. While I was away, he found someone else." Elaine looked at her hands.

Justin thought she was going to cry. He felt a little sorry for her, but when she looked up all of the pity he might have felt was gone. Her eyes were black with anger.

"So, okay. I decided I'd had it with men; I'd had it with everyone. Especially my oh-so-saintly sister and the asshole who'd loved her. I'd take care of myself in my own way and be damned to everyone else." Elaine shifted her position on the couch.

"What else?" Sarah asked. She knew there was more.

"Not much else to tell. I went on with my life; we all did. I stayed as far away from Tom-the-shit and my fucking sister as I could. And things could have continued that way forever. But, no. My crusading sister decided to mess with my prison."

"*Your* prison?" Sarah leaned forward in her chair as she squeezed Justin's hand.

"Yeah. Where do you think all my money comes from?"

"From your husband," Sarah answered.

"What? Are you kidding? I never married anyone. The only person I ever loved enough to marry was his father. And he proved he wasn't worth me." Elaine pointed the gun at Justin.

The gun aimed in Justin's direction scared Sarah. She wanted to keep Elaine talking until she could figure out a way to get help. Maybe if she could somehow turn on her computer, she could dial 911 that way. "Tell us about the money," Sarah commanded.

"I made tons of it." Elaine licked her lips and smiled.

"How?" Sarah asked.

"Don't give me that shit. You know all about it." Elaine pointed at the things on Sarah's desk. "You take such good notes. Which isn't too smart. If I would've gotten rid of you in Freeman City, you would've never found out. But better late than never, I always say. Sure, it was fun for a time to mess with you."

Sarah felt so much anger, she didn't know if she could breathe. She was as afraid to ask the next question as she was not to. "So I suppose it was you who gave the order to have Mom killed."

"Hell, yes, it was." Elaine laughed.

"She was pregnant. Did you know that?" Sarah wanted to strangle her. She wanted to cause her physical harm, but she couldn't move. Her body was frozen. She needed to hear the rest of the story.

"Why the hell do you think I had her killed?" Elaine sat forward. "I went to visit her just a few days before she died. I wanted to see if she was making any connections with the whores, but all she could talk about was that damn baby. You should have seen her. She was so damn happy."

"You monster! You killed her and the baby!"

"Big damn deal." Elaine scratched her cheek with the gun barrel. "You know, I wasn't going to kill her originally I was just going to rough her up a little. Scare her so she'd go away. Get her out of there that way. But, because she was so stubborn—" Elaine's voice almost had pride in it as she talked, "—I knew she wouldn't have given up. She would've kept digging. She would've known that someone was trying to get her out of the prison, and she wouldn't have let up. And then she told me about the baby. That made what I needed to do so much more clear. I'd let her live through her first pregnancy, hadn't I? Let her have you." Her smile made Sarah's blood run cold. "Enough was enough. She'd had her happiness. She'd had her baby."

*

Justin felt Sarah tremble so hard, he knew she couldn't force out any more questions. He gripped her hand even tighter and took over. "So you killed her and had your revenge for my dad loving her and not you."

Elaine's laser-like gaze went to him. "Oh, the story doesn't end there, Justin, I thought my problems were over with her dying, but then I remembered who'd help put her there. Good ol' Tom

Breslow had pulled strings with Simon to get her there undercover. Tom was one stubborn son-of-a-bitch. He wouldn't have stopped, either. So I took care of him, too."

Justin froze, his mind trying to catch up with what he'd just heard. As if it was happening to someone else, he felt Sarah's grip, trying to give him strength.

Elaine continued, "I was in your father's side closet when you came in that night. Ah, the boy you were made me cry. You were so strong and sad. I was a little concerned over how I was going to clean up the trash on that one, but you, you quick thinker, took care of it for me. You cleaned up the gun I'd used to kill him with and stuck it back in its case. And made the entire thing look like an accident." She smiled at him. "I could've kissed you, when you pulled out another weapon and the gun-cleaning equipment. Brilliant." She nodded. "Oh, yes, you could have been my son."

"You're crazy!" Sarah cried. "You destroyed so many lives. Justin and his parents. My dad. My mom. And—"

"Shut up!" Fury lit Elaine's eyes. "Your mom. The saintly Helen. She was always so perfect." Elaine stood. "Now I think we've talked enough." She pointed the gun in Justin's direction. "I think I'll kill you first. It'd be pretty easy for the cops to believe that she killed you when she found out you'd been lying to her all this time."

"Lying to me?" Sarah twisted to look at him.

"Sarah, I've wanted to tell you—"

"But now I will." Elaine interrupted, keeping the gun trained on Justin. She grinned. "He's an FBI agent. He's not a reporter from Dallas. He only said that so he could get close to you."

Looking shocked, Sarah dropped his hand. It felt empty without her touch.

Elaine laughed. "Ah, it's too bad the Breslow men keep journals. Though yours is quite boring. No sexy scandals to speak of." Elaine pulled the hammer back on the gun. "So where do you want it? Head or heart?"

Justin had no time to think. He knew his life was over. It had ended the minute Elaine had told Sarah who he was. It didn't really matter to him where he was shot. The heart would be best, though; then he wouldn't have to feel it break.

Suddenly Sarah yelled, "No! I'm not going to sit by this time."

At her words, Elaine blinked and flexed her finger. Before it could register with Justin what she was doing, Sarah jumped in front of him.

Justin hardly heard the shot, but he saw the bullet rip through Sarah's shoulder. She cried out, and he flung himself forward to catch her. Blood soaked his shirt. Her body went limp as he lowered her to the carpet.

He didn't hear the door burst open behind him or Pat's hurried entry. He was only dimly aware when Pat fired his weapon and silenced the woman who had ruined so many lives. He barely heard Sarah murmur, "FBI?" before her eyes closed and her blood pooled on her floor.

And he didn't feel the tears wet on his cheeks.

CHAPTER 28

Justin sat and paced and swore the night away, as well as most of the next day. He hated hospitals. The paisley printed chairs of the waiting room had become his best friends. The sweet, flowery deodorant spray trying to mask the antiseptic scent had become his oxygen. The tropical fish in the tank across from his favorite seat didn't dart away each time he moved anymore. He'd become part of their ecosystem. He had enough horrid hospital coffee in his system that it could replace his blood. He could identify which nurse was walking down the hall by the sound the shoes made on the hard-tiled floor. Eric had gone home saying that he needed a break, only to come back looking more haggard than when he'd left.

As the middle of the day approached, Justin sat in a tall-backed, padded chair beside Sarah's dad in her hospital room. It was a large space, not something Justin was used to when it came to hospital rooms. It was longer than it was wide. At one end, there was a table with a few chairs for visitors to sit at and play cards. It was currently piled high with flowers and cards and food. Justin didn't know Sarah knew so many generous people. The guys from the office brought in a container of peanuts and dried fruit, which Justin was grateful for. He and Eric had been snacking on it all night. Annie had brought in an extra blanket and a good pillow to replace the hospital's. And she'd brought some good coffee in a Thermos for Justin and Eric.

Pat came by several times. On his first trip, he brought Justin's duffle from Sarah's apartment. The last time, it was to say that the police had found enough evidence in Elaine's house to make arrests where the prison prostitution was concerned, but that they were still no closer to finding out who Elvis Peterson was or if Senator Ames was involved. Justin shoved his duffle under the table, not feeling like changing his clothes. It was as though he didn't want yesterday to end. He still wanted the chance to change things.

In his hand, he held two things. One was Sarah's birthday present, which he'd had made, and the other was the little horse he'd won for her at the street fair in Texas. She'd left it in the bunkhouse the morning she'd gone, and Justin had brought it with him, hoping to give it to her. Now he didn't know if he'd actually be able to even talk to her. The doctor had been in a few times, saying that even though it had been touch and go for a while, she'd wake up soon.

Justin looked at her pale face and closed eyes and doubted the doctor's words. She was sleeping the deepest of sleeps. Her eyes didn't flicker with the dreams she might be having. They were still, as was the rest of her. The nurses had tucked Annie's soft, green blanket under Sarah's chin. Her left arm lay straight at her side, with tubes and cords connecting her to all sorts of machines that beeped and paused every few seconds. Her right arm was bundled in a sling. Through the thin hospital gown, Justin could see the bandage that covered the wound the bullet had made as it had entered her body.

He'd seen the puncture. He'd held Sarah's sweatshirt against it while he waited for the paramedics to take over. The size of the wound hadn't seemed large enough to warrant hours of surgery and a night in intensive care. But Justin knew, even though the .22-caliber bullet had made only a small hole in Sarah's shoulder, once it entered her body, it could have ricocheted around inside, bouncing from one hard surface to the next. That knowledge had never bothered him, until he'd held Sarah in his arms as she fell, knowing what was going on inside her.

Why had she jumped in front on him? he wondered over and over as each minute of the night ticked by. It was a waking nightmare. No matter how many times he scrubbed his face clean in the men's room or drank a cup of horrid coffee, he couldn't make the image of Sarah leaping out of her chair as the gun fired go away. He couldn't erase the sound of her cry as the bullet entered her body or the feeling of her body jerking in pain. The whole scene played continually in his mind until he was sure he'd never see or feel or hear anything else.

"Son, you've got to stop torturing yourself." Eric patted Justin's knee.

"I'm not." Justin twisted in his chair.

"Could've fooled me." Eric smiled. "You'll be no good to her when she wakes up if you can't chase the demons away now."

"I'm working on it."

"I'm a pretty good listener. Do you want to talk about it?" Eric asked.

"No." Justin looked out one of the long windows at the gloomy, gray day beyond the glass. "She's not going to forgive me," he said without thinking.

"For what?"

"For lying to her."

"Why did you?"

"It's complicated."

"Well, I've got lots of time." Eric paused for a moment. "You know, when I walked into that office building and saw you sitting there beside her, I was proud of you." He cleared his throat.

Justin frowned at him. "What are you talking about?"

"I went to the office to meet you and Sarah yesterday, but when I got there, I heard voices so I just looked through the crack in the door. I knew that if I went in there, I'd be in trouble, too. So I went around the corner to the hotel where your friend is staying and got him."

Justin took a couple of breaths and narrowed his eyes at Eric. The truth slowly dawned on him. Eric Johnson was an FBI agent, too. Justin nodded his head.

"You got it, son." Eric winked. "We've all got secrets, but I'd appreciate it if you wouldn't tell Sarah. Not yet. I have some other things to work out. Then I'll tell her myself."

"Elvis?"

Eric nodded. "But we're not talking about me. We're talking about you. Why don't you tell me why you decided to tell Sarah you were an investigative reporter and not an FBI agent?"

Justin rubbed his face. "Well, I guess you could say I was mad. My mom died about three months ago." Had it really only been that long? It felt like a lifetime ago. "After all the arrangements and everything were made from the will, I received a letter and a key from my father's lawyer. Dad believed in being prepared. Anyway, when I was growing up, I always felt like there were things he wanted to tell me but didn't. And in the safety deposit box the letter directed me to, I found a journal. Dad put in the beginning that he'd hoped I'd never have to read it, but just in case I did, he had some things he wanted to tell me. Basically, it was a lot of advice and stories about things he did when he was kid."

"Sounds like a nice thing to do."

"Yeah. I learned a lot about him." Justin looked over at Eric. His blue eyes were trained on Justin's and were very interested. "He talked about Helen. About how much he loved her and how much she'd loved him. But something happened, and she just left him. He talked about how it broke his heart." Justin shook his head. None of what his father had believed was true.

"Helen did love him. They were good friends, but she loved her sister more. Helen left to go to school because she knew Elaine loved him more than she ever could."

"But he didn't know it."

"Helen didn't see Tom again until she needed help getting access to Freeman Prison and the only reason she did that was because she knew he was friends with Simon."

"What a damn mess."

"I'm sorry, son."

The details he thought he knew about his father and what he'd learned from Elaine mixed in his mind, frustrating him. "All the things Elaine said shifts everything. But staying with what I originally believed: the day after Helen was killed in prison, my father killed himself. I came home from the restaurant, where we were going to have dinner with my mom, and found him. I thought he'd killed himself. Only that's not true, either." He shook his head. "But that's why I was angry. I was furious that my father would kill himself over a woman. That's why I told Sarah I was an investigative reporter. I wanted to find out who this Helen lady was. After a little bit of research, I found out she was a reporter. I thought that if I was one too, I could get close to Sarah and she'd help me figure out why my dad loved Helen enough to kill himself."

"Sounds reasonable, knowing now what you believed to be true."

"But it's not reasonable. The more I learned about Helen, the more I liked and respected her. And the more I learned about Sarah the more I liked and respected her. But, I was using her. And I couldn't do it. So I decided I'd just see the whole case through with the women at the prison and then tell Sarah the truth and hope she'd forgive me."

Eric smiled as he looked at Justin's face.

Justin blew out a breath. "God . . . I love her. I didn't realize how a man could fall in love with some gray-eyed woman—" Justin snapped his fingers, "—just like that. Not until I read my dad's journal from when he was a kid, and not until Sarah smiled at me over a mountain of cotton candy."

Eric hadn't seen the gray eyes of the woman he'd loved for so long. "I know what you mean, son."

Justin looked at Eric and saw the glistening of tears in his eyes. "I guess you do."

"I think I'm going to take a walk. You make sure you tell her you love her when she wakes up," Eric demanded.

"Yes, sir."

Justin stood and walked to the edge of Sarah's bed. He thought he'd seen her eyes flutter just a little. But he waited and didn't see anything.

"Come on, sweetheart," Justin whispered. "I have something I want to talk to you about." He'd left the stuffed horse on his chair, but in his hand he held a tiny box. Opening it, he took out the ring he'd had made for her. There was a delicate arrangement of stones. A small ruby was in the center of it. Six, small, canary diamonds circled the ruby, and six more rubies circled them. He wanted to give her something that would remind her of the day at the waterfall in Texas and the flowers he'd given her in the shadow of the swaying trees. He'd intended the ring to be a belated birthday gift, but he'd changed his mind. He wanted it for something else.

He got nervous just thinking about it. It was a big step for him. He could hear Pat laughing at his hesitancy. But this wasn't just a simple question. It was *the* question on which the rest of his life hinged. Would she ever forgive him? Would she understand why he'd done what he had? Would she believe how much he loved her? Would she say yes? Would the ring fit?

Justin smiled at the last question. He felt as if he were on a precipice, waiting to decide which way to fall, and one of his worries dealt with the simplest of things, the ring fitting?

He shrugged his shoulders. Well, he could definitely answer that question. He pulled her left hand into his. The limpness of it surprised him. He saw her as strong and independent, but when he held her hand, she seemed frail, not at all like the woman he loved. The paleness of her fingers against his made his protective instincts kick into overdrive. He wanted to cradle her in his arms and hold her until she was well. The need to see his ring on her finger pushed at him until he slipped the warm band representing his love for her along her slender finger.

He snapped the box closed and slid it into his pocket. Seeing the ring on her hand made him feel as though everything would be okay. The future he hoped for them would happen. The ring was a perfect fit, just as she was in his life.

"Hello, Mr. Breslow."

He started.

A sharply dressed nurse walked through the door, letting it close softly behind her. "I'm Hope, and I just wanted to check up on our patient here."

"Okay," Justin said. He looked down at Sarah's hand, thinking he should take the ring off, but he didn't know how to do it with the nurse standing there. He didn't want her to think he was as crazy as he felt. So he turned and walked to the far corner of the room to look out the window, where he let his mind wander while Hope took Sarah's blood pressure and made quick notes on the chart in her hand.

*

Sarah felt as if she were in a fog. She could hear well, but her vision was clouded. She wanted to rub her eyes to clear them, but doing so seemed an impossible feat. She wanted to see. There were questions she needed answered, and Justin was the only one who could do it.

Sarah concentrated hard and blinked her eyes open. The bright light of the room hurt. She squinted against the pain. A form dressed in white wavered in front of her. She could hear the soft scratching of a pen on paper and her gaze found the face of the person who was writing.

"Hey." Hope smiled as she whispered, "Good to see you."

Sarah frowned.

"I'm Hope, your nurse. You've had a rough time of it. But don't worry. You and your baby are just fine."

"Baby?"

"Congratulations." Hope beamed. "You get some rest. If you need anything, just press that right there." She pointed to a device with a button. A sweet smile filled her face as she let the door close behind her.

Justin whirled around when he heard Hope mention a baby. Shock and terror and excitement raced through his body, all at the same time. He was so filled with emotion that he couldn't decipher one from the other. Wanting something to do with his hands, he picked up the stuffed horse on the way back to Sarah's bed.

"Hey, sweetheart." Justin smiled and set the horse on the bed next to Sarah's hand.

Sarah looked at Justin's ragged face and then down at the little, furry horse. Closing her fingers around its fuzzy form, she wanted to cry. Had all of the time they'd been together been a lie? What was she going to do now?

Justin felt as if he couldn't breathe. He wanted to make excuses for what he'd done so she would understand. But there were none.

Sarah tried to talk, but her voice was raspy and quiet.

"Here," Justin held her water cup while she drank.

"Thank you." She whispered. And then silence.

"You never taught me how to ride a horse," Sarah finally said.

"I know. There are lots of things I never did. I never took you to the movies or out to a fancy dinner." Justin took a deep breath. "And I never told you that I was an FBI agent from Texas, and that I was only pretending to be an investigative reporter."

"Why did you lie?" Sarah smoothed the ears of the tiny horse.

Justin shook his head. "Because I was angry. I wanted to get back at the person who'd taken my father's life and my mother's. The only way I knew how to do that was through you."

"What did you intend to do?" Sarah didn't know whether she felt more anger or pain. Everything Justin had felt toward her was for all the wrong reasons.

"To use you. I planned to get you to help me research Helen Johnson."

"I guess you managed that now, didn't you?" A few tears slipped down Sarah's cheeks.

Justin caught them with his fingers. "I wanted to know what kind of woman my father would kill himself for."

"But, it was never her."

"I know. Let me finish," Justin said when Sarah started to talk again. "I couldn't do it. The more time I spent with you, the more I learned to admire you and your mother. In all my damn plans, I never expected to fall in love with you myself. The whole thing backfired the second I looked into your gray eyes."

Sarah just looked at him.

"I'm sorry I lied to you. But I could never find the right time or way to tell you."

"Besides the apology," Sarah squinted at him, "are you saying you love me?"

"Yes, damn it. Why do you think I've driven myself crazy over the last damn month? Why do you think you have that ring on your finger? I couldn't love you anymore if—"

Sarah laughed. Her side ached, her head ached, but she laughed anyway.

"What the hell are you laughing about?" Justin yelled.

"You." A few more giggles escaped. "I've never heard anyone tell me they loved me while they were yelling."

Justin bowed his head. "Sorry."

"I should be mad at you. But I'm not really." Sarah bowed her head for just a moment. "I have a secret that I never shared with you either."

"Oh yeah," Justin leaned forward.

"My mom was undercover as an investigative reporter. She really was an FBI agent."

"That explains a lot."

"I'm sorry I didn't tell you. But the longer I kept the secret the less important it became. And then I got so wrapped up in what was going on with Aunt—Elaine . . . I just can't believe she killed so many people."

"I know." Justin slipped his hands along the side of Sarah's face.

"It was all for nothing." Sarah looked into Justin's understanding eyes. "We loved her. All of us."

"I know that, too." Justin smoothed the hair out of Sarah's eyes. "But there is something good that came out of all of this."

"What?"

Justin laid his hand on Sarah's stomach. "A baby." He smiled. "Our baby."

Sarah nodded. She didn't know what to feel about that now. Later, when it was quiet, she'd think. Now she just searched Justin's face for his feelings. "I'm sorry. I guess everything just worked out wrong."

"Why don't you let me be the judge of that?" Justin said as he knelt on the tiled floor next to Sarah's bed. "I love you Sarah Juliet Johnson. Would you be my wife?"

Sarah held her hand up to the light and let the diamonds and rubies sparkle. "This is our flower isn't it? The one from Texas? It reminds me of that beautiful day we had there."

Justin nodded.

"Yes, Justin, I'll marry you." Sarah laughed.

EPILOGUE

Almost nine months later

"Hey, Dad." Sarah looked up from her hospital bed. "You're just in time. Justin was going to go down and get the babies."

"Yup, it's about time for those little tykes to eat some lunch," Justin said from where he sat in a chair within arms' reach of her.

Sarah almost laughed. He looked so silly with his hair messed from the long night of ordering around everyone from the cow-eyed receptionist to the doctor who'd delivered his children. Piled high on the table next to him were twin teddy bears, tall presents, and bushels of balloons.

"I brought some people with me," Eric said.

"Who?" Sarah asked.

"Carla and Nathan."

"Oh." Sarah tried to sit up straighter in bed.

"Don't worry about it, honey," Carla said as she and Nathan walked into the room. "We'll only be a little bit." Carla looked at Eric and smiled. "I—we—have something for you."

"Why don't Nathan and I go down and get the babies," Eric suggested.

"Sure." Nathan smiled at Eric and let the door click behind them.

Sarah tucked her hair behind her ear and cleared her throat, not sure about what to say as she looked at Carla.

She stood tall next to Sarah's bed, her black hair piled high with a long-tailed scarf falling from it. Shaggy bangs curved around her face and the edges of her glasses. She wore a pair of old overalls and a big, baggy, tie-died T-shirt. Her dark, almost black, eyes were shining with happiness.

Justin, apparently feeling Sarah's discomfort, scraped his chair over to the edge of her bed and twined his fingers with hers.

"What did you name your babies?" Carla asked.

"We named the little boy Thomas Justin and the little girl Helen Hope," Sarah said.

"Oh, that's nice." Carla's voice cracked as she spoke. Turning, she folded her arms and looked at her feet.

Sarah frowned, wondering what she wanted, maybe needed to say?

"I wanted to do this here," she said, as she turned back to face Justin and Sarah. "I think you know that Eric was in the Navy years ago. And that he had special assignments where he learned a lot about technology and espionage."

Sarah gripped Justin's hand. "Yes," she whispered.

"The name that he went by then was Evan Peterson. His buddies gave him the nickname Elvis because he could dance. Really dance." Carla smiled as though it was a memory she had.

"He told us that weeks ago," Sarah said, wondering how Carla knew any of this.

"I know," Carla said. Sarah saw her swallow, then she took a deep breath.

"Eric said there were a few things he had to take care of before he could tell us the rest of it." Justin shifted in his seat so he was even closer to Sarah.

"It's taken care of. The people involved with the Freeman Prison prostitution activity have been arrested, and the women who were kidnapped have been released." Carla motioned toward Sarah and Justin. "The girl, Karen, you spoke with, went home yesterday."

"How do you know all this?" Sarah asked.

"I've known everything all along. I even talked to Jackie, Sherry's sister, and let her know that her father had nothing to do with Sherry's death or going to prison. I explained that she'd never committed a crime but was kidnapped like many of the other young women."

"That's good," Justin said, as both of them waited to hear how Carla could possibly be involved in any of this. "We were going to talk to her when the babies were a little older."

"Maybe you still can. I'm sure she'd like that. Just a minute." Carla turned and walked to the counter at the edge of the room.

The first item she removed was the glasses that had helped disguise her face. The next were her contacts, which had changed the color of her eyes.

"Today is sort of a celebration for me. I begged Eric the day you were shot and over the last months to let me tell you, but he insisted that you might still be in danger. So we had to wait until everyone involved was arrested," Carla said and pulled the dental retainer that had changed the shape of her mouth away from her teeth. She wiped away the heavy makeup she wore around her eyes. Then she removed her wig and turned to face Sarah. "Going to Freeman Prison was the worst mistake of my life." Tears spilled out of her gray eyes and fell down her cheeks.

"Mama?" Sarah whispered. She couldn't believe who she was looking at.

Helen nodded. She unclipped the fasteners on her bibs and stepped out of them. She pulled off the T-shirt and pitched it on top of the overalls. Beneath, she wore a silk shirt and pair of smooth pants.

Sarah stared at a thinner, older version of her mother. Her long, blond hair fell in a single wave down her back. Around her eyes were lines that showed age and the passing of time.

"We had to make the person who was in charge of the prostitution think that they'd killed me." Helen wiped the edges of her eyes. "I had no idea it was my sister." She looked out the window, vowing that the sun shining outside the window would shine in here today. "So Eric rigged a fast burning mixture and planted it in the light bulb in the cell. Everything happened just like you saw on the video, except that I didn't plan on Sherry wanting to be involved. She insisted, even when I told her what could happen. The people you saw outside the cell in the video were your father and one of his Navy friends. She was the one you heard on the recording. They were there to get me out. The whole event was arranged so it would look like I died. It's just coincidence, really, that Simon was instructed to eliminate me."

"Why did you do it?" Sarah asked. She didn't know whether she felt betrayed or proud.

"I had to. I had to save those girls' lives. Some of them were barely eighteen. I'll regret my decision to enter Freeman Prison for the rest of my life because it took me away from my family. But I can't regret the lives I've—we've saved." Helen smiled. "Someday, I hope you'll understand. Eric wanted me to go south. Live far away from you and him, so that I'd be safe. He wanted me to get plastic surgery so I would look different. But I flat-out refused. I kept hoping I could come back and be your mom, as your mom and not somebody else. So a makeup expert taught me how to change my appearance with just a few items." Helen held up her hands. "These were the easiest to change. They got burned in the fire, and so we just let them scar. While I was waiting for Nathan to be born, I did a lot of practicing on my new personality. After he was, we moved in next door."

"Why did you wait so long? Why didn't you keep trying to figure out who was behind all the kidnappings and the prostitution?" Sarah asked.

"We did try. We sent in several other agents, but one of them disappeared and two others were killed. The Bureau was having a hard time getting through all the red tape. Plus, Tom died; he was our main contact. We were in the process of sending in someone to be a prison guard when Eric realized he was being investigated. So we stopped. We didn't want anyone making a connection to you or Eric. Plus, the whole operation was getting to be very expensive, both money wise as well as in human life."

"What about your life insurance policy?" Justin asked.

"We were going to use the funds to further the investigation personally, but we never filed the claim. We couldn't, especially after we found out that Eric's identity was close to being uncovered."

"I can't believe this. Years have been wasted," Sarah said.

Helen nodded. "I know. And I'm so very, very sorry. Truthfully, I just wanted you and Nathan and Eric safe. Being where I was, I knew how all of you were doing. But I got worried when you told Eric that an investigative reporter wanted to do a piece on my last assignment. When we found out that the reporter was an FBI agent, we decided that if anyone could find the truth, it would be the two of you together. When we found out that the agent was Tom Breslow's son, we felt even better."

"How long have you known who Justin was?" Sarah asked.

"Since shortly after your birthday party," Helen said.

Sarah looked up at her mother. "I can't believe how I never liked or trusted you. I mean Carla."

"It was really better that way. You were always so smart. And with you disliking me as Carla, we hoped you'd never figure out who I really was."

Every minute of the past fifteen years had been a lie of some kind. *How do I even know this is the truth?* Sarah wondered. "You don't sound like you," Sarah said.

"I had a voice chip surgically implanted." Helen rubbed her throat. "It's me, darling. And I love you with all my heart."

With that statement, Sarah heard the mother she remembered. The voice was different, but the fact, the simple fact, was said in just the manner she'd said it years ago. Sarah didn't care about all of the details anymore. All she wanted was to have her mom wrap her arms around her. She couldn't believe she was standing in the same room with her. That she'd always been there, right next door, but she hadn't known it.

Sarah held out her hands to her mother. "Mama." She smiled.

"All the years of not hugging you or holding you or telling you how much I love you tore at my heart." Her mom's voice hitched on a sob. "Being able to now is the greatest gift I'll ever receive. My little girl. I'm so sorry. So sorry," she cried.

Sarah worked to find her voice. She wanted to tell her mom she understood and that it was okay, but truly feeling that would take time. She'd missed her so much, but telling that to her was going to take time as well. But there was one thing she was anxious to do. "Justin," she said, "this is my mom."

Justin stood. "Nice to meet you, Mrs. Johnson. I can see where Sarah got her courage and her pride and her determination. Like you, Sarah would have done anything that needed to be done to see that the girls in Freeman Prison were released and cared for, too."

Sarah gave Justin a grateful look. Over time, he'd help her forgive her mother.

"I'm sorry about your father. He was a good man. Just as I know you are." Helen reached across Sarah with her other hand and took a hold of Justin's. "I think he would be pleased to know that his son married my daughter."

"I think so too." Justin smiled.

"Hey, Mom, look at this. They look exactly alike except one's dressed in blue and one in pink," Nathan called as he came in the room, holding the door for Eric, who was holding both babies in the crook of each arm. "Oh, you changed." He smiled. Now everything was the way it was meant to be.

Sarah watched Nathan's face turn from boy to man, back to boy as he took a step toward her.

"Mom told me yesterday. I got to help her get in disguise this morning. I've known that you are my sister for only a day." He rubbed his arm across his face and looked at his shoes. "But I always sort of felt like it." He looked at Eric. "And it's really super to know he's my dad. Because I always wanted him to be."

Sarah giggled. "I have a baby brother." She pulled him to her. "Well, maybe not so much of a baby, but I still get to tell you to behave, because I changed your diapers. 'Cause I really did." Sarah wrapped her arm around his neck and scrubbed her knuckles across his head.

"Knock it off." He laughed back. "I'm gonna tell Mom," he yelled.

"Hey, you two, you're going to wake the babies," Eric said.

"He really sounds like my dad, huh?" Nathan asked. His face reddened and he looked as if was going to cry—and was very determined not to.

"Yeah. He does." Sarah smiled big, completely ignoring the tears Nathan was fighting.

Eric handed little Helen to his wife. "Here you go, Grandma. Isn't she beautiful?" He smiled. "I think I'm going to buy Tommy here a baseball glove." He softly bounced the baby against his shoulder.

Helen laughed. Sarah could tell she was overflowing with love. "I think you'd better get her one too. They're going to be a handful." She swayed back and forth in the age-old mother rock.

Justin linked his fingers with Sarah's. "I thought we were going to have difficulty with our family increasing by two. But now I can see how wrong I was."

"What do you mean?" Sarah asked as she smiled up into his eyes.

"I thought we were going to take two people home from the hospital. But really we'll be taking five." Justin leaned his forehead against Sarah's and grinned. "We're never going to get rid of them now, are we?"

Sarah's laugh filled the room. "No, we aren't."

"I knew you were trouble, damn woman," he muttered and pressed his smiling lips to hers.

ABOUT THE AUTHOR

Growing up out West, Rionna Morgan followed her love of horses to the rodeo arena and her love of English to the classroom and to writing. She has been looking forward to sharing her stories with you her whole life. Rionna is a founding member of Montana Romance Writers; she reads as much as she can possibly hold, and she loves most of all combining the chilling edge of a knife with the sweet surrender of romance. Rionna shares her home in Missoula, Montana with her husband, her four children and the mountains outside her window. Please be invited to stop by *http://rionnamorgan.com*—she loves the company.

In the mood for more Crimson Romance? Check out *Watching Whitney* by Jerri Drennen at *CrimsonRomance.com*.